TAMRIN
Merchant of Aksum

Tamrin, Merchant of Aksum Travels Through Egypt

(Illustration from an ancient Ethiopian scroll owned by the author)

TAMRIN
Merchant of Aksum

A Historical Novel

By
Harold M. Bergsma

Strategic Book Publishing and Rights Co.

© 2014 by Harold M. Bergsma
All rights reserved. First edition 2014.

No part of this book may be reproduced or transmitted in any form or by any means, graphic, electronic, or mechanical, including photocopying, recording, taping, or by any information storage retrieval system, without the permission, in writing, from the publisher. This book is a work of fiction. Names and characters are of the author's imagination or are used fictitiously. Any resemblance to an actual person, living or dead, is entirely coincidental.

Strategic Book Publishing and Rights Co.
12620 FM 1960, Suite A4-507
Houston, TX 77065
www.sbpra.com

ISBN: 978-1-62857-265-0

Book Design by Julius Kiskis

21 22 20 19 18 17 16 15 14   1 2 3 4 5

Contents

Prologue: A Personal Journey vii
Acknowledgments.. xiii

PART 1

1. 3
2. 33
3. 50
4. 53
5. 81
6. 95
7. 111
8. 137

PART 2

9. 153
10. 175
11. 188
12. 207
13. 225
14. 235
15. 254

Epilogue 264
Ethiopian Proverbs Used in the Text......................................267
Introduction to Glossary 268
Glossary of Words Used in Arabic, Hebrew, Urdu, Hindi and Amharic..269
Annotated Bibliography of Selected Sources 277

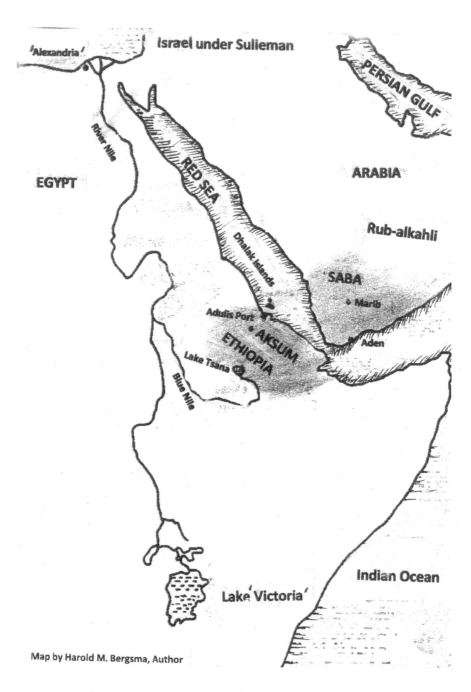

Map: Kingdom of Aksum under Queen Saba

Prologue: A Personal Journey

Tamrin: Merchant of Aksum is a historical novel of a remarkable man who lived at the time of the Queen of Sheba. The process of writing this novel was a journey which involved delving into ancient resources to find information, researching Ethiopian parables that have been used for many centuries and finally providing for the reader, a glossary of foreign words which Tamrin may have used in his travels in the Red Sea. Ethiopia, Yemen, Arabia, Jerusalem and India. During my lifetime I have traveled to most of the same areas that Tamrin did, which heightened my motivation.

Where did Tamrin, the protagonist of this historical fiction, live? This is the controversial part. Fictional history or historical fiction is an apt medium for what took place nine hundred years B C E, because records are vague and often the stories are conflicting, depending on the bias of the historian. The Bible has its account of Solomon and Sheba, the Qur'an has its version, (drawn from the Bible) but embellishes with a tale of a magical hoopoe bird that flew messages instantly from Solomon to Bilqiz in Yemen, the earliest form of email.

Archeologists and historians have argued about the meaning and validity of written accounts and have come to one firm conclusion. It is an agnostic conclusion. No one knows for sure because no one really has records that accurately depict the life or even the reality of the Queen of Sheba. There are archeological relics and these provide data that makes for many questions, and for writers, many stories. They all say with great certainty that the stories of Solomon and Sheba are simply accounts, myths, tall tales and histories. The archeologists have more to say. Artifacts and ancient ruins speak louder than old history books. The stone stellae at Aksum, like the pyramids, provide a glimpse into the past. There is a wonderful book called the *Kebra Nagast*, which is the official ancient history of ancient Ethiopia that tells a story of Sheba's affair with Solomon, their son Menelik, who was born of their union, and the return of the son to Solomon's Temple to bring back the Ark of the Covenant to Aksum, Ethiopia. This Ethiopian 'history' was written centuries ago, but twelve centuries *after* Christ. To many Ethiopians this is an indisputable history of the establishment of the Solomonic influence in Ethiopia and a history of its emperors from Menelik I to date.

History books, if in fact it is history, such as the *Kebra Nagast*, are themselves a mystery as to their origin, authorship, date and the validity of the manuscripts that were copied by scribes over time. Many sources state that it was written in 1270 A.D. If so, what transpired before that time for thousands of years in Ethiopia? Some sources say that the present *Kebra Nagast* was translated from an Arabic text, and other sources insist that that this version was translated from a Coptic manuscript. All may be correct; however, historical validation is not possible.

Three important "historical" sources for the story about Sheba and Solomon are The Old Testament, with its love poem, Song of Solomon, (based on its history and authors); the Koran, (with no original text to examine and fanciful stories of a magical hoopoe bird); and the *Kebra Nagast*, in its various linguistic forms. The rest is oral history. Each is held by believers to be the true history because "it is written" in their true document. Who dares dispute the Bible? Muslims, however, reject that history and the Ethiopian

Prologue

account, and place their Bilqiz (Sheba) in Yemen at her palace in Marib. Muslims have their versions from the Qur'an, Coptic theologians have others. Each version is different and all are held to be the absolute truth, now called "history."

The 'real' kingdom called Aksum may have begun, according to some historians, in 100 A.D. and the first 'recorded' kingship occurred at that time. My use of Aksum for Sheba's 'kingdom' refers to a time some nine hundred years *before* the first king of Aksum was said to reign. Both versions are in fact 'pre-historic' and lack solid historic documentation.

The Bible speaks of Sheba's country as Ethiopia in a general way. Sheba's rule in Arabic history only includes what is now Yemen, but hints at incursions into Ethiopia. The seaport village of Adulis was a very important port historically and has its own history, showing it to be the hub for trade and cultural integration in the Red Sea area. *Merchant of Aksum* is a marriage of two of the 'religion-historical' accounts, the Islamic account strongly infused with Arabian history, and the "correct" Ethiopian account placing Sheba's palace in Aksum with Sabaean influence. The Koran, (an Arabian version) written six centuries after Christ, and some fifteen centuries after Solomon, (636 AC) opts for Marib. This novel crosses borders and combines the Ethiopian kingdoms to include what is now Yemen and Ethiopia as the actual larger ancient kingdom of Aksum under Queen *Sheba* (also known as *Saba*, or *Bilqiz*) and later of her son Menelik.

The distance between the two areas is small. Only a narrow body of water separates Yemen from Ethiopia, a trip of mere days by dhows. Languages spoken at Aksum reflect the languages spoken at Marib. Written phonology, (900 B C E) may have been similar in both countries with the exception of the Ethiopian account, a phonetic south Arabian alphabet. (See ancientscripts. com). There are numerous charts available, which compare and contrast the old and newer versions of ancient alphabets. Some of the maps I studied showed that the Kingdom of Aksum does in fact include a portion of what is now Yemen. The distance between the narrows, which join the Red Sea to the Gulf of Aden, is only fifty miles, an easy link for early dhows.

"The Queen of Sheba" (by name *Bilqiz* in Arabic tradition) came apparently from Yemen, but she had affinities with Abyssinia and possibly ruled over Abyssinians in her kingdom. In the 10th or 11th century B.C. there were frequent invasions of Abyssinia from Arabia, and Solomon's reign of 40 years is usually synchronized with B C E 992-952. The Sabaean and Himyarite alphabets, in which we find the south Arabian pre-Islamic inscriptions, passed into Ethiopic, the language of Abyssinia. To reiterate, the Abyssinians possess a traditional history called "The book of the Glory of Kings," *Kebra Nagast,* which has been translated from Ethiopic into English by Sir E. A. Wallis Budge (Oxford, 1932). It gives an account of the Queen of Sheba and her only son Menelik I, as founders of the Abyssinian dynasty.

Queen Sheba may have traveled by boat, north, (down) the Nile, (*Al-bahr*) and then by camel caravan past the Nile Delta and along the coast to Jerusalem. In this fictional work Sheba was queen of the area on both sides of the Red Sea, had palaces in both Aksum and Marib, and used the Red Sea as the most convenient means possible to meet Solomon.

According to some histories, her son Menelik, son of the wise one, traveled to Jerusalem at about age eighteen and met Solomon his father. That visit and the return trip are crucial in ancient Ethiopian history because Menelik was said to have brought back to Ethiopia religious advisors and the Ark of the Covenant. Did he actually bring a copy of the Ark, which is still in Ethiopia to this day, according to Coptic Church

Prologue

proclamations? One can see that the fictional tapestry being woven about Solomon, Sheba, Menelik and others is colorful, of various fabrics and involving many weavers at different looms with gossamer historical threads.

Historians differ as to what constituted Sheba's span of rule. Some, reflecting the teaching of the *Kebra Negast*, place her in Ethiopia, an African country. This novel takes the point of view of more recent historical studies, which posit that Ethiopia at the time of the Queen of Sheba was an empire called Aksum and also included Marib, in what is now Yemen. Her palaces and their ruins are both in Aksum and Marib, which I have visited. A narrower view, one suggested by the Koran, is that Sheba, who became Solomon's concubine, was from Yemen-Sabaean origins, as revealed by the story in the Holy Koran. The controversy continues. Ethiopian historians suggest that the Ark of the Covenant was taken from Israel and placed in Aksum, and that Sheba's son became Menelik I, ruler of a political and religious empire that has lasted up until modern times.

Tamrin served his queen as the organizer of caravans. This is his story. Tamrin, the protagonist depicted here, serves the larger empire. As a merchant he brought trade goods from India (Hindush) to Aksum, including silks and porcelain from what is now China. Remember, the story takes place between 900 B C E. and 750 B C E. Records were few back then. Trade items, however, treasured by their owners and enduring over time, provide a history of their own. Who knows the actual time span of the Silk Route?

What is a historical novel? The two concepts seem to be oxymoronic, history and fiction. Fact and fiction are joined in the headlock of imagination in order to put life to myth, myth to history, and history to science, squeezing life from archeological findings. Quite an order!

Acknowledgments

Kathy Hughart; reader/editor, with thanks.

PART 1

CHAPTER 1

A strong bull is overcome when it limps.

"Take the afimi pipe master. Take it and sleep, Master Tamrin."

"No, take it away. I must keep some clarity. I can try to speak through pain, but not through the fog of opium. Go."

Tamrin closed his eyes but could not exclude the dreams of his mind.

To stare at death should frighten me, but instead it makes me sad. I look at the decaying part of the body that is poisoning me and do not relate to it, do not acknowledge it. But the pain is a different thing. It is that which now consumes me so that it is hard for me to rise above the threshold of it to speak and think of my life. Pain comes in waves on the beach that is my body, marching in high power as they crash on the sand of my leg, marching in deafening power as they engulf me. Death, yes, it will come and all too soon. There is the story I have to tell! If I don't, what was the meaning of my life and my passing here on this earth? I am compelled to speak, and if the story blurs from time to time, see the tale I tell as I see it, through the eye of struggle, the ear of fever ringing deafness and the halting voice of premature age that comes from eternal night, creeping closer. There is such a short time left for me to record my thoughts. My scribes will write day and night, that is, if I can stay awake and let the pain goad me, like the goad with the nail that makes the ox move forward, the goad that impels me to put my thoughts down. My life stories are intertwined with each other but I will try to sort them out, to separate the real from the improbable, the hazy from the crystal clear.

Can a matter of a few days change the matter of a life, fully lived, full of adventure, risk, and full of the satisfaction of having appetites assuaged? These eyes looked out on the world and saw infinite possibility, daunting challenges, and swept aside illusions, disdained weakness and the whining of others whose wills were weak or hesitant. Yet now these eyes become blurred by my own pain and weakness. It must be the poison in my leg which has moved to my mind that changes me so. I will not let the poison shrink my world to be very small, so small that it hardly encompasses this crude room and my cot and the huge swollen leg that, as it gets grossly enlarged and grows, seems to drain the rest of me. Even I, a strong man, cannot face the blankness of death, that sharp knife that will cut my frail thread, my cord of awareness. Will it be like it was before? I existed in my mother's womb but have no memory of it, yet it was I who cried in protest when I was born, I cried when the cord was cut yet I felt nothing. I have no memory of it. Will it be a similar cut, this death? Will it be like that, a single snip and then rebirth into another place as the Hindush say, or is there simply the foreverness of no more, no more? All the holy men speak of rebirth, even Solomon with his single god Yahweh, who sought after the other gods like Baal and Ashterof, a pantheon of gods of his women. Why? Just to make sure? My four scribes are kind. One whispers that I am repeating myself. Let me try again.

In my travels I have seen those who seek out the favor of the gods that they believe rule in the place called death. Each believer cries out to get the god's attention, to placate, to bribe, to shout the name of the god over and over. Baal, Moluch! Khudah! Vishnu! Ram! Yahweh! Lord! As if the gods are deaf, and cannot understand them the first time they cry out. I have watched the priests sacrifice animals to their god, make bloody sacrifices so that god will pay attention and grant their wishes. How many similar bribes have I taken from men who make the appearance of sacrifice to catch my favor? A thousand? Those who cried out, Tamrin, Tamrin, where are they now? I have eaten the banquets prepared by princes for me so that I will trade with them for their goods to make them rich, yet now I cannot remember their faces. I have taken the innocent girls, like lambs that they offered me but where are they now? I cannot remember their names or supplications or see them. These eyes now look out through a haze of pain, or is it the opium that is the haze that makes all of me so flaccid? Certainly the gods have no pain, yet they never replied. Could it be they never heard? Could it be? I can hardly speak it, could it be that all the gods are made in the minds of men?

I will not take the opium today until I have spoken about a certain matter about which I must not be silent. The men of medicine say I have but a week to live. One wants to cut off my leg now. Do I believe them? One thing I seem to know, that what I have left is my compulsion to tell my story before the haze blinds me and binds my lips to silence. Why, I ask, do I wish to tell my story rather than sink into the sleep of the poppy, which is so inviting? The gods, wherever they are, wherever they reside, must be very far away and very silent. Perhaps gods do not have ears. I will soon know why. They have been silent all my life, and so how can I now awaken them or get their attention? One can only make supplication to a close friend, to one who feels for the other. Is the god's silence telling me that that is what it is? The great silent one who has no friends of her own?

My compulsion: all I now do is talk, tell my story so that thousands of years from now a traveler, a camper making a nightly bivouac in some desert cave, will chance upon the sealed earthen pots in which the scrolls are kept, the story of my living, my passing, my meaning.

Oh, Sita, write on the stone hawilt that will lie on the sands near Aksum, write that my entire story written on papyrus will be hidden in the caves on the hillside. The other Stellae have fallen over because of frequent earthquakes and have broken into many pieces. Mine; construct it lying down on the ground. Someone a thousand years from now visiting the temple of Sheba at Aksum will see a stone obelisk, like a needle that rises up high made by some king, and perhaps while admiring it, sit on my Stella on which my story is carved. Instead of the stone pointing to an empty sky, arrange my stone so it points north, using the beacon star to position it. Someone who sits on my stone will by accident feel that words have been carved into the stone and cry out, "What is this? Is it a tomb? Did it fall over? Which way is it pointing? Toward the Temple of Solomon!"

Then perhaps I will find rest in the place that is beyond, the place of silence. My thoughts now are still caught up in a crack of regret, which leaks the smoke of the memory of my youth, my strength, and my joy in the small ecstasy that came with the experience of a new, young woman holding me. Sadly, I forgot her name. That smoke almost blinds me now; I must get on with my story.

The scribes are scribbling, but when I glance at them I can see that they are waiting for the real story, that what I am saying now is the ranting of one almost dead. They are being paid well, so they can afford to be patient. They can afford to pretend to scribble when I speak. Sita who writes in Sanskrit is the only one I really trust. The other scribes, especially the Egyptian, have to draw small pictures, and these are often not what I meant to say. How can a picture of a woman facing a man mean conflict?

Of my four sons, there is one who will carry out my wishes when I die and have my story preserved, and the account of it now being written on papyrus and vellum by the four scribes. Tamrin: Merchant of Aksum will be carved onto the shiny face of my stone. It will be read by others, long after the pyramids have crumbled, long after all the tombs in the necropolis have been opened and robbed, when the rulers' bodies have turned to dust. Kings seek to preserve their bodies and have them buried in caves or under massive pyramids, but I have seen the shriveled, dry remains of some who have been disinterred by grave robbers and know that that is not that which will travel to the endless days of tomorrow, that will speak from the grave. Mummies will be thrown aside, become dust. They thought they carried with them some parts of this world; food, servants, gold instruments of joy, to make the gods be pleased in the next world, but only the grave robbers were pleased. My voice will not be silenced by death; each reader of my story will hear it in his own language. All of the Stellae built near Sheba's temple will topple and break up, but mine will be protected as sands drift over and cover it. Two thousand years from now it will be read. Tamrin: Merchant of Aksum!

"Do not write now" *Rest your fingers for a while. This silk cloth that covers my leg is like the story of my life. The flies, some black, some the shiny, blue-feces flies, are running around on their grisly journeys, trying to find the meaning of the rotten odors that entice them, as men are enticed in their youth by the perfume of a virgin. The cloth, beautiful silk from the land of the Hindush, is printed with swirls and teardrop shaped patterns* which become the pathways for the flies to walk. There is pain, there is swelling and there is the quiet inexorable poison that rises swiftly to end my life, but I am still here, still seeing the great places I have traveled, the wonders of the earth that I have touched, the foods that kings and queens of other lands have never tasted. My wealth is my memory.

"Why are you scribes not writing? Write again!" *My story must give meaning to the living, the addition of all my deeds together that make the sum of what was my treasure, that until a week past, I did not even know I had. This will be recorded so that my tiny story is part of the bigger story, history. Strange, that as my life is now measured in mere hours, the meanings are so great, yet they are like the silk that cannot be weighed. But I must try to set down my thoughts so that my four sons and their four sons and their four sons will not have to traverse the rough, the narrow, the sharp and the putrid journeys of life that can be avoided. It is strange that wisdom comes from pain. Yet I know that most of those who read this chronicle will not learn more than what brings a smile to the face, a shaking of the head for the utterances of a fool who died from the sting of a fish. I may be wrong, but let time be put on the scales that weigh the meaning of this story. My sons may not even read this, but they will write their own stories of the women they have had, the gold they have hoarded. Or will they remain mute and become like mummy dust?*

The scribes glance at me again, impatient for the story. I ignore them.

If I turn my head to the side I can see the Arabian Sea. My bed, a simple, humble, cheap string cot, has been placed in the doorway of the house to catch the breeze. The cot will be burned after I die, no one would deign to lie on it, a place of death and rot. My right leg has been elevated with cushions and is covered with a silk cloth, to keep the flies away. The stingray, caught by my eldest son on an iron hook fell into the boat but I did not move away fast enough and was stung on my calf. That was ten days ago. I have summoned the best medical men from Aksum and each has sought his way to prevent the infection from spreading. One smeared on mixtures of crushed jasmine and wet clay. Another attached leeches to drain out the poison. The last ran his fingers over dark lines creeping up my leg and shook his head. I hear the healers and medicine men whisper quietly to my sons as they leave. They say that the infection has spread up my leg to my groin and that the wound will not heal because blight, a smelling infection, is rotting my leg; they call it gangrene. How strange. I have braved a thousand men, have a hundred scars on my body from the fights with mortals, fought against the intrigue and slander of my debtors, have struggled against storms that tried to engulf me in my dhows, and I endured. I have gone for days in the great desert of emptiness, the rub-al-khali without water, drinking the urine of the camels, and have survived. Now, a lowly sea creature, a stingray, has been sent as a messenger to signal the end of my days. What irony! My life has been one on the sea; now a messenger from the sea has spelled out the length of my earthly days.

"Scribes! Water!"

I have protected and guided our great queen, Sheba, ruler of all Ethiopia, which extends from the mountains and lakes to the south to the border of Egypt, across the Red Sea to the shores of Marib. My sons were leaders of the caravan; they rode with the soldiers in Sheba's entourage, protected the Queen who traveled from Ethiopia, all the way overland through upper Egypt, down the Nile to lower Egypt and then on to the kingdom of Solomon the Great, one who was known as the hakim, the wise, the insatiable, one who had nine hundred wives. Wives.

Perhaps in his language there is no other name for a woman taken as lover rather than wife. In my language we call such simply, women. How many hundred women have embraced me, I cannot count? Yet I, a civilized man of Ethiopia, have only four wives, the mothers of my sons. Four who have tied their lives to mine so strongly that their very name is my name, their very sorrow is mine.

Now, a sea creature with a brain as big as an almond brings me down. There must be a meaning to this that I have not yet understood. How can one who has tasted the bounties of Marib be brought low by a fish? How can one who has explored the great country across the sea, (a true descendant of Seth) of which the wisest historians tell the story, come to be rotting flesh?

For the past many months I have been telling my story to four wise men, those over there, all of whom can write things down on their scrolls, papyrus and velum sheets as fine as cloth. I hired those scribes almost a year ago. But I was in no rush. We met each day when the sun had risen, and I spoke, often repeating myself. But now time is evaporating like water on a hot stove. Others will use these scribes' notations to assist with the engraving of a massive granite Stela on which my story will be engraved after my death. I want no tomb, nor do I wish to have this body preserved. Let the ocean take it.

The scribes are shaking their heads, a sign I am repeating myself.

Let the Arabian Sea take my body, let the stingrays that swirl in the water there eat it. Cut up my leg in small pieces and soak these in poison. Thus I will deal with the brothers of the rays.

My story will be called Tamrin's Chronicle. My story, what does it even mean? But let it be told. Gold and wealth, fame and even favor of the Queen Sheba are all dust now. What does it mean?

Only gold can make this possible and only four loyal sons

will ensure that my wish is fulfilled. My story is to be written on three different surfaces, papyrus, and velum, thin and scraped skin of young cows, and on stone.

A small boy sits near me with a fly swatter, the tail of a buffalo attached to a stick. He flicks off the flies deftly without touching my infected leg.

"Baraka. I am ready. Record my words."

Tamrin was known from Northern Ethiopia to the delta of the Nile, from the land of the Hindush to the great city of Marib across the sea. His land was filled with treasure, black wood, ivory, gold and honey wine. Bees favor the climate and what grows here. The rulers of Egypt call this country, Punt Ta Netjer, and they are correct. It is truly "Gods' land." In Tamrin's sixty plus years, he made journeys across the waters of the Arabian Sea to the home of his father in the Tihama in the other half of the Ethiopian country of Queen Sheba. He traveled south with dhows as far as the coast of the Hindush to trade, and all of the citizens in Aksum know the story of his trip with Queen Sheba to visit the great King Solomon and see his temple built to honor his one and only god, Yahweh. Solomon was lavish with women and stingy with gods.

Tamrin traveled down across the land to the Nile and from there to the delta and then on to Al-Bahr Al-Abyad Mutawassit, which means in Arabic, the Middle White Sea. The Nile River runs 'down' to the sea, though it runs north where the floating iron needle points toward the North Star. It is the same star one looks at when crossing the Arabian Sea, always keeping it to the left. Its Hindush name is *Dhruwa,* the fixed star.

On clear nights when a fleet of dhows crosses the Arabian Sea, sailors put lanterns at the front of each of the boats. In the darkness the lanterns look like stars on the dark water. Camels wait in Hodeida to carry treasures, gold, frankincense and myrrh, ivory, Nubian slaves and opium seed worth its weight in gold. The Hindush in the celebration of *Durga Puja* use the waxy tops of the medicinal hemp plant, brought from the foothills of the *Himal* down the Indus River and sell it to pilgrims.

Tamrin's wealth was great, so great that he kept an accountant to record business dealings. His possessions in four cities, including Cairo, lay hidden where few would think to find them. Marib? Hodeida? Aksum? Wealth is thought to be in gold coins, but those are but the medium by which real wealth occurs."

His wealth was invested in huge land holdings along the eastern side of the Nile, invested in a fleet of dhows that fish the waters across the sea, from all the way to the other coast of the kingdom of Sheba to the village of his childhood called Hodeida. His wealth was in writs of credit from Hindush merchants and Egyptian farmers. Of course he gave his four sons both gold and silver bars, but Tamrin learned long ago from his father, a native of the Tihama in Saba, that each generation must struggle to find its own meaning. To flood his sons with gold would spoil them forever, since they would not strive, would not become devilishly clever in bargaining. Land, trade, and writs of credit, which control others, are the true meaning of wealth.

If Tamrin's sons had wealth they would abandon their mulvi, who instructed them in the ways of writing and accounting for money. Wealth is not just coins and gold bars but the trust and awe other men give, that one's writs and word are as good as gold. Most of Tamrin's investments were recorded and signed with fingerprints in blood of those who owed him, witnessed by four trusted friends, two from each side.

The Queen of Sheba gave Tamrin letters of insurance whenever he took boats to trade across the sea. If a storm destroyed one of his ships or pirates pillaged his bounty, the Queen's insurance would cover his losses. But he lost little, and his expeditions to the south toward the great Indus River of the Hindush made her wealthy beyond measure, and him the richest merchant in Aksum. An overly modest man goes hungry.

Tamrin recognized the ancient saying that it is not wise to mix business with pleasure, but he knew pleasure to be the grease in an axle that moves business. He was also mindful that health and strength were like gold.

Tamrin's sons, knowing his end was near, felt tension among themselves. His death would be sad, but it would be the beginning of change in the family. Wealth, debtors, and storehouses were foremost in their thoughts.

Tamrin's four scribes, each taking notes in his special way, were from different locations—two from Egypt, one from India and one, an Arabian/Egyptian who wrote in *Ge'ez*. The latter was from the deserts that border the great waters to the sea, Al-Bahr, white water between the surrounding lands. Each scribe's translation was unique. Tamrin considered the Hindush Vedic Sanskrit most useful, as it was written quickly by the scribe, and represented the oldest written language in the world. The Egyptian scribe wrote slowly, and Tamrin knew that few people would understand the meanings of the pictures used to transcribe his words.

A great stone tower would be inscribed from top to bottom with Tamrin's story which would reveal to future civilizations what existed in the past, the knowledge of the stars, the worship of heavenly deities such as Sirius worshipped by Aksumites, the wisdom to foretell eclipses, the understanding of the days of the year, the calendar, the very meaning of existence, revealed in the mystical meaning of the zero, the nothingness that comes before and after numbers, understood forever because of Tamrin's stella.

Tamrin's scribe Kala, from the Hindush people, had told him about the ancient people's language and great writings in Vedic. His love for the many Vedic hymns had also inspired Tamrin to choose Kala. When men, a thousand years into the future found Tamrin's story, they would wonder at the script on his stella in Aksum and explore its relationships to other languages. On one side of the stone the story would be told in Ge'ez and on the other in Egyptian hieroglyphics. And on the base would be written: *The Story of Tamrin, Trader of Aksum.*

Tamrin raised his palm toward the scribes, closed his eyes and rested a moment. Flies crawled on his face, but he ignored them.

My scribes look up at me now wondering what I am speaking of, but it will all become clear to them. My scribes are listening for any hidden meanings related to treasure, to my wealth. That is the curse of becoming ill. 'All lame dogs are bitten and eventually killed by stronger dogs.' Scribes write notes in the margins when they think they have discovered the hiding place of my wealth. I have for most of my life been Aluf, the first letter of the alphabet of Marib. Now a stingray has robbed me of my very position in life, yet, while I live I exert my will.

Tamrin opened his eyes, stared intently at the scribes, and spoke.

"All of you will be rewarded with land, gold and camels after the great stone has been carved. Write our agreement now on a small stiff parchment in Ge'ez. I will sign it and press the imprint of my thumb. Each of you will have a script of my debt to you for your work on this card of credit that is as good as gold when the agreements have been met."

The scribes scurried about, wrote on papyrus and velum, on leather and on a flat stone, then waited to be called to their master. As soon as Tamrin had given each scribe his signature and seal, he fell back exhausted, and rested.

His sons were now wide awake, realizing that a part of their inheritance had lessened. Tamrin turned to the sons and told them to come forward to print their thumbs on the back of each of the cards. Tamrin smoked opium and slept.

After servants lit oil lamps, the scribes waited. Breezes came from the sea. Tamrin awakened to the aroma of hot mocha coffee. He began speaking again as if there had been no time between his last words half a day before.

"The same day I was stung, there was a great omen predicted by Sabaean and Egyptian astronomers. The sky darkened as a shadow moved over the sun, now hidden as if a dark cover had slipped over it. Cocks crowed and sought places to roost, the temperature dropped and people sought cloths to cover themselves. Fools, who stared intently at the half-hidden sun, later became partially blind. I watched the sun darken in a mirror and glanced at it from time to time.

"My father once said that in ancient Egypt, when Jusef was administrator of the people of Egypt, such a thing had occurred, and famine soon struck the land. An eclipse signaled the end of something and the beginning of another. After the eclipse, the Egyptians' first-born sons died.

"My leg was already swollen like a melon from the strike of the stingray that day the sun was covered. My sons gathered around me and I warned them not to stare at the sun. They asked if it was magic, and I told them it was a sign of great changes, both good and evil. Magic, I told them, was simply the deception of the mind. Magic is the creation of deceivers. Magic, I told them, is a lazy man's way to understand life and death. The eclipse, because it was predicted, was only a comfort to those who understood that regularity of stars is what governs men, not magic. After the hyena has gone, the dog barks.

"Each of my four sons took charge of one of the four dhows the year of Queen Sheba's voyage. Each born of a different mother, the young men shared varying talents with their father, intent on making the trip successful.

"Setu, the eldest, was born of my first wife, a Nubian of great strength and beauty, tall, and with a quietness that came from her loneliness and sadness. Never able to return to her own people, she was circumcised when she reached puberty. She would no longer seek the pleasures of men. She bore Setu, who grew to be a giant, dark skinned man, a head taller than myself. No man challenged Setu. His skill with weapons made him a warrior of renown. He carried a scimitar with which he could slice a hovering fly in flight. He was leader of the caravans who guarded my bounties and fleet of dhows. He was first officer, a warrior from whom thieves and pirates fell back. Those who looked upon him would never know that my blood flowed in his veins, that it was I who taught him to read the stars, to read the flight of birds, to read the color of the seas and even the expressions of men and how they stood or held their hands.

"Ram, my second son, was born of a woman from India whose unsurpassed beauty of form and face he inherited. She danced for a ruler called Rajah of Sind. I had watched her dance and perform with great interest and lust, and she became a gift to me from the rajah. But that gift cost me dearly in the faulty gems the Rajah traded for my frankincense. Of all my women she was the most acrobatic, performing wondrous dances and moving in ways I had never seen in Aksum.

"On leaving Hindush land, I took her with me on my dhow.

She never returned home, nor heard a single word in her own tongue for more than twenty years. Ram's mother has been the wife whom I have loved; she has been my friend and shares my secrets, and only the almighty knows why I tell her everything when we lie on our bed in the early morning hours before dawn.

Ram is light of skin, quick with words, and clever with his mouth. He always stays by my side when I am selling and buying, for he can see if there is evil in a man's dealings. His weapons are bows and arrows, and his bare hands. He carries a shiny purple stone the size of an egg that he rubs with his thumb. A surprise blow from his hardened fist has disabled the strongest men.

"Aaghaa, my third son, was born in Aksum from Saba, named after Queen Saba (Sheba). From the far north, Saba was a desert woman who grew up with camels and understood the ways of animals - sheep and goats - and how to train watchdogs. Saba was born as a caravan moved across the deserts. She grew up in tents. She, even as I speak of her, is a trusted companion to me, not only a wife. She and I speak the same dialect and talk of all my adventures and plans. We two share a secret language that none of the rest of the family understands, the slang of our childhood. Thus she and I glance at each other to verify what we hear and then speak to verify our ears. Though she is my closest adviser and critic, I sometimes hate her sharp tongue. I tire of her company because she knows not when to be quiet, when to smile, when not to speak in her high voice that sounds like a myna bird. I seek her eyes and she holds my gaze and smiles.

Her son resembles her, lean, long legged and tireless on the march. As a child, it was he who always won races. Aaghaa, like his mother, is always first to seek me, tends to my needs, and speak his heart. He carries a jambiya, the short curved dagger of the land of Marib, never drawn from its scabbard unless it tastes blood. He carries as well a rope of woven ostrich skin leather tied to a heavy, grooved, black rock the size of a child's fist. He says this rock came from the stars. His skill with that heavy stone and thong are legendary; he can bring a camel to its knees with a single throw, a horse in full gallop crashing to the ground. He can throw this rope at ten paces and make it snake around a man's throat, strangling him. With his jambiya in his left hand and his rock from the stars in his right he is an opponent that few men will challenge. Most men are right handed, but Aaghaa uses both left and right equally, which confounds his enemies.

"Rinta, the youngest, seems to be my physical copy. His mother was the daughter of an Egyptian shopkeeper, a distant cousin of my father. Being the youngest son, he has learned the skills of many weapons from his older brothers, but simply carries a broad headed gala spear and a sharp, narrow bladed skinning knife which he hones daily. The shaft of his spear is made of black ebony wood with a heavy carved knob on the end. It is balanced so well that it can be thrown or tossed, or used as a close in-fighting weapon, which terrifies those who face him. Rinta understands that most men are prisoners of their habits and turn to the very things that harm them. When his brothers become ragingly drunk he remains sober; when his brothers seek new robes and colorful shoes with upturned tassels, he stands quietly in his desert sandals. When they squander their coins on ointments and perfumes, he smiles and watches their money disappear. This means he always has a bulging leather purse of gold and silver coins, while his brothers, usually broke, come to him for money, which he lends to them with great care, keeping records of each debt and charging them double to repay. Debt is like the imprint of a hippo foot in mud.

"My other sons are happy to get a loan, but when they see Rinta's face they see their own debt. It is better to be the creditor than the debtor. Rinta, the youngest, will probably be the second great merchant of Aksum.

"All my women were bought with gold in a business transaction, except the last one who was exchanged for three fine Arabian brood mares. Her name is Kenest. All the fruit of her fertile womb were girls, six of them, my burden. But when you see them all together, talking and laughing, working to prepare the food and cleaning the compound where they live, they seem to be as one. These six young women have a treasure that I covet, the treasure of each other's friendship, and seem to be able to speak and talk, even to cry together or laugh endlessly. The eldest will be married to a wealthy gold dealer in a month, and she is already beginning to look sad, but not as sad as her mother who was circumcised. It is now my eldest daughter's time. Camel herders turn their heads to look at her as they pass. She will marry, but her new husband will pay dearly since he agreed that his payment to me would be three years of service. Yes, I know you know the story of Laban, of Rachel and Leah. Thus life repeats itself. My fourth son Rinta will insure that the debt will be paid in years of service, or gold. He knows the abacus and carries it with him. It is his greatest weapon. His brothers are amused when he moves the round stones around on the tablet, but they frown when he calculates what they owe him. He is the only one of all the seeds of my loin that plants the idea seeds for the next generation. He writes in Ge'ez each and every day on papyrus scrolls and records his thoughts, but more importantly, what others have said and done. It is, he says, his *rooz,* which in Persian and Hindush mean day. His day book."

As Tamrin closed his eyes as if in a trance, all four scribes waited for him to continue. Leaning forward slightly, he extended his hands and arms.

"What is my race, my origin, and my country of birth? That I have not spoken of until now, because I am a citizen of the

Sabaean Empire. I speak the language of the southern Arabs, but I also can speak the language of the northern peoples of Ethiopia, Ge'ez, and I speak the language of Egypt.

"My father taught me to read their numbers and how to count and record numbers as high as nine thousand. He taught me both the numbers of the Arabs, the desert dwellers, as well as those of the Hindush, which I have used as my secret records to check on the accountants who have recorded all my wealth. My secret accounts are small histories of how money grows, how wealth is used. My secret *rooz* daybook confounds my accountants. Two accountants are no longer with me, for they tried to line their pockets with my money and lied when they wrote their accounts. There is no human act as base and evil as the cheating of a scribe, or one who records the strange pathways money takes, because treasure has been bought with the life of a man and stealing it thus must be paid back with the life of a man. Brothers kill brothers over money. Kings will start wars about debts not paid.

"Two copper coins heated to the melting point, were placed on the eyes of accountants who deceived me. Only when they felt the hissing of their own eyeballs were they put out of their misery.

"I have been amazed that many men place their treasures in the hands of men who tell fabulous stories about how they will invest and how the treasures will come, but who never give back in coin. Why? Perhaps men like to hear what they wish, that money and wealth will multiply by magic. The old Hindush proverb is true, 'Money makes money, or better yet, money produces its own little chicks, but you have to first sit on the eggs.'

"The Sabaean leader named Mukarrib Saba was a priest-king who stood at the head of the state, a long, long time before my father was born. I am also a citizen of that land across the sea. A castle called *Sirwah*, three full days journey from the

Saba coast by camel to Marib, was my favorite place on earth. How can you be a citizen of this land of northern Ethiopia and its Queen Sheba, *and* be a citizen of Marib, or as I mentioned before, a citizen of the coastal village called Hodeida? Because, though there is a great sea between the lands, the distance a running camel can travel in ten days, Arabia and Egypt are all one. Sheba, Saba, or Makeda as we call her with respect, rules all and has her palaces both here and there. This land of Ethiopia, where she was born, is the origin of all great learning, the first astronomers and mathematicians. This land is proud; it has never been conquered and made part of another land. Some have tried, but Ethiopia is the home of civilization, and the kingdom of Aksum is its jewel. It has taken the best from Egypt, the best from the land of the Arabs, all the way from the north where Solomon rules his country with wisdom, to beyond the great barrenness of the *Rub-al-Khali*, the vast empty desert of the southern country. I live in this great Sabaean kingdom ruled by a Queen, the sixth Queen, Sheba.

"With my own eyes I have seen Solomon's temple and his palace, but they are simply the expression of a man's personal pride inspired by a belief that there is only a single power, a god that talks with men, privately speaks to them, those who are of Solomon's tribe; imagine a creator of the universe who speaks to a king of a small kingdom of no great renown, a ruler ignorant of the stars, ignorant of the meaning of the great zero of mathematics and ignorant of the star of the north. Imagine a god who speaks to a slave personally, or a shepherd. Oh yes, I can imagine it about a shepherd or a camel herder because they are alone so much that their minds talk to their own minds and they know it as god. They design their own god from their loneliness and longing.

"My father, a dark skinned man from Ethiopia, settled in

the *Tihama* of Saba, the desert area between the sea and the mountains, and helped build the village of Hodeida on the coast. He traveled back and forth across the waters of the sea of Arabia which lies before me; he shuttled back and forth across the sea when the winds of winter blew to the south and the winds of spring and summer blew to the north; he sailed in his huge twenty pace long dhow a hundred times, but he always managed to return to Marib. Marib, the beginning of the end and the end of what all began."

While the scribes waited, Tamrin raised himself up on one elbow.

"Bring me sweet wine and dates. I am tired. Bring me small cups of Arabica Coffee so strong that it can only be sipped. Then I shall continue."

"There is a great desert called Rub-al-Khali, which means the great emptiness, where no one can live for long, where acacia trees barely survive and where a few antelope roam the sand dunes, food for the scrawny desert lion that is always at the edge of starvation. At the very border of this immense and great emptiness is Marib. It is the pride of our civilization. Its wonder is greater than the great pyramids of Egypt because more earth and stone was brought to make the Marib dam than six of the greatest pyramids combined. The pyramids were built for the pride and folly of rulers, built on the lives and backs of a thousand slaves, and these monuments are no more than massive markers of personal pride and delusion. Yes, they will stand for another thousand years, but what good does that do? What does it serve? In a thousand years do you not think the religion of the land will change so much that to revere the religion of the Pharaohs will be no more than blasphemy?

"From the hills behind Marib, once a year comes water, rain water, which floods down from the sky in sheets and runs down a streambed, a dry wadi. During my lifetime the greatest builders of Ethiopia and of this part of the Sabaean kingdom worked with ten thousand laborers to make a dam. Stones were brought from Taiz in the hills on camel back, earth was carried by ten thousand slaves in woven baskets and the final stone structure of the dam as it is now in Sheba's rule, was built in three hundred days! The dry riverbed had been picked clean of rocks and stones for as far as a man can walk in two days and these stones were brought to the site. At the narrowest part the wadi was first filled. Then thick papyrus and coconut mats from Egypt, brought by dhows across the water, were laid in layers across the stones, and earth was filled and packed hard. Limestone was burned to powder and this was mixed with the dirt around the river stones. For a distance of two hundred paces on each side of the river the stones were stacked and fitted by stonemasons so tightly that a knife could not be inserted between the stones. Again, mats were placed against the wall and earth filled in behind it. My father said that the shape of the dam resembled a cupped hand. The mats are now part of the compacted earth, but they served the builders well, holding back the water and binding the earth with the great pressure of the water.

During the years after the earth dam was built, great earth berms and levies were constructed and canals were dug for miles. Water gates were constructed of date palm wood, which is slow to rot. Then the people waited. Folly, said many, and scoffed. Sheba (Saba) the queen resided in her palace two days journey from Marib, and she and the entire kingdom waited and waited for the first rains to fall. Her priests who served her, the learned men from Solomon's empire that brought knowledge of the one and only true god called Yahweh, made sacrifices of perfect young rams, and blew horns to get the attention of their god so that rains would fall in abundance to celebrate the building and repair of the dam. But, alas, only sparse rain fell and the waters just reached the Marib dam, but there was rain for only a week. The dry riverbed soaked up the water, but little did the builders know that the dam now became compacted at its base, heavy with absorbed water. The weight of the stones sank a little into the clay and anchored it. Sacrifices were now made and messengers were sent all the way to king Solomon with gifts of gold so that there, in the temple of the land of Palestine, one hundred perfect young bulls, one hundred perfect goats, and one hundred sheep with the great thick tails full of fat were slain, so that Yahweh would send rain to the deserts near Marib. The priests of Solomon and their families feasted for weeks on the slain beasts. The price of meat in the markets fell and butchers went out of business. Those who dried and smoked meat smiled.

The people waited. My father was there when the skies darkened and the rains came. It rained for almost a month and the river was filled and the water backed up behind the dam and formed a huge lake in the natural depression behind the dam. There was dancing and celebration as the first waters were led into the canals that fed the fields, the new farms waiting for the irrigation water. That second year was a time of rejoicing. Yahweh had answered and had given the water of life. The great dam held the waters in its palm and not even a trickle was seen below it. The massive stone and earth structure larger than ten pyramids combined held the liquid gold, water, behind it. This water of the Marib was the new life of a civilization that now flourishes. When desert folk hear about groves of date palms, citrus orchards and green fields, they become moved to migrate. People from distant parts of the desert to the north in Arabia heard of it and moved south to plant their crops. Businessmen heard about the people that were moving and brought their goods: clothing, knives for cutting vegetables, silk cloths for the vain, dark eye shadow for the flirtatious, needles made of copper or iron so fine and valuable that after use they were kept in olive oil to prevent rusting. Saddles, sandals, pistachios and dried fruit were brought. Markets sprang up overnight. Those who could cook special food sold their delicacies to farmers who were starved for the savor of home; longing for *wat* and *tej* from the high country of Ethiopia across the sea, curries from the Hindush, and fragrant flat breads from clay ovens, a reminder of Cairo.

The water behind the Marib dam soon was filled with fish, those carried in clay pots across the sea in dhows from the rivers and lakes that fed the Nile, perch that would grow in five years so large that one could feed six men. Fish of various colors from the Nile were kept as pets. People brought these to Marib for their ponds! These joined the perch and feasted on each other.

Other fish are in the waters of Marib. Legend says that when rain fell hard one day and the clouds were black and the thunder deafening, the gods showered fish by the thousands from the sky. It must be true because the story is told that some landed on the sands and were eaten by the people. In the storage room of treasures of Bilqiz, there is a stone jar in which four of the fish, dried and salted are preserved for the skeptic. Yes, it rained fish of the kind that lived in the sea.

The land of plenty, but not milk and honey! Beehives did not fare well in Marib. The air is dry, the desert devoid of flowers for months on end. Honey is as valuable as gold, for without it the people could not make tej. From Hindush came sugar cane. Gunnah. It was grown widely near Marib when the dam was first built. Sweets are the joy of the Hindush, and strong drink made from sugar is the joy and primary need of the Sabaean. The

Marib dam made the city that grew near it the major producer of distilled liquor. My father gave me my first drink there.

During my childhood, Father and I visited the growing kingdom of Marib every year at the time of the harvest to taste the great long, white radishes, to drink barley soup and eat sweet dates and to drink liquor, the fiery *ghaal*. My Hindush wife Sita laughs when I use the Arabic name. She says the real name for strong drink made from sugar cane or grapes, a name from ancient times, is *sharaab;* so I have learned to use her word as well. A merchant such as me, (and all my sons), learns the languages of trade with the Hindush -- *sona* for gold, *chandi* for silver and sati for an honorable woman. My father's compound in Marib had all three.

Marib was then a green jewel, the emerald of Saba in southern Arabia, ringed by the golden desert sands of the great Rub-al-Khali. I will not return there again, this is my great regret. My son Rinta will return and bring back the treasures of Marib, frankincense and myrrh which will be traded in turn to the Egyptians for huge boatloads of grain, dates, thyme and slaves. Slaves from Nubia, the Gala, which the Egyptians prize, are the most hardy in desert climate as well as in the mountains to the south. These, particularly the women, are prized for their tall, lean black bodies and are worth much gold. Good slaves must be able to endure almost anything, any climate, any deprivation, any abuse and still at night when they sit together around their own fires they laugh, they dance and they produce more slaves. The slavers use them out of lust; they, like happy creatures use each other with grunting abandon. I have watched them working in the fields, men and women side by side, I have watched them glance at each other then move to a thicket and embrace in conjugal union, not bothering to lie down, then return to the field and carry on their work, the sweat of their wrestling still upon them. Then as if from a fountain of sound waiting to bubble up, the woman makes a whooping cry, a ululation of satisfaction and all the others laugh and join her, their tongues wagging left and right as they echo her pleasure, glancing with white eyes at the men next to them. The men, still bending over in the fields, weeding and digging become aroused and look around and grunt in anticipation. The slavers use them, yes, but they stroke each other's needs like coupling lions in the veldt and they copulate for sheer satisfaction, like the satisfying scratching of an itch. Do not smile! I was a young Nubian once.

Marib and Saba, the two are the sounding boards for each other. Marib, the fertile liquid of life, Saba the country and its queen Sheba, all of this soil which put together, created, brought forth a child of green in the desert to match the verdant hills of Taiz with their irrigated fields terraced on the slopes holding the precious crops of *qat* which all chew. Would that I had fresh leaves right now. I would ease the care of my pain, not the pain itself.

Marib was where I chewed my first *qat*, the bitter soft leaves that make the hot afternoons a time of social sharing, the men sitting in a circle, picking the green leaves, chewing and talking through a poetic haze that is forgotten once it is uttered, but while uttered, the words are so profound that all who listen nod and murmur, yes, yes! Yes, the leaves create poetry, not the quick lust of the Nubian but the enduring lust that erases other memory; the green leaves make the body at ease, not ill at ease with tension for women. *Qat* leaves the mind pliant, gentle, quietly excited. He who chews is like he who feels the small waves with extended fingers next to the side of a dhow in placid waters. *Qat* is like liquid that flows along stroking the planks of the Dhow but not disturbing the tranquility of the placid sea, moving through it like the giant otter moves through the water, gliding as if without effort. *Qat.* A man would rather give up a meal than give up his cheek full of the qat leaves. One becomes an apt listener of stories fed by qat. Listening accumulates power. But, unhappily the power lasts only as long as the cheeks are full."

Tamrin paused.

A scribe now offers me qat. Yes! Where did he get it? It may help me tell my story more clearly and not repeat myself. Sita my wife from Hindush tells me that to chew pan with betel nut is much better than qat and it makes the teeth red, the mark of person who is sharp with money and women. The red-orange spittle of those who chew pan does not please me because it stains. The decks of four of my dhows have red splashes that penetrate the wood and I have now forbidden its use on my ships. Our coffee from the Arabic coast is better for stimulation. What is swallowed does not dirty the floor.

Tamrin looked up at the four scribes.

"Dhows. I have mentioned these boats already because they are part of my life. My fleet of seventeen ships rests in the harbor, right down there in Adulis, below me on the Arabian Sea coast in the small bay. Do you see the small islands? Yes, there is Adulis. Each ship is as different as my sons are different. Each is a different length, each put together by different creative hands, each with its own personality. Some are responsive to the wind, others sluggish; some big of belly to hold huge loads, others slender and shallow to move in the waters near the coast to catch the elusive sting rays; some with one triangular sail tied to a bent pole which can be taken down, others with two masts called *jelbut* and two sails, able to stay closer to the wind, to make the sweeping tacks when the wind is not directly behind. Two of my ships have a new construction called a keel, a projection that is weighted at the bottom of the ship that makes the ship more agile in the wind. Some ships, which were recently sewn and carefully tarred, were dry enough to carry bags of rice in their holds; others built carelessly leaked so badly that slaves did nothing but bail the boat day and night. There is a lesson here. A poorly built craft cannot be rebuilt once it has been put into water. An undisciplined child is a poorly built craft and cannot be reformed.

"In my childhood I became a friend, almost a son, to a ship builder named Arif. He built ten dhows for my father. I would run to the waterfront of the small stream where the shipyard was located and play on the teak planks and watch the men work. I would play with the curled shavings of the wood, make small boats out of scraps of wood, sleep in the shade of the dhow being constructed when the sun was hot and be enveloped in smells of the wood and the bitumen. Arif showed me how the planks were joined. Holes were drilled in planks as thick as my wrist and woven string made from coconut fibers, slow to rot, were strung through the holes and tightened down with such force that the strings could be strummed like a musical instrument.

"The planks were cut and planed so that each met the next with a groove and a ridge that fitted perfectly together, smeared with black bitumen. The ship builder constructed a frame outside to hold up these planks. He had no drawn plan. The ship's design was in his head and it was fashioned like a baby is in the womb, built from the very fibers of wood impregnated with the plan of the designer. The largest boat was as long as twenty of my steps, a marvel to behold as its sides were sewn together and fitted to the keel. Then the carpenters made the internal beams, which fit so tightly to the sides that they had to be hammered with wood mallets to fit in the slots and joined with swelling wood pegs. Passageways were created through which I ran and played. Rooms were made for storage of the cargo, and finally a deck was made of teak wood that was grey and smooth, each joint sealed with the bitumen-tar so carefully that the deck looked like a grey woven cloth with black threads. Through the deck, attached to the supports, masts were fitted, each so large and heavy that twenty men with ropes and block and tackle were required to pull it upright as it slid in place into the hold below, squared and fitting so perfectly that it squeaked as it slid into its hard black wood receptacle. Then cabins were placed on the deck, which had box-like structures on all sides that could be opened to hold possessions and on which mattresses were placed in their rolls during the day and unrolled for the sleepers. Rails of wood were put all around so sleepers would not fall off the platforms in heavy seas.

"Last of all, the part I liked the best, was the box built into the deck, a container made of slate and limestone slabs, the open fire pit, over which all the meals were to be cooked, water to be boiled, and feet to be warmed on cold nights. This firebox had a double wall, so that the inner wall could become hot enough to make water sizzle if spilt on it while the outer wall was cool to touch. Between the two there were spaces that were filled with sand dampened with seawater that warmed but never boiled. When the ship was finished, the master builder, Arif, slept an entire night in the cabin alone on his virgin ship and intoned the gods of the water and the land with his songs and chants. A young he-goat was slaughtered and its blood poured on the new boards of the front deck, staining them forever. Arif had slashed a line across one of the boards of the deck, drawing a circle with his knife. The goat was then roasted over the fire pit. At dawn, exactly at the time when the first sun rose above the water of the sea, Arif shouted to the slaves, who began to pull the ship, now resting on palm tree poles, to the water. The boat slid into the shallow slip and floated. No one spoke, as the boat first tasted seawater, which would be its home for life. Arif sat on the dhow alone and talked quietly to the dhow which was the child of his mind, which had been born through the labor of his love, which he would name on the second month the same as when a male child had a tiny snip the size of man's fingernail cut from the skin of his penis so that the sheath could be easily drawn back.

"This practice of circumcision was first brought to Ethiopia when Solomon sent his priests to teach the people about Yahweh. The ship had the blood of the lamb on its decks. This stained the circle he made by the circumscribing knife. All of Arif's ships were male. He bragged. 'Isn't he just the most beautiful craft you have seen? Wait until you see how he cuts through the water.'

"The newly built dhow bobbed on the shallow waters and absorbed the salt water, making the sewn planks swell, sealing the joints with a force so strong that even the tar oozed out on the inside of the ship. When the ship was ready for the master, my father walked up the gangplank with me, holding my hand and greeting the builder who then took us to every part of the dhow and explained everything, including the use of the ropes, the rudder, and how it was attached to the boat's steering arm.

"Arif blew on a conch shell and the workers gathered for a feast. At last an artist came, riding on a shallow dhow, and wrote in blue-purple copper and squid dye-ink "ARIF of DMI" on the front of the boat, using the script from south Arabia. No paint was applied to the wood of the boat, but over the letters, the wax of bees was smeared thickly, and then buffed with a cloth. That blue paint was made by the artist from blue coppers scrapings, mixed with crushed quartz and heated in a bare metal pan until almost red until the two fused. Then oil and the ink from octopus and squid were mixed in and heated again. The blue-black remained true. The rest of the hull was painted with liquid bitumen.

"Sails were now hoisted on which the same lettering had been written, and drummers began to beat their drums, and people danced and shouted, 'Arif, Arif.' My father's name was not used on the dhow, but rather the name of its father, the builder who had a 'dhow son.'

"My fleet of dhows carried trading goods back and forth across the Arabian Sea and along the coast as far as Hindush land. My herds of camels in Aksum and in Hodeida carried goods overland, north to the deserts of the Arabian Peninsula and beyond. What now? Regrets? Yes!

"My greatest regret now, is that I will no longer sit in my desert tent next to a wadi in an oasis and watch the sun go down as a flock of desert quail, or thousands of *quela* birds bank and come to the water to drink. While camels groan and complain, I listen to the humming of my woman as she works over a camp fire to prepare the coffee for me that is so strong and thick, sweetened with spoons of raw honey still in the wax combs. Regret? Yes. Not only the sands beckon me but the waves and the gentle motion of the dhow on calm seas with the entire heavens above as dolphins rise and pause to greet me with their mouths in a perpetual smile. My memories are what I carry. All else is vanity. All is vanity. At the moment of my death I will ask my body be taken in Arif's newest dhow, south along the coast to Zeila, the place of my father's birth, and there feed me to the sharks so that I become one with the sea. I am not a person of the land, but of the sea and water."

The sun set behind Tamrin's back. He called for the opium pipe and dismissed the scribes who each had come before him and touched his unharmed leg.

Tomorrow. Tomorrow. That is our greeting, and a lovely one. Tomorrow and tomorrow and tomorrow, and then ...

CHAPTER 2

You can't put fire in your pockets without burning your clothes.

Tamrin drifted off, the drug easing his pain. An hour later he lay half awake, imagining himself focusing on the gate of Sheba's palace.

The grey stone walls were fortified with buttresses every twenty feet. He thought it strange that two goats were using these as their playground, running up and jumping down, then racing to the top and racing down. He imagined that the Queen would be on the raised dais in the center of the courtyard attended by her faithful women.

How can I tell the story so that the world will know about her, about Menelik, her son from Solomon, and the glory of Aksum?

He began in a shaky voice.

Queen Sheba had a palace in Aksum. The stones for its construction were brought many miles distant from the hills by mule, each beast carrying two heavy stones in back packs, their legs quivering from the weight. Sheba had asked the merchant Tamrin to supervise the purchase and transport of all the building materials for her palace. She listed such things as the procurement of the foods needed for her household, the purchase of cloth, perfumes, *khol* for the eyelids, jewels for the goldsmiths to work with, in fact most of her provisions. Tamrin transported the Queen and her goods. The journey from the Queen's palace to Palestine took six months. She delayed another five months there, living with Solomon in his household's women quarters. She was not allowed to sit with him in public, or to eat with him during state banquets. He visited her in her chambers and brought her only the best fruits of the land, except that she did not show her face in public, nor did she visit the great temple where only the priests were allowed into the holy of holies, which housed the Ark of the Covenant.

Tamrin was not with her during this time, but was given a *sarai* where he and his men stayed as honored guests, waiting and waiting for the day of return to Aksum. Tamrin longed for Ethiopia, for Marib, for his great dhows.

Sheba returned to Aksum only after the birth of her child. The trip, riding first an ass, and then a camel for days on end, was difficult for her during her pregnancy. It is hard to prepare good food as one moves along in a caravan. She remained in Lower Egypt for two months resting in one of Tamrin's properties on the eastern bank of the Nile, *Al-bahr,* on the return trip. It was here that her son Menelik was born.

Tamrin organized all the pack animals, the riding mules and the camels to take her retinue to the Nile. He organized the dhows for the Nile trip, which transported the Queen to Upper Egypt and thence across the 'sea within the land' to Palestine. Menelik grew up in the very palace in Aksum for which Tamrin provided materials. This child, the Queen's only son, became as Tamrin's own child. Tamrin took him everywhere; Menelik rode on the saddle in front of Tamrin on his stallion. Menelik's own first steed was a gift from Tamrin, a small Arabian mare on which he learned his first skills as a horseman.

By the age of twelve, Menelik was entrusted to Tamrin's care frequently because of Tamrin's own sons who knew the skills of many weapons. He practiced with his own small bow until he became skilled and learned to use the sling, bringing down hares on the hunt. He swung the flying stone tied to leather thongs and brought down goats and an unhappy donkey. Menelik was clever with weapons of all types and learned them in Tamrin's camps.

The Queen wished to harden her son's muscles, to sharpen his mind, to enhance the speech of his tongue. His tongue was not as clever as his hands. Give him a bow with an arrow and he could shoot brilliantly, but ask him to remember the letters of our Ethiopic writing or write his thoughts down and he tires, losing interest. He was entrusted to Tamrin so that he could be schooled in the recording of numbers and mathematics, the knowledge of the stars, and the ancient texts from the Hebrews. He was not a student, but rather an athlete and a warrior at heart. The queen confided that she wished Menelik to visit his father when her son first showed signs of becoming a man, when he had his first night emission. Only then would he return to learn from Solomon.

Menelik was truly a child of beauty and talent, and because of his weakness with the pen, with numbers and writing and reading, he was vulnerable to the scribes and those who kept the accounts of his land. To be the ruler of a great country one must have eyes as sharp as the eagle and a mind as curious as the mongoose. Struggling with reading and numbers, he hired specialists to help him. When Menelik came of age, Tamrin planned an extensive journey to take trade goods on the Arabian

Peninsula and sail then south to Hindush lands. Queen Makeda of Sheba and Tamrin talked at length about his plans."

Tamrin paused, spat out a wad of *qat* and replaced it with new leaves, then sat back, almost panting from the fever; yet his mind seemed clear. He reached for the opium pipe to ease his pain. The scribes had returned and were waiting. Tamrin seemed to be in a trance now. His body swayed from left to right and he spoke in a new way, too fast for the scribes, almost in a chant.

"All at once, the Queen's expression changed. The Queen adjusted her scarf and waited until Tamrin looked into her eyes. Then she spoke.

"Tamrin, you must take Menelik with you on this trip across the sea. He will become a man during the journey, learn to defend and care for himself, learn the meaning of being an adult, not just a pampered prince, learn to use his hands as a member of a team, not just be served by the hands of slaves who hover near him and spoil him. Tamrin, you have observed him, he is as soft as a girl. Like most of us who call ourselves royal, whose descent is from a line of marriages to our own brothers or cousins, many of us are soft of body, yet too clever in the art of deception. Brother marrying sister makes for either a dull fool, or produces a cripple with a mind that is cruelly sharp. Menelik is Solomon's son and his mixed blood has given him strength. But his hands must become calloused, his muscles hardened, his mind stretched by overcoming problems and learning to observe. He must know the meaning of being hungry and thirsty, and most of all he must observe the deceit in the faces of smiling men, merchants and those who sell to the wealthy and powerful because of their own weaknesses for self satisfaction, who see weakness as a means to obtain silver in their pockets. Menelik accepts all around him without any suspicion, with a trust that frightens me. He is truly a pleasant child with a smooth temperament, but naive. To become a strong king he must learn to judge, mistrust, even reject and punish. He who cannot walk can hardly climb a ladder.

Queen Saba reached across the small table and touched Tamrin's hand with her fingertips. "Tamrin, you have been like a father to the boy for twelve years. Take him with you. He must not wear royal clothing. He must be treated as a crew member and be as your own son."

She sighed, knowing the frustration Menelik would feel to be treated as a commoner and how hard it would be for Tamrin to treat him, not like an adopted royal son, but as a deck hand, an apprenticed seaman. Tamrin would worry about the crew, who liked young boys.

Tamrin was quiet for a moment before he spoke.

"But the trip will be long and there are many dangers. There are storms at sea; there are periods of calm that empty the sails, and the crew pants for a small breeze and all on board sufferer terribly from the burning heat of the sun. There are often battles against pirates in other ships that attempt to steal and take over our boats. We must battle them! Then worst of all, there are the sicknesses that come from bad water, tainted food, and night fevers from bad evening air near the jungles. Travel, my queen is dangerous for a prince and I fear for his safety and life."

He stood and paced back and forth in concern.

"If I agree to take him along, it must be kept secret until days after the dhows sail away. If not, there are those who will be sorely tempted to try to kidnap him if he is away from the protection of the royal palace and the guards. He may not return if pirates attack us. Most expeditions lose men. Your son may be one who does not return."

She nodded in agreement.

"Do you fear for your own life and the lives of your four sons when you travel to your other home in Hodeida? Do you tremble with anxiety when you ride your camels across the Tihama and across the hills to Marib to visit your other wives?" She smiled knowingly as she looked at Tamrin, her close, most intimate companion and faithful servant for many years.

"Not for a moment, my queen. I trust in the strength of my arms, in the plans I make. People say that I am fearless, but it is not true. I am simply curious and seldom think about the dangers that exist. Generally, I don't trust people and expect that they will try to cheat me or steal from me. If I dwelt on these thoughts, I would stay in bed." He laughed. "But I believe that my life is already planned, that my destiny is known, and even the day of my death is preordained. So I can do nothing. Therefore, I live my days to the fullest and I live them without fear."

Queen Sheba limped and shuffled about the room, pacing the floor, moving from the window, then back to Tamrin. If we live in a cocoon of destiny, so does Menelik, whose very conception was a mystery of impossibility, fathered in a remote land by a man who had had nine hundred other women, so he says, and me, a virgin queen from a distant land of Ethiopia. If I believed what you said, then Solomon and I joined together only because of my thirst for a drink of water."

Her face took on a look of stern frustration.

"No. Solomon tricked me. He insisted that a drink was precious and that I had violated the agreement not to take anything of value from his country without permission." She sat heavily on a cushioned bench and played with a silk string. "Yes, a cocoon of destiny wraps us all around. So, I ask you to take my son and during the next year help him become a man who knows hardships, who knows disciplines of team work as a crew member, who knows the sting of punishment that comes with disobedience."

Sheba limped to the open arched window, looked out onto the hills near Aksum and sighed, regretting that Tamrin would be gone so long, and that their long conversations would be ending. She was a worrier and held no ideas of destiny. She would not allow her mind to think that some power had made the jackal bite her and change her life. She wrapped the silk thread tightly around one finger and watched the finger begin to turn blue. She released it and looked up into Tamrin's face which was serious, almost sad. Tamrin spoke.

"This trip will be a long one; first to Marib, then back to the coast through the scorching *Tihama* to my home in Hodeida and thence south along the coast where the sun beats down mercilessly and reflects back from the sea, where there are days of being becalmed because there is no wind in the sails, where appetites fail in spite of hunger, days when storms rage and the waves are so high that all we can do is seek a small harbor and anchor, wait out the rough weather so we can continue down the coast. The dhows are prisoners of the wind; it pushes them, pulls them and sometimes drives them where they don't wish to go. We can't steer into the wind, we can hardly steer across it or it would blow our boats over. At times like these all of us on the ships pull into ourselves, into our misery and seek a quiet spot in the shade of the drapes hung over the deck and avoid heated conversation, avoid even hot tea. On one trip a sailor on one of the boats quietly slipped over the side into the water. The Arabian Sea can be smooth as a mirror or turbulent as an unbroken horse. When we are forced to wait out storms and seek shelter on the coast, there will no longer be fresh *Qat* to chew, and the mind will become depressed. Along the coast we stop to trade. We drop our anchor and let the small boats come out to us because there are few deep harbors along the Arabian coast. We look forward eagerly to these times to get our supply of *qat* which renews the very fibers of the body so it can perform in danger as well as upon the sheets. Only tobacco and the hookah are then of any comfort. Only strong coffee stimulates the mind. Your son will complain bitterly and rue the day he became part of the crew."

Tamrin sucked on the stem of the bubble pipe and became quiet. "I think you are wise to ask your son to learn about the hard and often cruel lessons that nature and people teach. One of my own sons is clever with writing and reading. I will have him share a sleeping place with your son so that he will learn the power of how to keep records."

Queen Sheba nodded. "What better schooling for a soft prince, Tamrin. I will tell him this evening about our agreement. Being young, he will have nothing but excitement as he prepares, but I will warn him of the dangers and of his new role as the lowest of the crew members." She turned and looked at her old friend the merchant, whose hair was already becoming grey. She smiled and hobbled over to Tamrin, avoiding pressure on the foot that had been injured so many years earlier.

He looked up to this woman who knew hardship and who knew also the life of leisure and luxury, knew that whatever she demanded she received. He smiled and reached out his hands and put them toward her. She took them and placed them on her waist and moved closer and embraced his head against her abdomen. They both were quiet for a long moment.

"Tamrin, the Palestine King, Solomon had one great fault." She sighed. He could hear her stomach rumble.

"Yes, my queen what was that?" he said with his cheek still against her abdomen. He could hear her chuckle and he too began to laugh.

She backed up. "Great wisdom? No, just luck. He did not know how to talk with a woman. He spoke to me, at me, but never knew my mind at all. He never asked me my feelings; it never occurred to him. Perhaps he had two faults, come to think about it. His second was that he never knew deprivation, never suffered hunger, never baked in the sun, and never learned to be subservient to any but his own will and his own desires."

She sighed again. "Perhaps a third; he simply used his lovers, and because he was quickly satisfied, he was a poor musician; he only played his own tune. Yet, he was a fair man, a strong man and one of insatiable appetite, without *qat*. I guess I can forgive him for not becoming my friend and talking to me about his ideas. He solved riddles well but not the riddle of how a man and a woman become intimate friends."

She laughed and stepped toward the window. "He was considered so wise, yet he was unwise to allow his appetites to be served whenever he wished. If he had loved food instead of women, he would be huge and fat. He was cursed with the power of his own position, his own wealth, his own idea that he was god-chosen; this cursed him, because all around him were for his manipulation and use. His harem was filled with unhappy girls and women. Have you ever tried to share a sweetbread with a hundred people?"

Again she wrapped the silk around her finger and left it that way until it became swollen. She looked at the fine silk.

"When you are in the land of the Hindush, search for scarves and clothing that are of spun silk, made in a place they call Benares, garments so fine that you can draw a large cloth through my ring. Bring these to me and you shall have a royal reward."

"I would know the reward first before I seek out your prize. What will my reward be?"

He stood now and looked down at the woman, a good head shorter than himself. She looked at his face and nodded, this woman who, though queen and leader, was also lover of many men. She was fiercely independent and knew her needs and satisfied them.

"You said earlier, that our lives are already determined in the cocoon of destiny. So until you return, how can I speak of what I will decide at that time?"

"I will find such Benarsi scarves for you, if that is what is destined to be. I will return with your son whose mixed blood is like mine own, the mingling of the Ethiopian with the Sabaean, and my reward will simply be, woman, friend, and my queen, that I see your face again and that you, in good health will take my hands in yours when we meet. I will kneel; I wish to hear the rumblings of your stomach once again." He put his head back and laughed.

"Tamrin, your words are fragrant as frangipani blossoms. You must write down your thoughts and your adventures before your hair is white and your tongue becomes forgetful. Before I forget, I am going to ask Aagha, Menelik's personal bodyguard and sworn servant and protector to also go on the journey with you. He would give his life for the boy. But I do not know if he knows how to swim. Aaghaa can support your four sons in battle if there is danger. He was chosen to protect my son because he is athletic, quick and does not fear pain. May all the gods protect you. A year is a very long time. I will miss our long talks, our discussions about our neighbors the Nubians and the Egyptians, and even the feel of your hard hands in mine. It will be a long time, Tamrin."

"My queen, yes, a long time. But at least you will be visited by prince Aalam, by the Imam Berhanu who comes to teach you about the stars and numbers and perhaps Amare, the tall handsome musician who is usually here whenever I come to visit you. I do not think you will be lonely. It is I who will suffer, stuck on a rocking, hot, crowded, stuffy, smelly dhow for months on end with a prince." He tried to look sad. "When I think of you with Amare, I will become very lonely."

She laughed. "When I think of Dehta, I become lonely. How many coastal towns did you say you would visit, more than twenty? Of course there will be no great feasts set out for you, at which dancing girls will sway and move their hips and invite you with their brown or blue eyes. Of course you will suffer." She laughed heartily. "Tamrin, did you not tell me that you had a wife in Hodeida called Dehta who will be hungry for your embraces? I can't imagine that you will lack affection. I have never met this beautiful talented, young woman, Dehta, but somehow, I don't like her. You said she played the lute? I dislike her." She chuckled and motioned for him to leave. "When your ships are loaded and ready to sail, see me once again, I will have a small feast prepared for you, and your crew, right here, and we will let priests invoke their various gods with sacrifices, just in case one or another of these is a friend of the real master of destiny and, the force that weaves the cocoons of our fate. Go well. Just to be safe I will have all the priests perform ceremonies and make sacrifices for your safety. Will one bull be enough to slaughter on the altar?" She watched his face. "Even the teacher that came from Solomon, the miserable priest called Kopt who insists there is only one god, may request more. His followers love sacrifices and roasted meat."

"My queen, since we are unsure of what force we are seeking protection from, let us just have a feast of an immature ram, roasted on a spit which we will consume totally ourselves. Let the priests find their own sacrifices elsewhere. If the cocoon of life has already been decided there is nothing we can do to alter it." He laughed, bowed and left.

Menelik stood before his mother, his robe half off, tied around his waist because of the heat. "Yes, mother. Aaghaa told me you wanted to speak to me. Before you do, I want to tell you that it was not I that tipped over the lamp last night. Well, in a way, but a fruit bat had entered the room and I was swinging a stick at it and the stick hit the stand on which the lamp was placed..."

"Stand still. Pull your robe up over your shoulders. Look at me, at my eyes. What would you think if I told you that you will be absent from the royal court, from this palace, and have to live the life of a servant for an entire year, during which time you will not have servants to hover near you, and during that time you will not have your juice of pomegranate nor fresh mangoes, nor see my face?" She watched his expression change from disbelief to fear, then to stubborn anger.

"I would say that I would have to do as you say, but that your punishment is unfair because of an accident I had. I will say that ..." and now tears formed in his eyes which he hid by turning his head.

"Sit down and listen. I was not speaking about a punishment. Tamrin will soon be leading a new trading expedition to the other side of the Arabian Sea in his dhows, with his four sons and a number of sailors on five of their ships. They will face terrible hardships, have to fight against pirates, endure hunger and pain as they travel. Tamrin has agreed with my request that you be taken along, not as a royal prince, but as an apprentice, a servant if you will, to learn the art of sailing, the ways of men at war, the ways of the merchants who bring wealth to themselves and this kingdom." She smiled as she watched the changing expressions on his young and beautiful face.

"He has agreed to take me along? How long will the journey take?" His voice quivered. "Will I sleep in his deck cabin?"

"No! You will sleep with the crew on the open deck. More

than a year. And yes, I have asked him to take you along as a ship's apprentice to learn about the sea, about a life of discipline, about yourself. Apprentices and crewmembers sleep on the deck, not in cabins. Do you think you are strong enough to be able to do this, to be away from the palace for a year, away from me?" Now her eyes began to fill with tears.

He stood taller now and nodded. "Yes. I will learn to live without fresh pomegranate juice and mangoes. What is an apprentice?" His voice cracked.

"An apprentice is one who learns by watching, doing, serving and obeying a master. An apprentice is the lowest rank in all the occupations, in the army, in the navy, in the ships that sail, in places that weave carpets. An apprentice becomes a craftsman only after he has proven his ability to learn, to act as a member of a team. Can you be one?" She was shaking her head now, as if this soft, spoiled prince would never be able to be what she had described.

"Yes. I will do it! Tamrin will teach me. Thank you." He bowed from the waist and turned to leave.

"Wait! You must teach yourself. You have played with foolish children of the royal court who fawn upon you. You must not be like them. He who lives with an ass brays like an ass. No one can force you to learn. You have to observe, obey, work, struggle and become a new person. I want you to live with tigers of the sea. Tamrin will run the ship, not be a tutor to a royal highness." She shook her head. "I will die, hopefully of old age, but I will surely die and you, Menelik, will become the first emperor of Ethiopia. Your blood father Solomon will soon die, grieving about the treachery of his son Rehabohm, but you carry his blood. After this trip, if you are a new person, a young man, not a boy, you should go and visit your father, take that terrible journey all the way to Palestine, but not without Tamrin. Your father was considered wise. But he was unwise to follow the gods of all his concubines. Women, young beautiful women, can persuade the most powerful of men to actions that are, frankly, stupid. It is history; your father now struggles with the intrigue within the palace between his appointed successor king, Jeroboam and his followers and his own son. He may well die, out of favor with his god Yahweh, and go to be with his fathers, a tired, confused, and unhappy man with his kingdom split between his son and his appointed successor Jeroboam. You must go there before that happens. When a man has too much of food, wine, and women, he becomes weak. It has been said that Solomon talks incessantly about many things now that he is in his old age. His mind is confused with a life of lust, wine and self indulgence. But you must see his temple and the Arc of the Covenant on which two gold angels sit. You must bring back the wisdom that first made Solomon to be called the wise one, and you are his namesake. Perhaps his wisdom was great when he was young. His greatest weakness as far as I can see is that he lacked self-discipline and disliked advice from others. He was preoccupied with women. But he was truly a beautiful man, of face and body when I knew him. You resemble him, all except for your color, which is from me. He wishes to see you before he dies."

She had never spoken about the private life of his blood father, and now, in spite of herself, in her voice there was anger and sarcasm. "Solomon gave up his belief and obedience to his one god, Yahweh, and romped his way through the beds and ceremonies of the gods of his women, creating jealousies and hatred among them and especially the priests and prophets of Yahweh."

Thinking of him and the time she spent with him, she hobbled back and forth, almost forgetting the lad who sat and watched her. She caught his eyes and took a deep breath, remembering why she had called the boy to her.

"When you return from this trading expedition led by Tamrin, the merchant of Aksum, you will understand that ruling means knowing what the lives of your people are like, knowing their struggles; and that will make you wise like your father was as a younger man. Have you ever observed my face when generals or common citizens come before me with tales of injustice, with rage or simple supplications?" He nodded.

"So what did you learn when you remember how I treated all these people?"

Menelik thought for a moment. "You did not smile, you did not frown, and you did not become angry. Your face was calm and your eyes fierce as a lion's as you stared at them."

"So what did you learn from how I acted as Queen?"

He looked at the ceiling as if to find the answer there. She waited until he looked into her eyes. "Did you find the answer on the ceiling?"

He shook his head. "I was just thinking."

"Look at the face and eyes of one to whom you are talking. Don't look around, at your hands, at the floor, out the window or the ceiling. It tells the one you are talking with that you are unsure, immature, and childish. Look at my eyes when you give me your answer."

Menelik looked at his mother now, at her eyes, but he could not read them, they were staring at him, waiting.

"I learned…I learned that the ruler, the Queen, does not reveal her thoughts, pity, or desire, anger or past friendship. I learned that commoners and even the highest general must be… must be in awe, must be a bit fearful of a ruler."

"Who is the ruler on a dhow who has the power of life and death?"

"There is no Queen or King on the ship. Just common sailors."

"You are wrong! When a ship is on the high seas the captain in command has all authority, to punish, to kill, tie up a person in chains and to reward excellent duty as well. Tamrin is that man. The ship is like a small kingdom. Who is the lowest in that kingdom?"

He pursed his lips, looked into her eyes. "The cook?" She shook her head. Without remembering he glanced at the ceiling, then back to his mother's eyes, embarrassed. "The one who cleans the refuse pail where filthy things are put to be thrown overboard."

"You are correct! That person will be you." She did not smile, just stared at the future emperor. "My words to you about going on a year-long ocean voyage sounded like fun, an adventure, because you cannot forget that you are royalty, spoiled and pampered by everyone, including me. Go on this trip as a boy, return as a man, a future ruler." Now there were tears in her eyes. "You may go now. I will call you in a week. Prepare yourself. There is one caution. This is a test. You must keep this secret! You may only go on this trip if you swear to me that you will not tell others, your friends, the servants, the maids, any one, except Aaghaa about this plan and only with him a week from now. He will have been foresworn, on the pain of death, to silence as well. This is to prevent evil men from planning to capture you. Do you swear?"

He nodded, yet his mouth could hardly form the words of agreement. He had been so eager to share this news with his friend Amin and the entire palace court and now he must be silent and say nothing. "I swear," he croaked.

"We are shielded here in the palace grounds from the rest of the world around us. We have all the best foods prepared for us without having to think about going to a market and buying the animals to butcher, buying the fruit we eat. Outside in Aksum there are men who are desperate for a good meal, eager to find ways to get money, even kill for it. Of this you know nothing. You have not understood that there are acts such as murder, demanding ransom, abducting boys and girls to sell as slaves; there is rape, pillage, theft, and simple cheating and lying."

She looked at her pretty son, so tall and almost girlish and worried.

"You may have heard gossip in the palace about men who become the lovers of boys like you. This will not make much sense to you now, but many men love young pretty boys better than women. Perhaps you will know more when you return from your journey. You have sworn to be silent. If I hear that there is gossip about your going on a long journey, you will not be aboard Tamrin's dhow when it sails! One of the most difficult skills of a ruler is to keep his own council, and that is very hard to learn. As future Emperor, you will have to listen well and also keep your mouth shut. A thoughtful face is superior to a blabbering childish mouth. You begin now! Your voice is beginning to change. Your life too will now change from that of an irresponsible child to that of an emperor within a decade." She walked to the lad, now as tall as she, and placed her hand on his head. "Ebna-la Hakim, I will miss you. You will be called Ebna. Live up to your name, son of a wise man. 'Gossip and bragging are weaknesses of kitchen women and insecure fools.' Your first test will be to keep a secret and not let even your best friend know what you are going to do. That is power."

CHAPTER 3

Don't be wise in your own eyes.

Menelik/Ebna wandered around his room and looked at his possessions, at his chest containing beautiful clothes, at the carvings in the wood panels behind his bed.

His bed was soft with its mattress of fluffed cotton, and the bright cloth spread on it was inviting. He lay back; he imagined having to sleep on a deck on a simple mat, imagined having to eat the food that the crew members eat, and dreading the idea that he would be as a servant to Tamrin, the master of the dhow, that Tamrin would be the ruler. Most of all he dreaded dumping the refuse container.

It is strange to think about something else, some other way of being, he mused. *I have never known anything except this. I remember riding with Tamrin on the back of a camel down the streets of Aksum and seeing boys my age running alongside us, shouting, boys with tattered clothing, bare footed and dirty. I remember looking down at them and knowing that the world was filled with many poor people and that was how it was. There are the poor, there are the rich, there are the powerful, and there are the weak. From my perch high on the back of the camel I knew* there was a separation that existed and would always exist. I was the son of the Queen and nothing could change that fact.

I remember that we passed a group of beggars sitting near the entrance to the gate of the palace. Usually I just glanced at them then looked away, but that day I stared down at one of them and saw that it was a girl. Her face was beautiful even though her hair was matted. Her legs were thin as sticks and seemed to be broken with the feet at right angles to her legs. Our eyes met and she did not look away. She raised her hand and saluted me and smiled.

I cried out, "Tamrin, give me a gold coin to toss to the girl there. Hurry. We are almost past."

"Master Menelik, if you toss one tiny copper coin, or one cowry shell to the girl we will be besieged by all the beggars. The next time we ride on the camel we will have an army of them following us. No. No gold coin now master." Tamrin urged the camel to move forward more quickly. "The poor and unfortunate we will always have with us. The ruler of every land knows that it is impossible to give succor to every unfortunate, to every beggar. To rule well is to find ways to make the entire kingdom prosper, to make the farmers produce more, to build monuments that employ the poor so they can have coins in their hands that they have earned. A ruler plans for more than his own feeling of generosity. Wait. Anticipate the good so that you may enjoy it."

I looked back over my shoulder. The girl was still watching us and again we caught each other's eyes. Her face was not sad. It was peaceful and gentle. She is the first girl that I ever loved. Her face comes to me when I am alone in my own room. I yearn to talk with her, to help her, to feed her.

Tomorrow is the day! I shall be dressed like a sailor. How will it feel to walk with others to the waterfront disguised as a commoner? Will I walk past the same beggar girl? I will look for *her and as I pass I will throw her a ... what can I give her? I am Menelik, yet I am a pauper as well. I have no coins or wealth of my own. Perhaps that silk cloth, there, the one draped over the toys of my boyhood. Yes. I will bunch it up and carry it with me and as we pass I will toss it to her.*

My room is dark now except for the single oil lamp that is burning. Shadows on the wall look like jinns moving. Will there be lights on the deck where I will sleep? It is stiflingly hot in the room; there is no breeze. I cannot sleep. Tomorrow!

It was dawn when Menelik left the palace courtyard with a small group of men and walked toward the distant dhows at the harbor. He craned his neck, looking around for the beggar girl, and saw her. At least he thought it was she. Yes, she lay on her back, legs misshapen and stretched out, face toward the sky. The memory etched itself in Menelik's mind. What was her name? It must have been Miriam. She died gazing at the sea of stars. Yes, Miriam, star of the sea.

CHAPTER 4

Don't withhold payments to him who loaned you money.

The unbearable, sizzling, debilitating summer months were almost at an end. The residents of Aksum looked to the skies for signs of a shift in the winds, which had been blowing from the southwest for weeks, stifling and humid. In far away Hindush land, the fertile area that surrounded the valley of the Indus River, rain fell. The monsoons were now pouring rain across the country bringing relief, but bordering the Arabian Sea the seasonal change that brought winds across the cooling landmass of coastal Ethiopia and Aksum were still; the monsoons were late.

Five dhows rocked on the calm sea, anchored off the coast in a small, protected bay. Pelicans clustered together and upended in the water seeking a school of small fish; terns and cormorants dove below the surface to catch their shiny silvery prey. Below, dolphins circled, bunching the school of baitfish toward the surface, and then dashed in to catch an elusive mouthful. Fishermen were hurrying to the site, hopeful of getting a net across the water above the small anchovy fish called wayra.

On board the dhows the crews were busy loading and tying down equipment. Each of Tamrin's sons was in charge of a dhow, which had its own crew of five or six depending on the size of the ship. Tamrin's dhow was the largest and the only ship with two masts. Some of the sails were flexible mats of tightly woven jute fiber, tied to ropes at the base of the mast, which could be used to pull the sails up and in place. Others boats had sails of linen smeared with mustard oil to make them more water repellent.

One crewmember of each of the dhows was called a mast-monkey. Selected because of his climbing skill, he used his feet and toes to mount the mast, hang to the rigging, tie up the ropes of the sails to the top of the mast, and make adjustments in the rigging. Most of the adult men could mount the masts in an emergency; however, it took a great deal of effort and strength to do so. The mast monkeys, though, could shimmy up the poles, their toes holding to the large knots on a rope tied to the mast and walk across the cross beams with ease and agility. Few of these young boys lasted more than three of four years in their jobs aboard dhows, not because of injury, or accidents but because of their declining ability to climb as they put on weight. In their prime they scampered up the masts to affix ropes, tie on sails, and repair minor damages even during storms when the sails whipped back and forth dangerously. A few of these youngsters were not only agile and strong but had been chosen because of their beauty, fair skin, and flashing smiles.

Times on the boats were often boring especially when, becalmed, the dhows, like squat old market women, sat motionless and flat bottomed on the water without wind. The heat was terrible. The water felt warm and smelled salty. At such times the men became restless and occupied themselves with games of *dara,* moving round seeds or stones around the carved depressions of the wood board to capture their opponents' stones. Others sat at the back of the ship and fished with hand lines, while others repaired sails and clothing with curved needles of copper and flat thin knife-like iron needles or crochet hooks of ivory.

The captain chose a mast monkey on each of the ships not only for ship's work, but also to perform body massages using fragrant oils. For this they would be rewarded separately by crewmembers with special food or a few coins.

The master of the dhow kept a compartment in the rectangular shed built on the deck as his personal cabin and sleeping place. Other crewmembers lashed matting across areas of the deck to spread out their mats and sleep, except during storms when no one slept. Some slept on top of the cargo in the hold, keeping the lids of the hatches open so the ship's cats could come and go in their constant pursuit of rats. But the ship's master kept a special place by his side for the mast monkey to sleep with him in the cabin.

Tamrin's mast monkey had been with him for three years. His name was Adesh, a name often given to girls. He was born in southern Arabia near Aden. His mother was of Indian descent and his father was an Arabian merchant to whom Tamrin had paid a shekel of gold for the lad. The boy was beautiful to behold, with large almond eyes, long ebony hair and a swinging gait, that to the beholder from behind, appeared to be that of a girl walking. Yet Adesh was all muscle and sinew when strength was required. The crew commented upon his appetite for food. In spite of the huge amounts of food he consumed, he remained slim, alert and taut, ready to move even when he stood idle. His special talent was cooking and preparing curries of all types, recipes he had learned from his Hindush mother. He was the only crewmember who did not carry a weapon. The entire crew spoiled him with gifts, smiles, and affectionate strokes. They watched out for his safety during times of battles with pirates or thieves. In reality, Adesh's "family" was the crew of Tamrin's ship.

At each port of call when the crew went ashore, Adesh never walked alone, but was accompanied by a couple of armed crew members. When fishing with a hand line, Adesh wore a pair of fingerless gloves made of sewn kid leather, which covered his palm so the string would not cut his hands. Those hands were agile and strong, hands that could hold on to ropes, hang from cross stays and untie the most difficult knots.

On the day before the departure of the small flotilla of dhows, Adesh hooked a shark. The concerned crew gathered around him as he struggled to bring it in. It was a hammer head more than six feet in length and very strong. Adesh let it take out some of the line wrapped around a short piece of bamboo pole, but then glanced back at those watching and asked for help. Two of the crew came to his assistance and struggled with the shark until it tired. Eventually it was gaffed and brought on the dhow amidst much shouting as it flopped around, it's strange eyes at the end of stalks on its head. The tail of the shark was hacked off and handed to Adesh. He smiled and hopped to the mast with the huge tail fin and nailed it onto the mast as high as he could climb, at the same time pulling off a smaller dried shark tail which had been caught by another crew member on the previous trip. As he did so, Tamrin returned from his residence in Aksum and all of the crew gathered around to tell him the tale of the capture of the huge hammerhead shark.

"Adesh, you have your work cut out for you, slicing up the meat from this fish and drying it on the ropes, and I mean those high above us. The sails are ready, so today you can work on this but tomorrow before dawn we set sail. While you hang shark meat to dry, check all the rigging, every knot. The winds are now starting to blow from the northeast."

Adesh nodded and again glanced over his shoulder to the other four sailors who unsheathed their skinning knives and began to cut up the fish. Already on the dock children with small baskets had gathered, waiting for handouts of the shark's fins, internal organs, intestines, liver and kidneys. Behind them were stray dogs waiting, and on deck two of the ship's cats sat quietly on top of the roof of the cabin watching hungrily.

"What is in its stomach?" asked Adesh.

A sailor slit open the stomach, and everyone stood back as a newborn baby, already half digested, slithered out onto the dock. Children gathered around staring at the gruesome sight. One of them shouted, "It is the slave woman's dead child. It was dead when it was born last night and she threw it into the ocean. My friend told me!"

Crew members pushed the fetus and offal into the water at the edge of the dock, and fish splashed in the water eating the remains. Adesh took pieces of thinly sliced shark meat sprinkled with sea salt and red pepper in a shoulder sling basket made of palm fronds. He scampered up the aft mast and began to hang the meat on cross-ropes to dry. The sticky meat became glued to the ship's lines in the heat. Adesh worked for an hour carefully putting out long strips to dry. The cats watched, waiting for him to come down. Though already sated with the scraps they had eaten, the cats climbed up the halyard on the mast toward the meat. Adesh jumped up and pulled one of the cat's tails until it tumbled to the deck. The other jumped away to safety.

With torches and lanterns lit, goods were brought to the five ships, first trade goods-- ivory tusks, rhino horns, gold from the mines of Africa in the south, leopard skins, cages of multi-colored wild birds, small monkeys and young baboons in cages, and coffee in jute sacks, almost worth its weight in gold. Rhino horns were prized. Handles of the curved knives, the jambiya carried by every Yemeni man, were made of rhino horn. The horns were sold to healers, medicine men who ground up the horns that cured half a dozen diseases and moreover, enlivened men who took the powder.

Next, in the spaces up forward toward the higher section of holds in the bow, foodstuffs for the journey were stored; onions, grains of many kinds in sacks; fruits, beans of various types, spices and oils for cooking. Last of all, the crew brought on board fresh water poured into animal skins that had already been used for fresh water storage. Each dark colored skin bag contained enough water for one man for a month. On the main deck in the shade, one of these bags was tied to the main mast so that anyone who needed a drink could tip the skin sack, untie the spout made from a skinned out leg, and direct the water into his mouth.

Wine skins of smaller size were stored last, filled by the merchants on the night of departure. These skins contained drinking wine and strong distilled spirits for antiseptic use.

The only crockery brought on board was large bowls for serving cooked food. Each person on board was issued a personal wood plate and wood spoon made of hard woods from acacia trees. These were cleaned after use, rinsed in seawater and stored with personal items. Food spoiled rapidly in the hot moist air and great care was taken to clean utensils carefully. Cooking pots and pans were scrubbed first with a paste made from seawater and ashes, then rinsed in seawater and sun-dried.

Each ship kept two female cats on board. These were put into the cargo hold each night to hunt for mice or rats. Vermin boarded the ships by running in on the mooring ropes, and in spite of copper discs attached to the ropes; some were able to get through. Rodents also arrived on board in the cargo itself, hiding in the bottom of baskets or in food containers. Cats were important because the rats gnawed many things, including the leather water containers and coiled ropes.

In the middle of the night the crews settled in, all except

Tamrin who awaited the final new crewmember, Menelik, who had a new name, Ebna. He was brought to the ship by his trusted servant and protector, both of them in disguise, dressed as commoners. Ebna carried his own clothing and personal items, the first time he had ever carried a load of any kind. The sack hung on his back and felt very heavy. He regretted having taken so many personal items, particularly two small, heavy statues from his room in the palace, statues of Hindush goddesses that Tamrin had given him as gifts from previous trading journeys.

"Welcome aboard my ship called Arif Dmi. You have been designated a place on the deck where the two mats are rolled just in front of the cabin, there. I will speak with you tomorrow. We will use a nickname for you, Ebna-la Hakim. Standing over there, is a person you will soon know well. His name is Adesh. He has been working on my ships for three years. If you have any problems about how to clean yourself, where to relieve yourself or when the food is served, ask Adesh. In fact, he will welcome your assistance after each meal is cooked, washing up the clay and metal pots, a task he has done alone for three years. Now he has you as his assistant, Ebna. Adesh will show you the ship and teach you many of his skills, such as how to fish and keep secrets. That skill on a boat is very important. Listen. Listen again. Speak little. Listening accumulates power."

The dhow, called in lower Arabic a *baghlah,* boldly carried the name of its ship builder, Arif Dmi, in deep blue letters, now slightly faded after decades of use. It was the third to leave the protected area of anchorage. Its foresail was lifted in place and caught a slight breeze from the north east as it pulled out into the Arabian Sea, soon followed by the last two ships of the fleet, badan, smaller craft with single sails, but with shallower drafts. These would be the first two of the five ships assigned to approach the coast. Crew members cast weighted lines with knots to determine the depth within the small sheltered bay near Hodeida, their first destination.

Each of the masters of the ships, Tamrin's four sons, carried charts, on which the major features of the Ethiopian and Arabian coastlines had been marked. On these charts were notations regarding where the sun rose in the morning and where it set at night during different periods of the year. Also charts indicated the location of the "pole star" or "faithful star."

Last of all, each master had with him an instrument called a *kamal*. On all five dhows the master kept this instrument. It was made of horn smaller than a human palm. It consisted of a rectangle of bone or horn through which a hole had been drilled in the direct center through which a line was threaded. Knots were tied at intervals on this line called *isba*. The operator of the *kamal* held the rope in his teeth and the lower edge of the instrument was placed on the horizon while the horn was adjusted to move along the string until it touched the pole star. The knot was then noted and the *isba* indicated the altitude of the star relative to the position of the boat and the horizon. Onl papyrus maps, locations were noted and what the *kamal* reading would be at that latitude at certain times of the year.

For the most part, each ship master would attempt to keep in visual contact with the other dhows, but if driven off course or a sail failed, then each would make its way across the narrow waters between the coast of Aksum and the Arabian peninsula, a journey, moving due east, of two to four days, depending on the winds. Once having reached the coastline, all the dhows would congregate at a given location, such as a small coastal village, and then proceed on their southeastern journey along the coast, keeping in sight of land. When the ships came into the Arabian Sea they would continue to hug the coast all the way to the land of the Hindush where jewel-turbaned rajas in the area reigned over small kingdoms, and battled with armor-plated fighting elephants. Along this coastal area the ships would seek out the Indus River as it poured into the sea. Here, in the rainy monsoon season, mud and sediment poured into the sea through the Indus River and colored the sea for miles, extending far beyond the coast. To the south was a terrible desert, the *sindh,* and beyond that, unknown lands, the ends of the earth.

One of the problems each master faced on this journey was keeping his ship moving forward to the east and south, riding the cross winds. The square sails of the dhows were moveable to the extent that one corner could be lowered and the sail slightly tilted on the mast to catch the crosswinds. Tamrin's double masted ship had greater reach than the other ships and also used a small square sail set out at the bow when the wind was from behind. In the Red Sea, known for its violent storms, and in the Arabian Sea, where the weather was variable and unpredictable, the dhows were often at the mercy of the elements.

Most dreaded were periods of prolonged calm when hardly a breeze stirred the surface of the water. Everyone suffered! Devastating heat and humidity literally cooked ships on the reflective surface of the water. Each dhow had a pair of long oars, which could be used in an emergency or during the entry to bays when the crew attempted to anchor. Using these long oars required two crew members on each oar. The work was grueling. On Tamrin's ship the oars were positioned amidships and operated through ports in the hull. These ports were kept closed and sealed most of the time, but were used when the ship had to be maneuvered in difficult situations. From outside, the ports were not visible, as the wood covering the openings was the same as the hull of the ship, and even had the appearance of planks sewn together with coconut fiber rope like the rest of the ship.

Dhows also faced Aribi pirates, whose small ships with lateen sails and powerful oars would harass trading vessels along the coast, trying to capture them for their cargo. In some districts pirates would threaten the ships and require their captains to pay a tax in order to carry on without being attacked. Each dhow, therefore, had trained its crew to fight and repel pirates with Ethiopian bows of wood three cubits long which were hardened in fire. The arrows had quartz, metal and even glass shard points. They were made of bamboo and had feathers placed on three sides to create straight flight. A few dozen arrows were made with kapok fiber wrapped around with cord, dipped into burning tar, and used to shoot at the sails of the Aribi ships.

Unfortunately, pirate ships also had the same type of fire arrows and threatened to use them if their demands were not obeyed. Young Nubian and Ethiopian boys were trained to use these long bows and various types of arrows. Others used slings, which, if handled correctly, were deadly at close quarters.

Finally, crews were trained in the use of spears and swords. Sharp bronze axes were set out to sever any lines thrown with hooks onto the decks of the dhows. If attacked, all five dhows formed a united front against the pirates. Pots of tar were heated to the point of smoking and held as a last resort if pirates attempted to climb aboard the ships. The tar was scooped in hollow coconut shells attached to small wood handles and sprayed onto any who attempted to board. The sight of two or three tar throwers on a ship standing ready to fend off pirates was an effective deterrent in most cases. Tamrin's ship still bore splashes of such tar from previous battles. These marks alone halted pirates who were otherwise willing to risk much for material gains. Attacks in the face of such defenses seemed suicidal.

Often small boats drew close to the dhows and hailed them, asking to do trade while at sea, holding up items of value, their crews smiling and friendly. The rule aboard all Tamrin's dhows was not to drop sail or trade at sea. To do so could result in a treacherous pirate attack.

Menelik had to get used to being called *Ebna-la-Hakim* by his new acquaintance Adesh, a lad four years older than he.

"Does your father live in Aksum?" shouted Adesh from the top of the mast where he stood adjusting lines.

"No, I have never seen him. My mother said he may even be dead, but I don't think so. She only said that he was a hakim, a wise man. My mother told me she was only one of many, many wives he had."

One of Ebna's tasks was washing the soiled decks after goods had been brought aboard the day before. He scooped water in wood buckets from the sea, splashed residue off the decks and swept the debris away.

"Where did you live in Aksum?" shouted Adesh from above.

"Near to the Queen's summer palace. Where is your home?"

"I live on this ship. This is my home. I have not seen the home of my birth for more than four years. The master, Tamrin, purchased me when I was a boy as old as you." He held to the knotted rope with his toes and hands as he made his way down the mast and jumped to the deck. "Tamrin has told me that you will help me to prepare the food and clean up the pots. We have only one main meal in the day, which is just after sunset. I cannot cook in the darkness so all the food must be made at least an hour before sunset. I will show you."

He motioned for Ebna to follow him to the back of the ship where there was a fire pit, an opening in the deck for a stone lined box where there was a fire and metal bars placed to hang the cooking pots. "Here is where I do the cooking. Do you know what charcoal is?"

"No. I have never seen it."

"This stuff. You must come from a very poor home if your

mother never uses charcoal. It's made from slightly burned wood that turns black. It makes a very hot fire and does not smoke as much as wood. See, there are some coals still glowing. I will put fresh coal on the hot coals and they will all begin to glow in a short time. Then we will make the food for the day. I have a fishing line. We will sit at the back of the ship, called the stern, and try to catch enough fish for a feast tonight. I caught a shark last week."

Ebna nodded and kept quiet. He had seen fishermen trying to catch fish but had never held a fishing line.

Adesh attached a piece of squid to a copper hook. "These hooks are very costly and come from Egypt or are made by the Hindush people. The line I have here is made of silk, six strands carefully braided and woven together. Near the hook a small thin piece of hollow bamboo has been slid onto the line so that the teeth of larger fish do not cut the line, which is protected by the tube that way. I was lucky with the shark I caught. The hook was only snagged on the side of its mouth and its teeth did not cut the line. See!"

He pointed to the hundreds of strips of shark meat drying in the rigging.

"Wear these gloves. The line can cut your fingers or palms if the fish is large and moves quickly. Like this." He demonstrated how to wear the soft leather glove.

Ebna put the gloves on and waited. Adesh held the spool of thread wound around a bamboo section tilted slightly up so that when he cast the line it would unravel from the small bamboo reel. He stood sideways and swung the weighted bait round and round, then let it fly. It fell far behind the ship and sank down. "You hold the bamboo with two hands and if a fish grabs the line you pull hard, then begin to wind the thread onto the wood spool. If the fish is too large, hold it like this in your palms so it can rotate and let the silk line out, then you squeeze the bamboo with your hands to slow it down like this."

Ebna held the section of bamboo tightly in his fingers waiting for a fish to bite the hook. He waited for a long time and began losing interest. When a fish took the bait he almost lost the spool of thread. To him it seemed like a huge fish because of its weight. Adesh took the spool and tried to wind the thread, but then decided to wait and let the fish get tired. He handed the wood spool back to Ebna.

"Just hang onto the spool and the fish will swim around; it is not very big, perhaps as long as my arm. I think it is a small shark."

Ebna felt the fish move first in one direction then another. Then he tried to wind the silk thread around the short section of pole by using his hand to hold the line and wrap it. Adesh took the spool from him and, holding tight to one end with both hands, twisted the thread around in small circles, thus wrapping the line on the crude spool without having to actually hold the line itself. When the fish was on the surface, near the boat he handed the tackle back to Ebna.

"Keep winding it, and then pull it up out of the water onto the deck."

The fish was soon flopping on the deck. "It is what we call a slit-eyed shark. This is not full grown but it is very good to eat. We will make a stew of it for the crew tonight and put in dried onions, flour, red pepper, and palm oil. Is this your first fish?"

Ebna nodded and bent closer to examine the eyes of the shark, which in fact did have eyes in a slit on the side of its head. The pupils seemed to be black lines.

"Kill it and clean it. I will cut it up into six portions."

"How do I kill it? I have never killed anything before."

Adesh shook his head in impatience, took a skinning knife from a scabbard, stepped on the body of the small shark and, leaning over, impaled the fish's head. The fish shuddered and then lay still.

"Well, I will show you how to clean a fish this time. From now on, that will be your job, to catch, kill and clean all the fish. Watch. It is obvious you are an orphan. Your father taught you nothing!"

He placed the knife in the vent of the fish and in one motion slit it up its belly, keeping the blade just under the rough skin. Then he reached down and with one motion pulled out the entrails and liver, gutting the fish.

"Like that. This fish has no scales, just a rough skin which I will cut off. Other fish have scales that must be cleaned off. Catch another fish."

The wind was favorable, and the five ships moved as one, largest in front and the other four following, spread out within hailing distance of each other.

After the crew had eaten spicy fish stew with *enjira*, sour, soft bread, they all sought out their bedrolls placing them where they could catch a breeze. The sun set astern, wind was in the sails, and the crew relaxed. Two oil lamps were lit and set up, consisting of a ceramic bowl with a spout in which a wick was inserted. These were placed within a shallow ceramic dish so that in case there was a spill the oil did not fall onto the deck. Lamps were set in front of shiny silver plates so the light would be reflected backward. The plates helped keep the moving air from blowing out the flame and acted as a crude windshield. When viewed from behind the dhows could be seen at a good distance if the weather was fair, seas were calm, and rain didn't fall. Other ships behind the largest dhow could steer in its wake. The smallest at the back of the little flotilla was the fastest and had the shallowest draft. From time to time the helmsman would race forward to one of the other ships and shout a message across the water, then circle and return to his place in line. This ship had special orders, that if pirates attacked, it would run forward and beyond Tamrin's slower ship. The small ship had been specially fitted with a copper ram, now greenish in color, that protruded three feet beyond the bow of the ship just above water level. Pirate ships used small boats with large crews who could fire arrows, particularly flaming torches, at the sails of the ships they attacked. Thus Rinta's boat had a teakwood triangular shield built into the bow, behind which five men could wait, protected from arrows, and repel any who tried to board if the two ships rammed. Rinta, Tamrin's clever and highly athletic son, commanded the crew of four. He was supple, quick, and had a short temper.

Tamrin stood at the highest part of the deck and looked at the North Star, then moved his sighting to the star nearest it, the *Thuban,* brighter and easier to sight with his instruments. The architects of the great Egyptian pyramids had used *Thuban*, a star in the constellation of the Dragon, for their north star as they aligned open shafts in its direction. Tamrin took out the *kamal* and moved the bottom of the rectangular instrument so that from his point of view it rested on the horizon. Then the horn was moved along the string until the upper edge touched the star he was staring at. He counted the knots of the string. The star he called the billy goat, *al-jadiyi,* was directly to his left as he faced the bow. He was satisfied that the dhow was moving directly east, toward the Arabian coast. He knew his sons were performing the same exercise, even though they were able to see the dim lights of his lantern reflected in the silver mirrors aft.

Men posted at the steering oars were rotated each time the water clock was emptied. A tiny hole had been drilled in the bottom of a large earthen pot through which water could drip. On the inside of the broad pot, dark lines were marked, corresponding to the number of hours indicated by the lowering water level.

The water clock on Tamrin's ship had been made in Egypt and required special care so it did not tip over. Only fresh water was used in it. Salt water was not used because it created small crystals as the water dripped through and eventually upset the accuracy of the device to measure time. Fresh water was poured in each night and the ink of a squid was squeezed into the water, making it easier to see as it reached the marked lines in the vessel. Each time four marks had been seen on the inside of the jar, those assigned for that watch rang a gong to call the next, their relief. The water clock had no use during storms and rough seas.

A copper hourglass was kept in Tamrin's cabin. All the sand in the top portion of the glass passed through a tiny opening above to the container below in exactly one hour. An assigned person noted when the sand was depleted. There were always two men assigned to each shift, both to keep an eye on each other and to discuss any problems that could arise before awakening the master of the ship. The senior of the two made the decisions. 'Better a single decision maker than a thousand advisors.'

The first night on board was unusually smooth and Ebna-la-Hakim slept soundly, hardly awakening at the sound of the gongs. Walking aft to the back of the ship, he performed his morning toilet, squatting over an oval hole in a board that extended beyond the ship. He looked up at the stars above him. Near the ship, porpoises splashed, leaving phosphorescent trails with their movement. Not seeing Adesh lying on his mat on deck, Ebna stretched out on his own mat. As he fell asleep, he heard Adesh laugh, his voice coming from the cabin of the master Tamrin. Listening carefully now, he heard Tamrin's deep voice in conversation, and Adesh's replies, then silence.

Ebna tried to imagine how the two would lie side-by-side, touching each other's faces and smiling, laughing. Strangely, thinking of Adesh's beautiful face, he became aroused, and then upset with his own arousal. He got up, tied his cloth around himself and walked to the back of the ship where he sat staring at the stars and looking at the shimmering sea. The moon rose over the sea, bathing it in silver light. He stared at the moon, trying to imagine the meaning of the dark marks on the surface. He almost fell asleep sitting with his back against the rear mast when he noticed that clouds covered the moon and the stars dimmed in the night's darkness. The small light from the mirrored lamp box was just an orange glow. Then that too went out, blown by a gust of wind that came across the ship. He quickly went to the sleeping area sheltered by a large tarpaulin and noticed that others of the crew had awakened. The two men on watch at the steering oars were now alert. One sailor retrieved and stowed the water clock and rang the bell three times.

Tamrin stepped out from under the shelter of his cabin and looked around into pitch-black sky. One of the crewmembers prepared to cover the fire pit with a metal lid which had a hole in the center and a series of small holes on the sides for air. First he took a small piece of wood and held it in the glowing coals and blew until he obtained a small flame. He protected this with his hand and re-lit the lamp, moving it into the cabin area out of the wind. That tiny light was sufficient for the crew to see dim outlines as they prepared for rough weather.

Adesh came and stood next to Tamrin.

"Lower the mainsail. Untie the bindings," ordered Tamrin. "Keep the ship into the waves," he yelled to the oarsmen.

Adesh climbed up the swaying mast and began to work on the sail as others stowed their bedrolls and items in the hold.

The varnished wood hold cover was placed securely, wood pins inserted to keep it in place. The ship began to lift and fall with the waves. One cat that had climbed the mast, now cried from a cross bar. The men ignored it, looking instead at the approaching storm front.

Tamrin looked back for the other ships following in the small convoy and could only see one small light. The other ships were dark and lost to view in the storm. He carefully took the mirror lamp to the back of the ship, shielding it with a cloth exposing the light toward the other dim light far behind him. He covered it again and waited. The following ship's dim light disappeared for a moment, and then he could see it again. He recognized the signal to be that of Rinta, his youngest son, master of the smallest dhow. He had moved forward to second place in line. Tamrin signaled in reply, trying to keep his own light from blowing out, hoping Rinta could advance closer.

The waves became choppy and tossed the dhow violently. It rose and fell from the crests to the troughs in sickening swoops. Each of the crewmembers tied a rope around his own waist and tied the rope to the rail, which ran around the edges of the deck amidship. Tamrin's rope was rigged with a brass ring at the end, which allowed him to move the length of the ship. He moved aft to the oarsmen.

"Try to keep into the wind and directly into the waves," he shouted.

"The wind is shifting and the waves seem to come from two directions," one of the men called back. "We will try, but the darkness is complete and from where we stand it is hard to tell the direction of the waves."

"I will stand near the stern and watch. If I notice we are moving in the wrong direction to the left, I will tap the bell once. That means steer slightly to the right. If I ring twice, steer slightly to the left." He hurried away.

Only one small sail now was unfurled at the bow to keep the wind behind the ship. Tamrin glanced at its flapping material made of fibers from palm fronds. He hoped the sail would hold. It was tied with tight small ropes to two bars, but where the ropes penetrated the material it was already beginning to rip.

He saw that the ship was heading broadside to a huge wave and rang twice. The ship trembled as the oarsmen tried to correct. Then it began to rain. Now there was no differentiation between seawater and the sheets of rainwater that sprayed over the boat. The deluge engulfed them. Lightening gave Tamrin a momentary glimpse of the sail in front of him, now tattered and flapping. He hung on to his safety rope, trying to make his way aft to help those at the steering oar, and suddenly stumbled over a body, almost falling to the deck. Reaching down, he felt Ebna's thin body and smelled vomit; the lad was bending over in violent spasms as the nausea came upon him. Tamrin pulled the boy to his feet and shouted in his ear.

"Hold to my waist and move with me toward the stern. There's a sheltered place near the steering gear. Come! Hang on!"

They moved together slowly, Tamrin shouting encouragement. The rain lashed Tamrin and Ebna so hard they could hardly take in breaths, their faces spattered with water from the sea and storm. They stumbled to a small hollow section where the steering oars were anchored and huddled there, Tamrin holding the boy from behind as they sat hunched over. Ebna lay motionless, limp and tired from violent vomiting.

The ship moved like a beetle upside down on a hot stone; it rose and spun and the wind howled in the rigging of the masts. Another wave hit broadside, almost making the ship capsize. Every unsecured object skidded across the deck, plummeting into the black water. The ballast, round stones from Nubia, saved the ship, which slowly righted itself as the oarsmen tried to move into the next wave.

Exhausted, the two men at the oars noted the ship's new movement. The storm ended almost as quickly as it had begun, and clouds scudded by, revealing the moon once more. The waves were still huge, but now moved in more regular patterns. As the skies cleared, Tamrin took out his *kamal* instrument and tried to place its bottom edge on the horizon, but the waves were still too violent. He looked up and sought the pole star. It was to his right!

They were heading northwest, opposite from their planned course. He shouted to the steering crew to reorient the ship, but the ship had no frontal movement and bobbed on the surface like a cork. A steady wind began to blow from the south, the dreaded capricious southerly monsoon winds of the Hindush. Dawn came and the sun rose behind them. Already Adesh stood at the base of the foremast waiting for orders from Tamrin.

"Trim the main!" Tamrin shouted into the wind. Adesh understood and adjusted the mainsail, securing it as the wind caught the sail with a booming snap. The boat veered, wind filling the sail. Now the ship was under control, but they were moving north, away from Hodeida, their desired destination. Two masts gave the ship some degree of maneuverability, allowing the crew to use both sets of sails, only one set, or in the case of very heavy winds, a small sail set low on the foremast. The crew tacked in a northeasterly direction and again trimmed the mainsail, then the jibs.

The sun came out and began to dry ship and crew. As the sun set in the west they had their first glimpse of land, a rocky coast with cliffs, sandy beaches, and reefs. The sounding line was thrown again and again as they approached the coast until the lead line touched a rocky bottom.

At the bottom of the line was a lead weight with a cup-like cavity filled with tallow. The tallow picked up material from the bottom, telling the sailors what kind of bottom they were over, sand, rock, gravel or coral reef. They crept closer, hoping to anchor for the night, looking for any sheltered cove. A small spit of land appeared to the north. Still sounding for depth, they approached, hoping to enter the mouth of the bay.

"Sandbar! Shallow. Only twenty knots on the cord."

"Drop anchor!" shouted Tamrin, and the heavy rope hissed against the grooved hard wood block as the anchor sank down. The boat swung and bobbed gently on the shallow waves as the anchor dug in. The men saw nothing but sand and rock, no sign of human habitation.

Two of the sailors took out their fishing gear and fished off the stern. Small fish teased the bait, and then a larger fish took the hook and struggled against the line. The men stood and watched as Adesh brought in a blue fish with a large flat body and tiny mouth.

"It is a fish that eats coral. Catch another," shouted Tamrin.

The winds did not shift to the southeast the next day, or the next. The men swam and washed their clothing. Two made it across a shallow reef to the beach more than a hundred yards away and began to explore. They returned within the hour with a piece of driftwood, which they showed Tamrin. The wood had holes drilled in it and had at one time been part of the hull of a dhow. The men gathered around and held the small bleached relic, looking at each other, and thinking that their own ship could easily have had a similar fate, crashing on the shallow reef in the night. One man handed the wood to Ebna.

"This is for you as a reminder of your first crossing to the Aribi coast. Keep it for good luck. It may help you during rough weather so you do not become sea sick."

They laughed as Ebna took the wood and walked away to sit in the shade of the tarpaulin, thinking of his mother, his home in the Aksum summer palace. He longed for pomegranate juice. He ran his fingers over the wood. Yes, he thought, I will place this in my palace meeting room on a low table for all to see and comment about.

Tamrin ordered that everything be removed from the storage hold and brought to the deck. All hands, including Tamrin, worked, toiling and sweating in the scorching sun. Only the ivory tusks and ebony wood was left below. Each item was sorted, wiped clean, and checked for possible water damage. There were sealed jars of green ginger, asafetida, turmeric, cloves, aloes and palm oil. Tamrin had labeled each with a brush and black paint but only he and Adesh could read the script. They checked each item against a manifest.

One item was missing! It was a small sandalwood box about the size of a loaf of bread. This had been kept lashed with a leather thong to a beam in the hold, high above the other goods toward the front of the vessel. It was hidden away there so that in case the ship was stormed and overtaken by pirates, this precious cargo would go unnoticed. All the crewmembers knew of this box and its contents and all were sworn to secrecy not to reveal it. It was heavy and contained a variety of crudely shaped silver coins from Egypt, Aksum, and even Palestine. The gold bars in it were from Egypt and had been hammered with numbers on one side to indicate their weight.

During Tamrin's journey with the Queen of Sheba, many gold bars had been taken from the mining area near Kush where the gold was extracted from quartz crystals. On the return from Palestine, the Queen gave Tamrin twenty small gold bars as a gift. He always carried these in his ship when they journeyed to India where gold was highly prized and where *sona* jewelry was fashioned for the women of many of the small rulers called rajahs. Gold was called *nub* in Egypt and this name was also used in Aksum. In the entire land of Ethiopia, on both sides of the sea between, *nub* was called the 'shit of the gods.' In the land of the Hindus it was called *sona* and was highly prized because there were no gold mines there and people relied on traders to bring the prized metal.

Six crewmembers were lined up on the deck, and then told to squat and wait until Tamrin came out of the cabin. He stood in front of his small crew.

"This is my sixteenth trading journey to the south. During all the years I have been a merchant, my crew has never failed me and has never stolen anything from the ship. For this reason, after every successful journey, I give each crewmember gifts of silver and cowry shells. Today I saw that the box, which contains the gold and silver for use in our trade in the land of the Hindu is missing. Someone here is responsible. After we left port, the very night we moved into deep water before the storm I went below and checked to see if the sandalwood box was securely fixed on top of the beam at the very front of the ship. It was there. Adesh was with me and held the light when I checked." He looked at the serious faces in front of him, all of them friends and to whom he would trust his life. None avoided his stare.

"I will cast a lot and choose one from among you who will go with me to search the entire ship. I have six cowry shells and one is larger than the others. Reach into this cloth bag and pull out one shell quickly. He who has the largest shell will be witness to the search."

Each man reached in and removed a shell and they all held the shells in their palms, glancing left and right to see who had the largest cowry. It was the oldest crewmember, Sabu, who had been with Tamrin for more than twenty years. He held up his hand.

"Sabu, while the crew remains here on deck, you and I will search every corner of this ship from front to back, from top to bottom." He glanced up at the masts, then to the men. "Move to the shaded area under the tarpaulin and rest."

For more than an hour Tamrin and Sabu searched the vessel, checking every beam in the hold, all the places on the deck and all the sacks of personal belongings. Finally they searched the cargo goods on the decks, which had been set out earlier to clean and dry. There were ten sacks of coffee beans from Mocha remaining. They stood and looked at these, then at each other. The crew watched them as they turned over each of the sacks. Then Tamrin looked up at the front mast and the rigging as well as the bunched sails. He sighed, removed his sandals and shirt and was about to climb up the mast.

Adesh called out, "Master Tamrin, let me do it for you. You may fall. I am the mast monkey. Please, Master."

Tamrin hesitated and looked at the boy's beautiful and earnest face, a face that he had kissed the night before. He smiled.

"Adesh, if you were the guilty one where would you have hidden such a box?" he asked.

The boy frowned, and then stood. "If I was the guilty one I would hide the box high up on the cross beam where folds of sail are tied in a bunch. The most dangerous place to walk, where sometimes, even I lose my balance. But Master Tamrin, I would die before I would deceive you or steal from you. It is not I." He sat down and tears streamed down his cheeks.

"Sabu, you are too old to go up the pole like a monkey. I will do it." Tamrin moved to the front mast, grabbed the heavy rope tied to it, placed one of the knots between his big toe and the other toes and lifted himself up, one step at a time. He moved slowly, his body not used to lifting itself repeatedly. When he came to the cross beam he rested and looked around. At the far end, he saw sail cloth, bunched together and tied with a thin rope. He knew his balance was not that of a monkey.

"Adesh, come up and go to the end of the beam and untie the rope as we all watch."

Adesh scrambled up the mast, paused, then with amazing balance moved to the end, sat down and wrapped his legs under him. Holding to the beam, he began to untie the knots, using his teeth to undo the tight bindings. The crew gazed, spellbound. He reached into the sailcloth, paused, and then began to extract an object, a small inlaid wood box, which his mother had given him at the time he had been purchased as a slave by Tamrin. Now he opened it and tears streamed down his cheeks. He took out a length of braided black hair of his mother, and held it up.

The crew glanced at Adesh's face and the braided hair and looked away, feeling the grief of the boy, feeling his frustration at having to reveal this small personal secret. They knew he had not seen his mother for five years and that perhaps he would never see her again.

"More precious than gold!" shouted Tamrin. "Replace it Adesh. We have to move to the next mast before our work is done this day."

They climbed down and walked to the rear mast and looked up. From where they stood it did not appear that any box the size of a loaf of bread could be hidden.

"Go up and run your hand on all the surfaces while we watch." Tamrin moved aside as Adesh climbed, then watched him as he sat on the crossbeam and felt it with his hands the entire length. Then he glanced back at Tamrin and shook his head. Tamrin motioned for him to come down. Adesh did not return to the mast, but swung out and held to a rope and came down hand over hand, his feet squeezed on to the sail. He jumped to the deck. Tamrin walked to him and placed his hand on the head of the boy and motioned for him to join the others.

"Sabu, do you have any ideas?"

"I don't think the thief would throw the gold into the sea. I don't think his anus is large enough to hide the bars there. There is only one place left, the sacks of coffee. They must be emptied."

Tamrin motioned to two of the men to assist them. He cut the rope holding the top of a sack and the men poured the coffee onto the deck. Nothing.

"Get the small flat shovel used to remove ashes from the stove."

The coffee was carefully scraped up and returned to the first sack. It took an hour to search the twenty-nine sacks and refill them. Sabu looked at the last sack and shrugged his shoulders, discouraged. Tamrin nodded.

The coffee poured out onto the deck and with it the wood box, which landed with a thud on the teak wood deck. No one said a word. No one glanced at his neighbor. The crew stood like statues. Tamrin bent over and picked up the box, opened it and closed it again, turned and walked to his cabin and placed the box on his own bedroll.

"One of you is guilty. One of you has betrayed the rest of us. Will you all agree to submit to the test of the heated sword?" He studied their expressions.

All of them feared this test. A sword tip heated until its end was blue was touched to the tip of the tongue. The guilty one would be burned. Others with saliva in their mouths, would be spared, would feel the sword sizzle, much like a cook checks the heat of a pan with a wet finger to see if it is hot enough to put in the oil. Tamrin took his sword and stuck the tip into the glowing charcoal in the fire pit. He waited for a minute then withdrew it and pointed to the first man to step forward. He did so, shaking.

He was the newest crewmember, named Set, and not counting Ebna was the first in line. He was breathing heavily now, almost panting; terrified of the heated sword. Tamrin, his face serious pointed to the boy Ebna, the next Emperor Menelik to be, and motioned for him to come first instead.

"Open your mouth when I tell you to and stick out your tongue. Do not move. Close your eyes." Tamrin brought the sword toward Ebna's mouth. At that moment the crewmember that was first in line screamed, ran to the rail and jumped into the sea and began to swim toward the beach some one hundred yards distant. All the crewmembers now lined up and watched him swimming furiously. He almost reached the beach when a hammerhead shark rose from below and slashed his leg and pulled him under. No one spoke as the shark thrashed about, then released the body, now missing a leg. They turned away as the water turned red, then pink.

Tamrin spoke so softly that the crew had to lean their heads closer to listen. 'Where there is no shame there is no honor. My box of gold will be under my own sleeping bag. I will use it every night instead of my usual wood pillow. Remember this day. We are all brothers here. I will die for you if the time comes. You too must die for your crewmates or me if the time comes. Each ship must have a family of trust and loyalty. One who would cheat, steal or lie about the other should be a shark's dinner. Return all the items to the hold and prepare to sail tomorrow if the winds are favorable. Those of you, who call on gods, call on them now to give us clear sailing and favorable winds.'

Adesh and Ebna returned to their task of preparing the food for the crew. Ebna turned to Adesh. "Do you think that Tamrin would have placed the hot sword on my tongue?" Adesh nodded, yes.

But I am me, the future." He looked away, having almost given his princely name.

"What did you say? You are me, the future...What do you mean?"

"I am just a boy. Would he touch a boy's tongue with a hot sword?"

Adesh smiled. "On the ship, the master is the emperor of all. His word is law. No one disputes him. It must be so with all leaders or they are not masters, rather only people who act a part. Tamrin served our queen, though she was but a girl, a young virgin woman at the time and did her bidding the long year he protected and cared for her when she went to visit Solomon. His men were loyal to him, as are all the men, and his sons on the ships of the convoy."

The next day the winds shifted and they set sail and moved away from the coast for a short distance. The bell rang once and the men gathered.

"I have called you together because we are now a lone ship, a target for pirates. Our fleet of five was dispersed in the storm. During the day, the first watch, Adesh will remain up on the mast seat to look for sails. He will take Ebna with him to teach him how to climb and help him watch. Later when Ebna's hands and toes are strengthened he will take a watch by himself. Know where your weapons are. Be vigilant."

The ship hugged the coast and moved south. Ebna, as he was now called, helped Adesh prepare the meals of fish that were caught. Then Adesh looked up at the rigging on the masts and shook his head. Not one strip of the salted shark meat had survived the storm. He moved to the mast and crawled up as a lookout.

Tamrin did not recognize any of the features of the coast but knew from his sightings that the storm had driven them far off course. When the coast of Saba would be sighted he would know it well, its small, shallow, sand filled bays, its sand bars sticking out into the sea, its rocky cliffs near to Hodeida. South to the home of his youth!

CHAPTER 5

Walk and work with wise men; don't have fools as companions.

Rinta the youngest son of Tamrin was master of the smallest Dhow. He lost sight of the glowing light on his father's ship ahead. The storms lashed the smaller dhow and the waves tossed it like a cork. Rinta took down all the sails and threw out a canvas sea anchor and sealed the decks as best as he could. Each of the men tied themselves with a rope to the mast so they would not be swept overboard.

They had almost given up hope for survival as the small dhow reared and fell into the troughs between the waves. They were not able to get to the goatskins to drink water, fearing that they would be knocked over. Thirsty and cold they waited out the storm. Then the storm moved north and left them in seas that were rough and choppy. There was no light for more than an hour. Then the clouds parted and the moon was revealed and they could see each other and the black sea around them, glistening and wild.

As dawn broke on the eastern skies the shallow draft ship was under sail and moved slowly south. The color of the water changed and Rinta yelled for the weighted rope and threw it into the water. Only fifteen knots passed through his hands before the weight hit bottom.

"Lower the sail and get ready to drop anchor!" he screamed. As he spoke, the ship ran across a sand bar below them, scraping and then somehow lifting beyond it. "Drop the anchor!"

The rope ran out and the anchor tipped on its metal point and dug into the sand. The dhow swung around and rode on the waves. All the crewmembers lined the rails and looked down into the water. Directly under them there was a dark object that looked like a black stone.

"Who will dive under and see where we are anchored and if we can move out and away from the hazard of the sand bars?"

Two men stood up. He nodded as they undressed. They dove over the side naked and swam down toward the dark object, and then needing air came to the surface, blowing like porpoises.

"It is the hull of a sunken ship. Very old. Most of it is covered with sand. There is a channel directly to the west. Just ahead is another submerged sand bar which has coral in it." The men shouted at those on deck and then swam back to the ship and climbed the rope ladder slung over the side.

They stood, naked and dripping before Rinta. "If we had gone a bit farther we would have crashed against the coral in that sand bar. To get out to deep water we will have to use poles and row. It will be difficult."

"The wind may swing us around if we weigh anchor. How deep is the water over that sand bar that reaches out into the sea?" Rinta began to climb the single mast to get a better view of their options.

"The sand bar has rough coral below it. If one of us wore shoes, it would be possible to swim to it with a line and stand on it. There is about three feet of water there. Then the line could be pulled to move the ship forward." One of the sailors who had dived to see the sunken ship looked up at Rinta, now at the top of the mast. "Is there a channel clear all the way to open water?"

"It looks clear, all except at the end of the channel. The boat may not float above the sand there. I think it would take three men pulling the line to move us ahead. We could raise the anchor slightly while the men move the ship forward. If the waves bring us too close to the reef we can drop anchor quickly."

Three men dove into water. A line was thrown to them, attached to a longer thicker rope. The men waded onto the sand bar, put on their sandals and pulled the rope toward to them. All three strained against the rope until it was taut.

"Weigh anchor until it is just above the sand!" shouted Rinta.

The anchor rose as the men strained against the rope, leaning forward so far that their chests were under water. The boat moved forward and they struggled to take another step in the sand. The oarsman steered so the boat would head away from the reef. At last the men reached the end of the sand bar.

"Drop the anchor!" Rinta shouted.

"Walk out onto the tongue of sand. I want to see how much clearance there will be for the bottom of the boat to pass over." Rinta pointed to the partially closed channel.

The tallest of the men waded out onto the tongue and the water came up to his neck, then at the next step his head went under. He came up blowing water and swam back. "The ship may be able to pass over, or barely touch the sand. The wind is with us. Hoist the sail and weigh anchor at the same time as the bow comes across."

The ship's sail slapped as the wind caught it and the anchor rose. The dhow moved forward slowly and gained speed, then the bow touched the sand tongue, paused and scraped by. The men cheered as the ship moved into deeper water.

"Drop the anchor!" There was a splash. "I did not want to talk about it while we were trapped. Now that we are safe I want to explore the sunken ship. How far down is it?" He looked at the two men.

"As deep as five men together."

"Could you see if any part of the ship was open?"

"Yes, the ship must have been grounded and holed on the coral reef. As water rushed in, it leaned over on its side, stern up, and sank. Fish were going in and out of it."

"Each of our ships carries a small box with coins for trading, as do we. You all know about it. It, like on my father's boat, is hidden on the beam at the triangle toward the stern. No pirate would think of looking there. Perhaps this ship sunk at night in a storm. Some few may have survived but in rough water one can't see into the water below. I hope we can find some treasure."

Four of the men were swimmers, and one, Salman, was an oyster diver and could hold his breath for a minute of two. The swimmers prepared to dive overboard and swim back to the wreck.

"Tie a light cord to your waist, Salman, and a sharp light knife. If there is a box hidden on the sunken ship, tie it to the end of this line. It may be heavy and weigh you down. Give three tugs to the line and we will pull it out. If I see sharks I will give you two tugs."

The men dived overboard. Their shipmates watched them swim to the sand bar; then again the swimmers took deep breaths and dove down to the wreck. In less than a minute two surfaced and blew air and swam back into more shallow water.

"Salman is inside the ship. He should surface any moment," they shouted.

As the men yelled Rinta saw two small sharks enter the bay in shallow water. He gave two tugs. He was amazed to feel the rope answer with three tugs and a moment later Salman surfaced, treading water and breathing deeply. He watched the line tighten and begin to move. Then it stopped, and Rinta shouted, "It must be stuck on something. I don't want to break the rope."

Salman waved, upended, and dove again. He could not see well because the box moving on the sandy bottom had thrown up a cloud of debris. He held the line and descended. The box had caught on a decayed hunk of wood just under the surface of the sand. He freed it, pulled three times and swam to the surface.

The men on the deck watched the line become taut, as the object moved toward them on the sandy bottom, stirring up a cloud of fine sand. They were in fairly deep water as Rinta slowly pulled up the line, worried that it might break from the weight.

"Dive down and wrap another cord around the box, hurry!"

The crewmember swam to the cord, held it gently in his fingers and kicked his way down, another cord attached to his waist. He wrapped the rope around the box, tied a knot and rose to the surface, his face purple as he blew out, and inhaled loudly.

Rinta and another crewmember hauled up the box carefully. Many hands reached for it as it came near. They set it on the deck and watched Salman swim the last distance through deep water. He held his knife in his teeth. A small shark the size of a man approached him from the side. He stopped swimming and faced it, his own face under water. The shark swam forward to investigate and he could see it was a slit-eyed shark. When it came close to him he stabbed it in the snout. It splashed and moved away. Salman climbed up the ladder and stood before Rinta and the crew of four men, a broad smile on his face, his chest heaving in and out for air.

Rinta stepped forward toward the men. Each of them held wrists in greeting.

"You have done very well. You now have the honor of opening the box and taking one of the first things you see."

The box had been in the water for a very long time. The teak wood was black and eroded; the metal hinges and straps were intact but appeared to be fused together. Salman took his knife, put it under the hasp, and snapped it off. The box was the size of small cooking pot. Now he pried up the lid, and the hinges snapped and broke. All the men in a circle peered down to see the contents. On the very top there was a large gold coin. Under it there was dark material. Salman reached down, picked up the coin, and held it up to the sun, then put it between his teeth and bit it gently.

"Gold!"

"I swear, the coin shall be yours. As master of this ship, I award it as a gift from the traders of Aksum." Rinta reached forward to take the coin and looked at it closely, then handed it to the next man.

"It has the shape of a scarab, not round. It looks like there is a person standing up, but, no, perhaps three persons talking." Rinta was very excited and had forgotten about the box and the rest of the contents. Now he leaned over and took out silver coins fused together. He set the silver lump on deck. It was the size of a large mango. Again he reached into the box and slowly, very slowly, lifted out a gold bar slightly shorter than the length of the box and as wide as his palm. It too was stamped with a strange mark. He held it up and the crew cheered. On the very bottom there were carvings of scarabs in colored stone, Egyptian scarabs. He held them in his palm, then passed them around to the crew.

"We shall put everything back in the box as we found it. When we meet with my father we will say nothing at first. Then when there is a time of feasting and rejoicing, we will surprise him and ask him to open the box! We may have made the entire expedition worthwhile. How can a man in ten years earn enough to buy a large gold bar?"

He and Salman returned the items to the box, talking excitedly as each object was returned.

"This box will be tied together with our box in the hold. We shall all witness how we hide it. Bring an oil lamp."

They fished for their dinner with hand lines using small minnows caught with their fine net for bait. Their catch was unusual: a very small slit eyed shark, a grouper, and two yellowish snappers plus a fish they did not know with sharp teeth that appeared to be misplaced and hideous. They boiled some barley grains and stewed some of the fish; others were roasted over the coals in the firebox. A small flagon of wine was brought from the hold and the men ate their fill and drank until they could no longer stand and lay on the deck with faces to the stars and slept. Rinta ate well, but drank only a single cup of wine. He leaned against the mast and kept watch for four hours. After he had turned the sand filled marker over four times, he awakened Salman who took over until dawn.

"We will hug the coast and head south to see if we can catch up to one of the other boats. Pray that my father Tamrin's boat is safe. It could not have survived if it had been here." Rinta turned to his men. "We have to go through the entire cargo and bring up anything that has become wet or damp."

The cargo in the hold had not been inspected since the storm. It was a bright windy sunny day and the temperature soared, making every move an effort. The four men and the young apprentice, their mast monkey, carried the cargo to the deck; baskets of bronze ingots, sacks of coffee and their major cargo, timber, the teak and Ethiopian hardwood planks that were used to construct dhows. Special rope woven from coconut fiber was stacked in the lowest area of the hold in case there was a problem with leakage or a violent storm during which water got in the hold. The coconut ropes, resistant to moisture, would swell, however, if wet for a prolonged period. The deck was covered with baskets and the hold covers opened to air. The ship moved along in blazing sun, drying out as the men sought shaded areas to rest after their labor.

Toward evening the wind shifted and the sail hung limp. The ship made little headway as the crew tried to catch a side breeze by lowering the sail at one corner and tying it down to create a partial triangle. With the changing breeze came sea birds, flying with wind from the southeast. Also with the breeze came the smell of smoke and a hint of cooking meat. To a man, the crew became alert.

"Get out your weapons, bows, and arrows, and have your swords ready. We are nearing an encampment on the shore somewhere to the southeast. I have not been here before and don't know if we are approaching a village or a camping place for pirates. Each person must take a large drink of the warm tea now. Fill up with liquid. You will pour sweat. If we fight it will be to the death. None of us wishes to become a slave. We will perspire terribly in this hot weather and will have no time to drink, so drink lots now."

Rinta scooped a calabash cup of the tepid tea and drank it, then another, and handed the cup to the mast monkey. "When you have drunk your fill, climb up to the top of the mast and keep a lookout for sails, or for land."

The sun was setting when the boy, Berhanu, shouted out. "There are two sails toward the south, lateen sails. They are brown. I can't see the ships yet but they will probably be small from the size of the sails."

Goods on the decks were once again stacked into the hold. The light with its reflector stayed unlit. A sea anchor was put out and the ship rode the swell up and down, hardly moving. Under a full moon, the men moved about easily on the small deck, preparing for a meeting with the smaller boats.

"There are two small lights to the south. The dhow's crew may have seen our mast or our sail and are moving with the wind toward us." Berhanu's voice piped high and clear.

"Make no noise. We carry no light. Pull up the sea anchor and move with the wind. If they head to where they thought we were, they will not find us. We will move up the coast and try to outrun them by morning. Do not make noises. Berhanu, don't call out signals. I will watch you. If you see the boats approaching, come down right away."

The dhow's sail filled with wind as the ship reversed its direction. Rinta was at the tiller now, trying to steer the ship northwest into deeper water, thus cutting across the path of the following boats. The men sat on deck, their faces grim. Each man held his weapons, tested his bow strings, placed his arrows in the calabash quivers, and waited. The smell of wood smoke became stronger. Berhanu slithered down the mast rope and came to Rinta.

"The boats are passing us to our right, between our boat and the land. See their lights. They are cooking food but not using charcoal, rather firewood and dried cow dung. There must be a settlement not far from here."

The moon was their enemy. Their light colored, sun bleached sail under reflected moonlight was a beacon. As the smaller boats passed in the distance, the men sighed and relaxed slightly. Then suddenly there was a shift in the position of the small lights, which in an instant were extinguished. Now in the distance the sails of the two small boats could be seen moving toward them to cut them off. Rinta leaned on the tiller, and the ship heeled, running with the wind. All at once, deliberately jibing, he steered toward the two small boats. Their action confused the men on the small boats who in turn moved parallel to the larger ship.

The wind shifted and died. Caught in the lull, all three boats hung on the water, hardly moving. The lull persisted. Again lights appeared on the other two boats and the sounds of faint voices came across the water.

"Put charcoals on the fire and cook a pot of rice with *ghee*. They know we are here. We will feed well again and be ready with energy when the sun comes up. Usually before dawn there is a shift of wind, and if it is favorable we will again head southeast and away from these boats. Trading boats usually pass one another without aggressive movements. These boats may well be those of pirates. They often carry tar or oil used to dip the tips of fire arrows. This is what they usually shoot first to busy their victims with burning sails or a burning ship just before they come aboard. If a fire arrow lands near you, pull it out and shoot it back at them. The sail is most vulnerable. There are two pots of water here. Extinguish sail fires. Remember, our ship is twice as high as theirs, so we are looking and shooting down at them. We have that advantage. But there are only five of us. They may have as many as ten on each boat, and that is a great problem in hand-to-hand combat. Use your arrows well. Do not shoot at hazy targets. Only shoot when you know you will impale your enemy. If they threaten us I will take advantage of the wind and move toward them fast, turning at the last moment to crash into one of their boats, sinking it with our ram. The others you must handle. Give our mast monkey a machete. He will be responsible for cutting any ropes thrown across to draw us near enough to board. Fight to the death!"

They waited for dawn and a change in wind direction. When the moon had set they could hear a squeaking noise coming closer in the first blush of dawn.

"They are using oars to approach. Get ready. Remember; only shoot your arrows when you know you will hit your target. Don't rush. Wait until you know you will kill, only then, shoot. They are coming!" Rinta held his own bow and nocked an arrow. Both smaller boats approached to port. Rinta's crew could see the fires clearly now. Men were dipping fire arrows, getting ready to light them. Across the water there was a shout, hailing them.

"If you want to live, give up now. Surrender or we will burn your ship to the water line. Surrender or we will burn you down!" The language was Southern Arabic.

The men on Rinta's dhow remained quiet and tense, waiting for a hail of fire arrows. "Most of the arrows will strike the decks. Pull them out and shoot them back. Their sails are still up. Shoot for them. Watch out for our own sail. It is going to be their target even though it has been taken down and wrapped tight. The small sail in front is half unfurled. I will use it to turn and run with the wind and turn at the last moment to ram the boat using oars."

The first fire arrows arched into the sky like meteors and then fell toward the dhow. They seemed to hang lazily, their fireballs blazing and settling down on the boat like a swarm of flaming locusts. Two of the arrows overshot the dhow, one hit the rolled up sail and five stuck onto the hard wood deck but three hit the walls and roof of the small cabin, which immediately began to burn. Rinta's crew pulled the burning arrows from the decks and shot these back at the two lateen sails. All of their arrows hit the large targets of the pirates' sails. These began to burn, slowly at first, until the woven matting caught and blazed in fire that swept up the sails in an audible whoosh.

The fire on their deck cabin began to burn rapidly. Rinta rushed in and pulled out the stored goods-- clothing, boxes, trade items and even a small trunk with cowries. His men stood on deck, taking aim at figures running on the boats below them, who were trying to prepare ropes and hooks to board the dhow.

They shot at these men at close range hitting their targets. But they in turn fired up at Rinta's crew. Two of his crew were hit and fell head first into the sea, impaled with arrows.

Rinta ran to the back of the ship so he could see the helmsman of one of the pirate ships who was steering the boat alongside the dhow. He took careful aim and his arrow hit the man in the back. He staggered forward, tipped over the steering arm, which moved the boat away from the dhow. Now Rinta moved the arm of the steering rudder and headed for the second boat, which had lowered their sails to stay near the fighting. They saw the boat coming at them and hurried to hoist the sail but the copper battering ram on the bow struck the boat and tore a huge hole at water level. Three men from the pirate ships now threw boarding ropes with hooks and scrambled up, hand over hand toward Rinta. He waited until the first pulled himself up on the railing, and shot him at close range. The man screamed and fell back. Before Rinta could prepare another arrow, the second man climbed over the railing and rushed toward him. Rinta drew his short curved sword and waited, knees bent, his body leaning forward. The man slashed at him and he leaped aside, but not fast enough. The sword cut his abdomen, opening a three-inch gash. In one sweeping motion Rinta's arm came around and slashed the arm holding the sword, almost severing it. The man fell back screaming, blood spurting across the deck. Rinta picked up his sword, rushing back to see his young apprentice standing with his back to the mast as a pirate approached him with sword drawn. Rinta threw his own sword, which turned once in the air and hit the pirate's head, handle first, knocking him out. Nearby the other small boat sank. Two men had jumped overboard and swam desperately toward their remaining boat.

It was over as fast as it had begun. One pirate boat drifted away from the dhow, its sails in cinders, and the remaining crews battling fires on deck where crewmen's personal things had been stored. Rinta and his three crewmembers stood steadily and fired one arrow after another at the pirate crews, wounding a few. Their own deck fire still burned. They drew seawater and battled the blaze for an hour pouring bucket after bucket of water on the fire until it was extinguished. By now the sun was up. Its rays scorched the men as they worked. Exhausted, the three of them lay stretched in the shade of the partially burned sail and poured buckets of water over each other.

Finally they had enough energy to hoist the damaged sail and catch a breeze from the northwest. A hole the size of a goat had been burned out of the sail. The men worked together to free the lower part of the sail, wrap it up, and lower the top half of sail, achieving about three quarters of the surface to catch the wind. Their dhow moved with the wind sluggishly, hardly making way. The pirates' ships had raised small cloth sails and were trying to maneuver their boats toward the distant shore to the east. Smoke was rising from the burning sail material that had fallen to the decks. Rinta watched, hatred rising up inside. If his ship had been larger, if he had more crewmembers and weapons, he would now pursue the pirate boat and attempt to ram it.

"Raise the Aksum flag!" he shouted.

The yellow banner blew in the breeze, in its center a brown colored lion with right paw raised, holding a spear. The crew of three did not cheer in respect to their dead, but rather stood sadly looking up at the flag. Then Rinta took a whistling arrow and pointed it at the sky in the direction of the small pirate boats; he pulled the string back to his chin and let the arrow fly. It screamed as it flew; a high-pitched whistle of pride, of challenge and warning. The, blood streaming down his legs from his wound, he collapsed on the deck.

"In the box from the cabin are the needles for repairing sails.

Bring them to me."

His two companions watched as he stitched his wound, pulling the lips together. They were amazed that he seemed invulnerable to pain.

"The stomach area has the least pain of the whole body. It looks terrible, but the wound is in the skin and small layer of fat. Bring me salt." He groaned as the sea salt was poured onto the roughly stitched flesh.

"We almost lost the ship. By preserving the egg, we ensured that a chick with legs will walk."

CHAPTER 6

The glory of a young man is his body, an old man his white hair.

Three days later Rinta's ship sailed sluggishly into the small harbor near Hodeida. Only two of Tamrin's dhows were anchored there. Their crews were working on the rigging and sails. Rinta blew a conch shell and the crews looked up and waved, yelling at them for joy. Tamrin was not present, having left to make arrangements to visit his properties and see his family and one of his wives there. He had informed the two youths that when he had things arranged he would blow a conch and call them to come bring a sack of their own clothing.

One of the larger dhows was still missing. Rinta dropped anchor and his ship swung around, hardly a ship's length from the largest dhow, Arif-Dmi. One of its crew slung a weighted string across. Rinta and the crew pulled on the cord attached to a heavy rope, which they tied half way up the mast. Tamrin's crew attached the rope to a block on their deck and slid on a rope seat with a wood pulley. Rinta sat on the rope chair so the crew on Aif-Dmi could pull him across.

"What happened? It looks like you were in a war!"

"We were stuck on a sand bar. Do you have any *tej*?"

replied Rinta.

A small skin of the wine was brought to Rinta who drank until he began to choke. He wiped his mouth and pointed at the flag. "We fought off two pirate boats, killed half their men but lost two of our own crew, Amare and Aalam, who were shot with fire arrows and died when they fell overboard. The bodies of all those who fell overboard were bloody and attracted sharks. There was no way we could save our own. We saved the trade goods and the ship. Is there no news of Setu's ship?"

"None. The storm drove us all to the northeast. We all fear for him because his ship was the oldest and the masts were the longest and heaviest. Setu wanted more cargo and less ballast stones. That may have been his problem. Our own boats almost capsized. We are not allowed to speak of it for a week! Tamrin is sick of heart. He left the ship in haste, his face like a stone. He ordered us all to take special precautions to place reflective lights at night and to insure that we all have a watchman who is awake and vigilant day and night."

Tamrin bargained with a camel driver for the use of three camels for a week. The man brought forward thin and old looking beasts. Tamrin stared at him and said nothing at first, then spat on the ground.

"I want running camels that can move across the sands with ease. My home would be a full day journey from here by my own camels. All I need are three sturdy beasts, one for me, two for my companions and one of your men on his camel to follow along to take the beasts back when I reach home. I have dozens of camels of my own. Look at my face. I am Tamrin. Are you so young that you have not heard of my travels and me? Have you not heard of my journey to Palestine with the Queen of Sheba?"

The young man shrugged and walked away with his camels. He returned after an hour, bringing five camels for Tamrin to choose from.

"I will hire four. You ride on the fifth and follow us. I will take my apprentices with me to see my home in Hodeida. Wait here, while I call my crewmembers. He blew four blasts on the conch shell.

Later Ebna and Adesh joined Tamrin together with two other crewmembers. They stood around the camels and watched as the herder ordered each beast to kneel, groaning and complaining. Tamrin, first to mount a large male, waited while the young men, each in turn, got onto his camel. Ebna had never mounted a camel and watched carefully to see how the other crew members mounted. He was last and watched anxiously as each man got on his unhappy and complaining animal. Ebna was hardly in place when his beast began the ungainly process of first getting to its back legs, then heaving itself onto its front legs. Tamrin rode his camel next to the smaller animal that Adesh was attempting to mount and held the rope. Adesh was small and athletic and made a show of leaping easily onto the saddle.

Each of the animals was tied to one in front of it with lengths of rope. As Tamrin moved off, the entire group of five camels with their riders strode onto the sandy trail full of boulders and rocks. The grunting camels made their way around obstacles, lumbering along, no longer loudly complaining and increasing their strides, faster than a man could walk.

By mid-morning the sun was hot and blinding. Tamrin pulled a white cloth over his head and was surprised that he had forgotten how hot and humid the coast of southern Arabia, part of larger Ethiopia, could be. He urged his camel forward with a slight tap of a stick and clucked his tongue. The beast groaned and increased speed for almost a minute, but then it went back to its original swinging stride.

Ebna rode the smallest animal, tied directly behind Tamrin. It never ceased to complain, wanting to travel at a slower pace. Ebna saw that the wood saddle that was placed over the hump had lost its padding and that the rocking motion had chafed the animal's skin to the quick. She groaned constantly. Stinging flies followed them and settled on the spot to ride with them and bite the bloody surface. His camel was a female that appeared to be rather fat. He wondered if it was pregnant.

He pulled a cloth over his head to shield it from the sun but opened the front of his clothing so air could circulate against his bare skin. He had never experienced heat like this in his life in Aksum and pitied the family of Tamrin who had to live their entire lives on this part of the coast. He had been given a small skin of water filled into a wine skin that had been emptied. He lifted this to his mouth and drank. This agitated his mount, which could smell the wine flavored water. It groaned and shook its head against the restraint attached to a brass ring in its nose.

Tamrin called back over his shoulder, "Hit the beast with your staff. It is a miserable creature. I should never have accepted it. Hit it!"

Ebna pulled his bamboo staff from the side of the mounting saddle and tapped the camel's rump behind him. It did not seem to notice. Remembering Tamrin's advice to hit it, he turned sideways and raised the stick high and hit it forcefully. It leaped forward shaking its head, almost tearing the flesh of its septum where the copper ring had been placed years earlier. This action dislodged the loop of rope tied to the back of Tamrin's saddle and the camel now turned right toward the desert and tried to run, making all the others attached to it veer with it into the hot sands away from the firm sand of the beach where they had been traveling. Tamrin's camel tried to turn and follow the others, heading away from them. Tamrin let it turn as well and he smacked its rump to speed up to catch up to Ebna's mount.

Adesh rode directly behind him. He shouted out, "Ebna put your legs over the side of the saddle, like this. Hurry!"

Ebna frowned but did so. At that moment the line leading from Ebna's camel that had been attached to Tamrin's saddle mount passed between its legs and Adesh's beast stepped on the rope as it came under its feet. It was hard to see what happened next. Ebna's camel's head was pulled down between its legs; the pressure against the nose septum ripped it free, the camel went onto its neck and Ebna was tossed from his side-saddle position onto the sand. His camel lay sprawled on its side its lungs heaving for air, but other than that it made no movements.

Tamrin stopped his own camel, ordered it to sit, pushed a metal rod into the sand, tied the lead rope to it and ran over to Ebna, still sitting on the sand, his head in his hands.

"Look at me Ebna!"

Ebna turned his head, completely covered with sand, his face bruised and scraped by a desert plant. Blood ran down his cheek. His eyes were not injured. Tamrin told him to stand up and lean over. Now Tamrin poured half a skin of water over his head. "Wash the sand from your face and wound." Adesh stood next to them with a serious face.

After much noise from the remaining camels, tying and untying of ropes and adjusting of loads, the caravan once again moved forward. Tied to two sides of the saddle of the owner's camel at the end of the procession were two of the rear legs of the camel that had fallen on its neck, breaking it. It had been slaughtered. The owner, on his return journey would cut off all the rest of the meat left on the carcass and take it back to the port town where he lived, that is if jackals, vultures, striped hyena and Asiatic lions had not already stripped it clean.

Adesh and Ebna rode together directly behind Tamrin's camel. The delay at the site of the accident had robbed the caravan of two hours of light. The sun set and darkness came rapidly with little twilight as the caravan moved forward toward Tamrin's village of Hodeida. They kept the sea to their left and kept moving carefully. In the distance a lion roared and far to the west another answered with a low rumbling coughing sound. The two young men looked at each other and Adesh smiled.

"That is a lion's roar. Is it the first time you have heard it?" Ebna nodded his head yes and stared into the night.

"Do you think they have already found the dead camel?"

"The first to find the camel will be the jackals. When one finds something to eat it calls to the others like this. His voice changed as he shouted like a jackal, 'Here, Here Here!" Its friends shout back, 'Where? Where?' and they listen for the reply, 'Here! Here!'" He laughed.

"Why did my camel fall forward on its neck?"

"Because my camel stepped on the trailing rope which pulled its neck between its legs. I have heard of this happening but it is my first time to witness it. Always be prepared to leap away from your mount with your feet against its body if it trips or falls. It is only ten feet to the ground, you will land on sand or a cactus plant, but you will not be crushed under the camel which would break your bones or kill you."

Ebna nodded and whispered, "Thank you. I am in debt to you and will repay you. I will not forget it?"

"So what do you own Ebna, a robe and sandals? How will you pay such a debt? You have no gold, no power. You are lower than I am." He laughed.

"I will…." He paused thoughtfully. "I will try to save your life some day."

The moon was high when the caravan arrived at Tamrin's

village. Dogs surrounded them barking wildly. All the camel's kneeled and the men stretched their backs and legs. Two men of the village, the brother's of Tamrin's wife stood in the darkness and called out.

"Your name? Your business here? Beware we are armed!"

In a loud voice Tamrin cried out, "Tamrin the Queen's Trader from Aksum!" In one of the houses there was a high-pitched keening as Tamrin's wife shouted out in joy, her tongue moving from left to right. Other women awakened and picked up the welcoming call, children cried out, and men quietly scurried away in the darkness to other parts of the village.

Ebna stood next to Adesh watching and listening. He looked up at the face reflected in the moonlight and saw the tears were flowing down Adesh's face; he had never returned to his own family, had never had the women ululate a welcome for him since Tamrin had bought him when he was a young boy.

Tamrin joined his family and bid the others good night, indicating to the members of his crew to find shelter in a room that was set aside for visitors. Adesh and Ebna unrolled their sleeping cloths, drank a huge cup of camel's milk, ate cold unleavened bread and fell asleep in their clothes. Both were sore and tired, but Ebna's bruises on his left side made sleeping difficult; each time he turned over he groaned and returned to his back or right side.

They did not hear the wind howl outside. The room was dark and they did not notice the coming of the light of dawn, obscured by a violent sand storm. When they both ventured outside for their toilet the wind tore at the door and sand flew into the room. The two young men closed the door quickly.

"Cover your entire head with a cloth. Make two small holes with a twig to see through. We must go outside but it is not good to inhale the air, and the flying sand will blind us. Look do it like this." Adesh took the white head cloth and put it over his head, put his finger over his left eye and held it at that spot. His small *jambiya,* a curved dagger was under his belt. He took it out and poked a tiny hole through the material and peered through it. He replaced the cloth on his head and could see through the pinhole. Then he helped Ebna with his cloth.

The two friends bent over and moved with the flow of the wind and sand to reach the outskirt of the village, which was the garbage dump area. There a group of camels were tethered and hobbled. Each had one of the front legs bent back and tied so that the animals only had three legs to walk on. All of the camels faced away from the sand blasts and wind, all chewed their cud and ignored the men at their morning toilet.

Within the village hardly a person stirred. Dogs did not bark, donkeys stood miserably in the lee of buildings. The dust in the air was so dense that the men could hardly find their way back to their room. They closed the door and fumbled around in the darkness and found a skin filled with wine. In the darkness they sat on their mats and passed the skin back and forth and then lay back and tried to sleep. Now the roaring of the wind against the flat walls of the mud brick building sounded like a small waterfall. The wind shifted when they were asleep and the dust and sand stopped as abruptly as it had begun. A loud knocking on their door and Tamrin's booming voice awakened them.

"We have been waiting for you. Others are eating. Get your morning food before it is all eaten."

It was like nothing Ebna had ever seen. On the floor set on a carpet were six plates of hot flat breads, small cups of Mocha coffee and at least a dozen people were reaching and eating, not saying much. Three women brought the food to the men and boys, their heads uncovered, their loose clothing flopping around them. Around the perimeter of the room were low couches and chairs and many cushions. Under them waited the Guinea Pigs, squealing and begging for another handout of bread. There were more animals running around than people in the room. The men watched and laughed as the guinea pigs rushed to get a piece of bread tossed to them, squealing and wiggling their bottoms.

Ebna said nothing, waiting until the meal was over to ask his friend about the rat like animals without tails. Adesh laughed when he heard the question about the animals.

"In the large room they keep these small animals and feed them there regularly. They actually run about in other rooms as well, but usually stay here where they are fed. Tonight we will eat their meat. It is very good, firm and soft and better than chicken. They are easy to care for. Look, over in the corner. That is where they shit. Once a day the sweeper cleans up the small pile of their pellets. Very clean animals."

"Why don't they eat cow meat or goat meat?" asked Ebna.

"Cows give milk, milk makes cheese that can be dried and stored. To kill a cow would be to kill a source of food. A few young bull calves are killed, usually for celebrations. One good bull is kept for breeding. Females make babies. They are not killed." He shook his head and looked at Ebna strangely. "What did you eat in your house?"

Ebna was quiet for a moment. "Goats and chickens and beef…" He was quiet for a moment, his face hiding a concern. Finally his resolve broke down.

"Adesh, I am called Son of a Wise Man. I will tell you a secret I have told no one else. I was forbidden to speak of it but you are my friend. Can you keep a secret?"

"I am not sure. It depends on the secret. All right, I promise I will keep one secret. Tell me just one thing I must keep secret and I will not tell Tamrin or anyone else." He licked his index finger and held it up.

"I am Prince Menelik, son of Queen Makeda and Solomon." He whispered it softly.

Adesh stepped back and looked at Ebna's face, his eyes to see if he could detect a lie. "I understand now. You have lived in the palace and know nothing, nothing about life, food, people, animals, nothing. I believe you. Now I have a real problem." He walked away a few steps with his back to Ebna, thinking. "I have a secret as well. We must both have important secrets about the other. I will tell you my secret but you must never tell anyone and by action or by how you treat me. Do you agree?"

Ebna looked at the beautiful face, long black hair and tall slender body of his friend. His eyes were sharp and bright, steady and still, staring at Ebna. "Yes. I agree. I swear." He made a sign, running one finger across the other as a knife would cut across a throat.

"I am Tamrin's lover. I sleep with him like women sleep with men. I am not like other men. I love men. I love Tamrin and would die for him. He bought me because of my beauty and because I was castrated at the time I started to become a man. There, I have told you three secrets. You may never tell."

"I have promised. I don't understand how you are Tamrin's lover. I don't know what it means that you were castrated. Everyone knows that you always sleep in Tamrin's room and even in his bed. But..." He sat on a large rock and stared at Adesh.

"You know what castrated means. They cut off my balls! I think you know, but you do not want to know. I have seen how you look at me. It is not the way you look at any other crewmember. You look at me as if I was a girl. Even now your eyes move across my body. Do you dream about me, Ebna?" He stepped forward and stood so close to him that Ebna's knees touched his own.

"Yes. We have shared many secrets. Yours is the most

important. You cannot change back. I cannot change whose son I am. Why did they castrate you? That part is strange to me. It sounds terrible and cruel. Why?" Tears formed in his eyes.

"To make sure that my beauty does not change, that my voice remains the same, that I resemble a half woman. I am two years older than you and have no facial hair like a man. I will never be able to have children. The real answer is that some men love boys like me better than women." He reached forward and placed his hand on Ebna's cheek. Ebna recoiled.

"But Tamrin has many other wives, many children. Why?'

"That is the secret he has, but it is not really a secret. Some men think about sex all the time, want their bodies satisfied all the time. Want …" He sighed.

"Tamrin could take one of his young wives on his boat with him." Ebna's imagination was now running wild.

"Imagine the trouble that would cause for the other crew members. Then they should be able to take their women. Imagine! The ships would have bad luck. We could not repel pirates. You understand?"

"Yes, I understand. I don't know why you touched my face. But I will tell you one more secret without an oath. When I look at your face, see how your body moves up the mast, look at how you walk and talk, I really admire you."

Adesh sighed. "I understand. Beauty is a blessing of the gods. Beauty is a curse. Heads turn wherever I go and that is a problem for me as well as the head turners. I am never just an ordinary boy, a person, but a target for eye arrows, all the time. All the time! I am aware of it and there is nothing I can do about it. Some crew members whisper to me, very carefully lest anyone hear, 'Adesh I love you.'"

Ebna nodded. "Tell no one, Adesh, but I am afraid of the storms, of the times when there will be no wind, of pirates, of moving farther and farther away from Aksum. I am afraid that I may never return from this journey." Ebna closed his eyes to avoid the stare of his friend. "I have nightmares. Adesh, I have never fought with anyone in my life. I don't know how to use a sword. I have never shot an arrow. You carry the curse of your beauty. I carry the curse of my being the next Emperor and I am like the guinea pigs, protected, fed and …"

"I am afraid we may stop going on trading expeditions, and that Tamrin may just be content to remain in a house in Aksum with one of his wives. What would I do? This is all I have known. The sea is my life, the ship is my life, newness and strange places and people are my life. I would be terrified to think about a life as a king, in a palace, with all the officials, with all of the country looking to see how I would behave." Adesh got up and motioned for Ebna to follow him. "I will borrow a bow and some arrows. Today you will begin your training as a fighting man. I will ask Tamrin to give you your first jambiya that will make you a man of honor because every man knows that the blade must taste blood if the owner is dishonored. Come."

Ebna was amazed that more than thirty people lived on a small farm in three tiny houses and as many shacks, that somehow the land made do for them. He watched and saw that even small children worked, worked at planting, worked at gathering dry grass and twigs for the cooking fire, worked at cleaning out the dung from chicken pens and guinea pig dung piles to put on the small vegetable plots. He had never thought about where all the food came from when he lived in the palace in Aksum. Here he saw that sweat and work were the ingredients that made tomatoes grow, that cooperation of every person made everything possible. It was much the same as sailing a dhow, there was a destination, a crew and storms to battle, with insects, with wild animals, with sandstorms and drought. What amazed him most was that each night he ate a meal that had come from the land, prepared by the people of the land. When small children played, they played cleaning, picking, and gathering. Everyone was always working.

Adesh's skill with a bow and arrows was truly amazing. Ebna practiced by himself when Adesh was called by Tamrin to assist him. On the fifth evening after the meal of *enjira* and *wat,* Tamrin reached under the mat and pulled out a short curved sword, a jambiya. Its scabbard was worn leather, torn in few places, but sound. He held the scabbard with his fingers away from the edge where the blade rode inside and withdrew the sword. It too was old, but the handle was dark brown. Many years of use gave a polish and shine to the rhino-horn handle. The blade was inscribed, not shiny and new, but very sharp. Tamrin held up a small twig and brought the sword down across it, neatly slicing it in two. All this time every eye was on him and he had not spoken. He pointed to Ebna and motioned for him to come, his hand upside down and fingers moving in a small scooping motion.

"Ebna, son of a wise man, be a wise man, an honest man, a fair man and a fearless man. This is your symbol, your heritage. Keep the *jambiya* in your belt always. Not only is it a tool for most uses, but reminds others that your pride and worth will not be challenged." He passed the sword to Ebna who was deeply moved to receive the gift.

"*Shukran! Shukran!* I am not worthy, but I will try to live deserve this. He drew the sword from the scabbard, but its curve made the blade slide on the open inside of the scabbard, which was worn from years of the blade passing. Instantly his finger bled as the sword sliced the skin. He looked at his fingers, then at Tamrin who had remained silent but now spoke.

"The first lesson of becoming a man is to keep a secret." He paused and looked around the circle of faces until his eyes came to rest on Adesh's face. Adesh looked back at his master, then at Ebna but kept a bland expression. "The second lesson is to observe well what happens around you. You did not watch how I held the scabbard, nor perhaps, hundreds of others who drew their swords. You took little interest in what common men did. Now you will have a tiny scar on the fingers of your left hand and you will see it and remember to observe. Observe life around you, your school is here, your own people. Learn by serving, learn by doing, and learn by watching. Your wound is small. Our people say, a fool is thirsty in the midst of fresh water. " He spoke to him as he would speak to any young crew member. The others all nodded in agreement.

The last dhow, whose master was Setu, pulled into Hodeida harbor two days after Tamrin left for his home by camel. The mainsail was half burned, portions of the deck were charred, the small cabin on the deck had been destroyed and the ship rode high in the water. It had lost its cargo.

Setu and his three brothers sat together on a small dock in the harbor. They were able to dangle their feet into the seawater from where they were perched, but the temperature of the water was the same as the air. There was not a breeze. Setu now told his story to his siblings and revealed for the first time since his arrival what had happened to his ship during the terrible storm.

"Let me start by saying that I will never again go without significant stone ballast. I believed that the load of heavy black ebony wood would take the place of stones, but I was mistaken. The cargo shifted, the boat tilted to the side two times, so far that I did not think it would right itself. It just hung there balancing on the fine line between capsizing and recovery. It seemed forever. Finally it righted itself. We had no option but to put out a sea anchor and ride out the winds and storm. The mainsail ripped so it was taken down to repair, and the spare, smaller sail was rigged which hardly gave us enough wind for steerage. Our bearings were difficult to figure out. At dawn we heard the watchman cry out from the crow's nest. Land! We approached slowly, trying the lead line and finally cast anchor a couple of hundred strides from the shore. The entire cargo was brought up to dry out and the sail was spread out to repair. To our west, four small boats appeared headed our way. We armed ourselves and waited. The boats drew within hailing distance. We were told to surrender or be burned to the water line. Already we could see pots of tar boiling and archers ready to shoot flaming arrows at us. We replied that we were traders and did not seek hostility and asked what they wanted to trade. They laughed at us. They had a dozen bowmen with long bows to our three bows. They approached and let off a salvo of flaming arrows. We worked feverishly to pull these from the wood of the ship. Two hit the furled small sail and it caught fire. The men pulled in closer and again warned us that they would destroy us if we did not put by our weapons. Two of our sailors had burned their hands and could not handle swords and we were greatly outnumbered. We put down our weapons, hoping for our lives.

"Men swarmed aboard the ship. Three of them stood guard over us with arrows nocked to their bowstrings. It took them two days to unload the cargo of the ship amidst much shouting and rejoicing as they found the elephant tusks, the ebony wood and the hundred pots of honey still in the combs. After the cargo was removed they began a search for the money that all ships carry. That took another day and though the moneybox was well hidden behind a beam amidships near to where the mast is set, it was found. Their leader, Shaitan, spoke southern Arabic to his crews about burning our ship and killing us. They argued about killing us and keeping the ship for themselves, but decided not to because the dhow is old and slow. After much talking nothing more was said, they simply moved their boats and sailed away. As the last boat left a singing arrow from it screeched into the sky and our own flag, with the lion holding a mace was flown upside down, at half-mast from their ship in derision. They took everything except what we were wearing. All the ropes, the water clock, the navigation instrument, bedding, cooking pots, everything! We were left with one small half-sail and struggled down the coast like a bloated sick toad. No water, no food. Nothing. Before the attack each of us drank at least a small skin of water, which saved us. We are alive, but have lost all the profit for Tamrin's entire expedition."

"Did you say the name of the pirate was Shaitan?" asked one.

"Yes, the devil; and his boat's color is orange-yellow and has a blue eye painted on the hull, the evil eye."

"Then Tamrin will find him. On our return journey there will be a war of revenge. We will seek out the devil and burn his boats and village to the ground. Tamrin's anger will be terrible."

CHAPTER 7

It is better to have little than to get wealth by cheating.

Upon Tamrin's return, his son Rinta greeted him with assurance. "I have good news, father," said Rinta.

Tamrin regarded his son with pride. "The best news is that you and Setu are alive and well. What better news can there be?"

"My crew and I located a sunken ship and have something to show you!"

Rinta motioned to his first mate who approached, holding an object wrapped in canvas.

"Here. Open this."

Rinta's crew stood in a circle around the canvas covered box. Tamrin took away the cloth and saw a water-stained box. Looking quizzically at his son, he held the box up and asked, "What is the meaning of this?"

"Open it." Rinta and his crew watched Tamrin's expression change from curiosity to amazement. He exhaled with wonder. "Gold coins! Silver bullion. Gold bars—ancient gold bars… A treasure! Rinta, this will restore all we have lost during the storm. More than all!"

Tamrin held out his arm to his son. They clasped wrists

warmly as the crew laughed and cheered.

The reunion was complete as Setu walked toward his brother and father, having waited out of sight until Rinta made his presentation. Next day, it was time once again to unfurl the sails and head out to sea.

The convoy of ships approached the ancient city at the mouth of the Indus River called Kolachi, a protected port and trading center. The dhows' approach was hardly noticed among the hundreds of boats moving about in the bay. They dropped anchor near each other, each boat within jumping distance of the other. Sausage shaped bumpers made of woven rope and filled with kapok or silk cotton fibers; these were tied on the sides to prevent bumping wave action. Tamrin's dhows were among the first to have these resilient bumpers. On his first trip to Hindush he had seen the tree and its seedpods filled with water resistant white fluff and had brought back hundreds of seeds, which had been planted in many areas of Aksum. On the top of the mast of each boat their flag of the lion holding a torch was hoisted.

Tamrin hailed a small boat to take him to shore. He knew the name of the trader whose warehouse he had used on a previous trip. The first boat did not know the place. After a couple of tries a boat selling fresh fruit came alongside and after they had purchased the precious items, Tamrin and two of his sons, Ram and Rinta accompanied him, leaving Setu the Nubian and Aaghaa the Aksumite to guard the ships. Oil lamps were prepared and set at both ends of the ships to be lit at night. Those on the ships were constantly on the lookout for small boats that came to trade small items such as fruit, prepared foods, small birds in cages, and prostitutes. The girls offered for hire were very young and had cosmetic paint on their eyes and lips. The crew had been told that the boat girls were the worst ones to hire because they only stayed on a ship for less than an hour before they moved on to the next ship. The girls selected for such work, though very young, brought disease, but also took small items. Sailors warned each other to carefully watch every item when a girl was on board. Their favorite hiding place for coins, gold, jewelry, spoons, in fact any small thing, were their body cavities. In spite of all the warnings, the men on the ships who had not seen a woman for months took risks, as youth does, feeling invulnerable and wishing immediate satisfaction for their cravings. Their men remained in the boats when the girls climbed aboard the dhows and tried to trade sex for other items, particularly ivory and gold.

Tamrin and his small retinue were the focus of attention, being of different races and wearing spectacular clothing from Aksum. Their guide had a small whip, which he used to drive away urchins who gathered around the men like flies to feces. The owner of the warehouse, Poocho Sahib, was absent but his son prepared *chai* (tea) for the men and ordered sweets of various kinds to be brought while they waited. The men watched as the cook rubbed black leaves from a block of tea into a pan of boiling water, then added cardamom seeds and ginger. Finally, milk and *gur*, a brown sugar, were stirred in, and all were brought to a boil, united in one fragrant drink.

Tamrin remarked to his sons that they should find out where the black block of tea leaves came from and trade for these to take back to Aksum. With pantomimed speech and drawings their hosts revealed to the men that the tea came down the Indus River all the way from the mountain area of the snows. They drew sketches of men on horses crossing mountains from a high plateau. Finally one young man got an idea and hurried into the living quarters and brought a silk scarf. He wrapped the block of tea in the scarf and drew a rough map of the two originating in a far away country called Chin. To the amusement of the visitors he put the two in a small pack on his back and 'hiked' around the room. Exhausted, he climbed furniture and finally, after great labor deposited the bundle at Tamrin's feet.

"We must explore this drink of the Hindush. We have known the story the young man tried to tell us, of a route across the mountains far from here to the East, so high they are covered with a substance cold to touch which they call *buruf,* unknown to us in Aksum. But other traders have tales about this substance they call *beredo*, which they say falls from the sky in light flakes, and cover our mountaintops of the Mountain of Dabat. With my own eyes I saw a substance like it when I was a child. While traveling in the north part of Ethiopia my parents rested in a small village. A terrible storm with dark clouds and lightening terrified us. A substance like small pebbles fell, hard like rock. We ran outside and picked them up and they were in our palms only a few seconds before they became water. The natives there told us that at times this type of beredo falls from the sky in large balls which can kill animals if left outside."

Ram laughed. "So a rock can become water? I have never heard of this. Can water become a rock?" He did not challenge his father but gave his comment as a joke.

"I have never heard of water becoming such a rock. But I can tell you that I sucked on the stones from the sky, and they became water. This is very strange. Perhaps the gods of the Sun, Moon and Stars prepare the cold stones to remind people that to live too high on a mountain and approach their realm is dangerous." He laughed at the idea.

Ram smiled. "It is a good idea. We have no idea how far up the sky gods reside. Your story sounds true to me. If I were a star god, I would like the earth to remain distant. If I were a moon god I would warn the beings on the earth below to remain humble and not try to climb so high that they approach the heavens."

"The merchants of silk tell us stories of mountains that are white on the top, covered with such a substance all year long. If that is true then our idea of the sun god must not be correct. If one climbs high it becomes colder, not hot like the sun. It is confusing." Tamrin and his sons leaned back on cushions and became sleepy with their talk.

Poocho the Hindush merchant arrived, out of breath and apologetic. He greeted Tamrin with handshakes and bows at the waist. With him he brought an elderly white haired man, a person who had been a native of Aksum in his youth and who had been exchanged in slavery decades ago. He greeted Tamrin in halting Ge'ez and squatted on the carpet.

"How long have you lived here among the Hindush?" asked Tamrin.

"I was a man, a strong man, actually a wrestler and I traveled with my master, a trader from the coast of Aksum. Our ship reached this port, but its bottom boards became rotten. The dhow leaked and could not be repaired. While trying to arrange for getting hard wood for the repair, my father was killed in an accident. A log fell on him and smashed his legs and he became sick and died. I have been here since that time. My name here is *Dari*, because of my white beard."

"Dari, you were not here the last time I came. Do you work for other merchants and traders?" asked Tamrin.

"I have a farm north on the river in a small town called Sujawal. Usually I live there. I have a family and sons to help me. We grow sweet cane that is made into gur and Poocho ji purchases my product."

"I will pay you to help us. You can translate while we bargain. If our negotiations result in good gain for us I will reward you with an amount equal to what your new master here pays you. Do you understand?" He nodded and bowed.

"What is he telling you?" asked Poocho.

"My master wonders what we are talking about."

"Tell him about your conversation dealing with Sujawal and your farm, nothing else." Tamrin smiled at Poocho.

Dancing girls and musicians were brought in to entertain the visitors. Tamrin's sons watched spellbound as the girls gyrated, stamping their tiny feet, bells on their ankles jingling, and their hands moving at impossible angles. They did not make eye contact but looked above the heads of the men.

"My mother? Was she one of such girls that you bought many years ago?" asked Ram.

Tamrin nodded. "To this day she is the most beautiful woman I have seen. Your mother's gentle nature and care for the family is like gold. I only regret her sadness of never having been able to return to her people, or speak their language, except the few words she shares with you. Shanti! Yes, she was a girl like that one over there."

"With my share of profits from this journey I wish to take back two girls from here, one for myself and another small child who will speak my mother's language and be like her grandchild." Ram's eyes followed the dancing girl's gyrations. He appeared to be hypnotized. "These women are so much more beautiful than our own. It is their eyes. Like almonds. Their smooth skin and straight black hair!"

His father laughed. "Old man, translate for Poocho what my son has said and see how he reacts."

The translator spoke to the wealthy merchant for a moment, asked questions, glanced from time to time at Ram, nodding his head. Then he spoke.

"It can be accomplished. I can approach the fathers of young girls who may be willing to arrange a marriage. The dowry will be very high because the girls will never return to their families. Certainly you do not wish to obtain slave girls such as these dancers. They serve other men. You wish virgins from wealthy families. It would not be a good idea to obtain sisters from the same family because their bond is so strong that they would have a hard time becoming Ethiopian wives. It shall be done, but it will cost four gold bars."

"Tell Poocho that the girls must speak the same language as my Sindhi wife," said Tamrin. "This will please her because she will be able to tell jokes and have secrets with the girls. She is lonely. Tell him that we will choose from four girls and select two. You speak of four gold bars. That is like speaking of catching the moon. Part of this arrangement will be that you hire small boats to bring hundreds of large round stones to be put into the bilge of one of my ships as ballast, and that you hire the best sail makers to fashion new and spare raw silk sails for our ships."

Tamrin drank his tea but found the strong taste of cardamom unpleasant and set the cup aside. "The sails should be of woven of raw silk mixed with cotton that is from the cotton fields near Sujawal where the best cotton grows. The sails must then be made resistant to water and the sun. The oil must be from small whales that are killed in the harbor, the oil in the head near the brain, must be used on the fiber as waterproofing. So, for our first day I have spent four gold bars. You will provide me two stunningly beautiful girls and make new sails for my ships and tomorrow the rocks can be brought to the fourth dhow, the largest in my fleet." He stretched and got up to leave.

"A small item. I must see the gold bars and weigh them before we can proceed. Tomorrow. *Kul subha.* Tomorrow morning. But I will arrange for the ballast stones today." He did not extend his hand. He put his palms together and bowed slightly from the waist, avoiding contact with the black Ethiopian barbarian trader. Their habits were unclean.

Ebna could hardly sleep. From his place on the deck he could hear water slap against the bow of the ship, along with strange calls of sailors from one dhow to another late into the night, arguing and drunken brawls and the snoring of fellow crewmembers. Twice he got up and walked to the end of the small ship and looked at the lights of Kolachi, circling around the waterfront of the bay. He was surprised to see that a rat made its way from the ship tied next to them and boarded their dhow. He looked for an object to kill it but the rat sneaked under a pile of merchandise already piled on the deck.

Dawn came over the bay as the sun crept across the land from the far away Himal and across the vast expanses of Hindush. To Ebna it seemed to come abruptly, first light, then a hot orange orb lifted from the horizon. Immediately the temperature began to rise. He stood astern and urinated into the sea. When Adesh greeted him from behind, he jumped.

"Ebna! Good day. Today we will go with master Tamrin to bargain with the merchants who are interested in our goods. I will stand behind Tamrin to brush away flies and attend to his needs. You should sit next to me and tend to my needs, fetch things I ask for and keep out of the way."

"Good day. I didn't hear you coming. I saw a rat. It came aboard our ship." He looked disgusted.

"Did you hear what I said about our trip to Kolachi today?" He drew a bucket of water from the bay, stripped naked and bathed with salt water.

"When is the last time you bathed your body? I notice that you smell. You should bathe every day to prevent sores and lice." Adesh stood naked, but like most Africans had tucked his penis to the side between his legs while bathing or standing naked.

"I will bathe when you leave. I do not smell. When I lived in Aksum I…" he began to take off his tunic.

"Yes? You did what in Aksum?" "It is what I told you about before. The slaves bathed me daily, pouring oil of jasmine in the water and anointing my body. I should not speak about that time." He stood half naked waiting for Adesh to leave.

Adesh laughed. "I can go and get some scented oil and after your bath I can anoint you if you like."

Ebna turned and looked at Adesh angrily. "Go! Anoint master Tamrin. My name is Ebna now. Don't taunt me!"

"I forgot, wear your best and clean clothing and oil your hair. You will see that Tamrin will dress like a prince, and that I will have on a many-colored light silk robe. We must impress the merchants. They are impressed with wealth, gold, fine clothing and pomp. They in turn will dress like rajas to impress us. Watch carefully, keep an eye on me and my hand signals and never look the merchants directly in the face. You will be most humble. Do you understand?"

Tamrin's servants carried examples of all their trade items in jute sacks. Larger items such as ivory and ebony were carried openly on the shoulders of the servants. A procession of more than a dozen people left the boats and was greeted with drummers and flute players of an instrument called *bansuri*. Ebna heard the word *tamasha* and asked Adesh what it meant.

"They are putting on a show, we are putting on a show, and everyone is looking and they are excited. That is a *tamasha.* These people love *tamasha* because it is like a special show, an entertainment. Look at the hand-held drum that has small strings attached to it that has heavy beads, which swing around and hit the leather, making a rattling noise. Those drums are used to announce every *tamasha*, acrobats, snake charmers, dancing girls, and special visitors like us." Adesh walked next to Ebna and spoke to him softly, pointing out the wonders of the coastal city.

"That is a beggar's row. Each beggar is special and more hideous to attract people to be generous. Look over there. That entire street is called a *chiriaghar,* or *chirikhana.* See all the birds in cages, many different kinds from many countries and very expensive. I bought one on our last trip but it died. Perhaps it was lonely, or I gave it the wrong food. Look there. They are preparing for a wrestling match. See the huge men with oiled skin. They will slap their inner thighs and shout, *kabadi kabadi.*"

Their group walked through various markets. They approached shops that appeared to sell carpets, but behind these in back rooms was the real purpose of their trade, ivory. The servant that carried a large elephant tusk stopped at a signal, put his load down groaning as he stood upright. The merchant looked up from where he was writing on rolled papers. Tamrin and he had met before in previous years, yet the matter at hand was not one of welcoming a guest. They kept serious faces and greeted each other. Through the interpreter they began to speak of ivory.

"It is not a good year to buy ivory. A number of Hindush elephants in the terrain were killed this year and, look behind me; I have ivory to spare and a small market. The rajahs are content with what they have." Ebna did not understand the words but he seemed to get the meaning. Their trade item was not desired. The face of the *dukan wallah* looked almost sad as he spoke and he mopped his brow with his cloth and motioned for Tamrin to enter and eat sweets that were now set on a small carpet.

"Since we have traded before, I came here first," said Tamrin. "I know you to be a fair and honest man. I have many tusks of ivory, most of them larger than this one, most of them harvested this year, but I have two that are almost yellow from age and very hard, perhaps having lain in the jungle for years before they were found. I greet you and wish your household health. I regret I cannot eat, a sensitive stomach." He turned as if to leave.

The shopkeeper motioned with his hands in a gesture that was almost stroking. "What did you wish in return for your ivory? Perhaps I may be able to find a market for it. I am not sure."

Tamrin held up a silver bar the size of small brick. "This is one silver *deben* as you know. For a tusk that weighs as much as a man, like that one, the price is four deben. Weigh them both, I have little time and must move on. Perhaps your neighbor will have a greater interest in ivory from Africa, different than your Hindush ivory, little hollow and greater girth." He motioned for the slave to pick up the tusk.

"Let me weigh both, just to see what your *deben* is worth," said the merchant. He made motions with his fingers to hold the silver bar. "There is a new substance that is mixed with silver, also found in Africa that is very light and shiny but worth little. Let me see." He took the small bar, placed it on a scale, set weights on one of trays and the silver on the other, and then placed a few smaller weights until the bar was balanced. He reached for his abacus, a board with lines and round stones of different colors. He looked at the tusk, then at the silver, then at Tamrin. From his box he took a ruler made of ivory on which tiny marks were etched. He wrapped a string around the thickest part of the tusk, noted the length and then measured the string with his ruler. He reached for a small box and took out oblong silver bars shaped like tiny bananas, each with punched markings. These he put on the scale opposite from the bar that Tamrin had provided. Three of his smaller punched bars equaled one of Tamrin's bars. Tamrin put out his hand and one of the punched bars was placed in his palm. He passed it around to those in his group including

Adesh and Ebna. The bar had not been polished and was heavily tarnished.

Cushions were set on the carpet and Tamrin's party now sprawled comfortably in the background while the merchants talked. Tamrin never changed the expression on his face; it was always serious but pleasant with slightly raised eyebrows. The merchant's expression was at one moment joyous, the next apologetic, then sad, and finally friendly and defeated. His arms moved constantly. Ebna watched the process, entranced by the trading. The interpreter was magnificent. To Tamrin he expressed the meaning of the Hindush merchant with almost the same facial and body expressions; to the other he appeared to be Tamrin, even the depth of the tone of his voice.

The sun was directly overhead when the negotiations changed to serious nodding, and finally the jotting down of numbers and weights.

"In two days, send fifteen slaves to my ships to carry the ivory. On my own ship, away from the eyes of the crowds we will finish our transaction. Your payment will be in silver as agreed, plus a letter of credit for me to the gold dealer who is your brother. I am sure you will bring your armed guards, and my ship will be armed and protected. As you know your guards will have to beat back the crowds that press close to see."

Tamrin got up and prepared to leave. "I will bring guards, but oxen driven carts to carry the tusks. It is easier to carry larger loads more quickly. Until tomorrow then, at sunrise."

That night Ebna and Adesh slept on the deck because of the intense humidity and heat. They talked for hours, rehearsing what they had seen.

"My mother has many silver items from different countries. Some were given as gifts from Solomon, my father, bars of silver like those we saw today, but coins of different shapes stamped with numbers. One was stamped with the design of a bull. I played with these on the carpets during the winter months. They were my first toys."

"In my home I made toys out of clay which were baked. I had an entire farm of animals made of clay. My friend made a lion and I exchanged it for four of my farm animals. Clay and silver." He took out a small silver mirror from his shoulder bag. It was highly shined and smaller than half the width of his palm. He moved the candle so it reflected onto his face. He looked at his image, his beautiful eyes, dark long hair and perfectly formed lips. He pointed to the image, that of an amazingly beautiful person. "Silver," he said. He handed Ebna the mirror.

Ebna looked at his own image, his tightly curled hair, his broad face and nose and large teeth. He smiled broadly and pointed to the image. "Silver," he said. Adesh laughed and waved his finger at Ebna, then at the image. "Clay." He remained quiet to see how Ebna would take his remark. Ebna was initially stunned, then looked at himself again and nodded and said, "Clay." He put the mirror on the blanket and pointed to Adesh's chest and said, "Slave." Then to his own chest and said, "Emperor." Now he waited to see how Adesh responded. His friend's face remained sober but tears ran down his cheeks. Ebna reached forward and hugged Adesh who shrugged him away.

Tamrin, walking barefooted on the deck came across the two embracing boys. He stopped, turned around quietly and returned to his sleeping mat. He lay on his back and stared at the moon now rising. Three words that rhymed in his language came to him and he said them over and over. "Servant, Merchant, King."

Tamrin took the two young men with him on all his trading missions. At first they were amazed and enthralled by the sights, sounds, tastes and variety. After a week of getting up at dawn, returning at sunset, tired, hot and sometimes irritable, Ebna dreaded the next day. Tamrin seemed tireless and energized by the trading. Ebna was amazed at the information that he knew, the figures of weights, and the values of a huge variety of objects. Now, on their return trips to the ship there were oxcarts of materials that had been obtained to take back to Aksum: foods of a great variety, particularly dried fruits, spices of all kinds in bulk packed in huge clay pots and sealed with leather and wax. Ebna perked up when Tamrin visited and traded with the gem dealers. He knew the names of topaz, sapphire, ruby, emerald and garnet. The beauty of the gems was amazing to him. His mother had some jewelry, necklaces and rings, but what he saw in the markets astounded him. He could hardly imagine such wealth in one shop. The merchants took out only one or two stones at a time, and unwrapped them, removing their tiny papers and placing them with reverence on a black velvet cushion. Tamrin had one type of gemstone in mind that he prized above all others. It was a star sapphire that he had once seen in the turban of a rajah. On his third visit to the jewel market a jeweler placed a cabochon ruby on the black cushion, and then held it out so the sun's rays could catch its surface. The star shone back brilliantly, the light reflecting back so that a star, hidden within the stone revealed itself no matter what angle it was placed from the eye. This purchase took three days. Ebna knew it was of high value because six of the sailors accompanied the party back to the ships with hands on their swords.

Ram was told that four girls had been selected and that they were to be introduced the next day. All four brothers, along with Ebna, Adesh and Tamrin hiked to the warehouse of the merchant called Poocho. It had begun to rain and the streets were a quagmire of mud and filth. By the time their party reached their destination they were drenched, their legs dirty and covered with mud. Poocho was prepared. All the shoes were removed to be taken away and cleaned. Perfumed water was provided to wash their legs and feet, and slaves bent, washing each foot carefully and drying it with cotton cloths.

First there was a meal. Ebna had never seen a meal like the one spread before them. A roasted peacock was brought in, tail feathers spread out as if it was alive. Tiny roasted pigs, still sizzling on hot iron plates, curried eggs, piles of rice with raisins and coconut, topped with a fine silver foil that could be eaten. Musicians played different instruments, and the *tubbla* player pressed the leather of his drum in ways that made it sound as if it were speaking.

Dancing girls in thin *Benarsi* scarves gyrated in front of the visitors. Ebna's eyes were drawn to one girl who had a dark complexion but whose body was so perfectly formed, proud breasts, rounded buttocks and long lean legs; he became aroused, and could not turn his eyes away. He had never in his young life been so totally drawn to a woman. He turned his head to follow her movements. When she moved closer to where they sat, she saw his intense eyes; then danced in front of him. Ebna looked sad, yet he smiled. He had a gold coin his mother had given him for good luck before he left on his journey and without thinking he motioned to the girl who came close, glistening with sweat. He pressed the coin onto her damp forehead. Tamrin reached to stop him, but was too late. The coin was on the girl's forehead for a moment, she twirled and when she looked back it was gone, but her eyes flashed. All four girls danced before Ram, all of Sindhi origin, fair of complexion and light eyed. Each was more beautiful than the other. Three caught Ram's eyes as they danced by, but the fourth, dressed in green, danced to perfection, stamping her small feet, the silver bells jingling, but she looked above his head, her face a mask. She did not smile or make eye contact. Two girls were selected, one of whom was the one who did not look at Ram. They were brought before him and fell to their knees, their heads on the ground. Ram spoke in their language.

"I am seeking a wife and her attendant. I live in Aksum. My mother is from the *Sindh*. She will rejoice to have two girls such as you as part of our household. I will not make slaves of you. I wish to marry one of you and take the other as a concubine. Look up at me."

The girl in green looked up at Ram. He spoke directly to her. "I would like you for my wife. I already have wives in my country but none from the country of my mother. I will pay your father the marriage fee if you are willing to come to my country and leave Hindush."

She shook her head. "No, great sir. I do not wish to leave my county, my family and my life. I am from *Sujawal*. I would die of grief if I were forced to leave here and go with you to Ethiopia. I beg of you, remain here, buy a huge farm along the river near *Sujawal* and become part of our land and people. I beg you, do not ask me to give up my aged mother, my brothers and sister and my land and never return. I would die of grief." She was crying now.

Ram was stunned. He had never had a woman speak to him like this one did. Yet his yearning was great. Now all he could see was the girl in front of him, how she would be a companion for his mother, an honest person who spoke the truth of her mind. He looked at Poocho the trader and shook his head. "I have made a choice but I will not force her. My mother left her country here and had no choice and has grieved her entire life though loving my father Tamrin. No."

"Come tomorrow, come tomorrow. The girl's name is Shanti. She will change her mind. Tomorrow." The merchant stared at the girl with hard eyes.

She spoke in Sindhi, the language of his mother. "Lord from Aksum, if I am taken against my will tomorrow, I will not reach your country. The sea will take me. Do not force me, lord." She knelt on the carpet. Ram was quiet for many minutes and stared at the girl's back. Finally he spoke. "I will go with you to your city of Sujawal and stay with your family for a week and marry you there. Then I will return with you and we will go back with my father Tamrin to Aksum. I promise you that each year in this season, just as the monsoon winds are coming from the north to the south that we will return to your family for a month so that your mother can see your children and you. Each year, as long as I am a merchant and have the health to travel. After five years, if you no longer wish to stay with me in Aksum then you may return here to your people. After five years I release you from marriage to me. But only your daughters may accompany you back home. Look at me. I do not want a slave. I want a friend for my mother and a young and beautiful and honest wife for myself. You. It is pleasant to speak in the tongue of my mother. I always thought it was just our secret language."

The girl in green looked up at Ram. "I believe you. The merchant Poocho, there, would receive much gold from you for me. He does not own me! I was taken from my village six weeks ago against my will. I will agree to your offer but half the gold must be paid to my family when you visit *Sujawal* so that they can purchase land and no longer be tied in a bond to their landlord. It would make the people of my family land-owners, not bonded workers with little choice."

Ram nodded. "Tell me truthfully for I will know. Have you slept with a man and know any man carnally?"

She turned her body quickly and stared at Poocho. "Ask him." Ram did not ask any thing of the merchant, but the merchant replied as if he had been asked a question. "When she was purchased from the uncle in her village, I asked the same question. She is a virgin. My own woman tells me this. I believe it. Because of this, her value is double the other beautiful girl you chose, who is not. If you go to her village, you must pay me a percentage of the dowry for finding her."

Ram told his father what had transpired and what he desired. Tamrin understood the urgency of Ram's selection and fixation on the girl. The merchant could not understand their Ethiopian speech. Tamrin warned his son to leave the negotiations to him. Already the merchant was trying to double the price for finding the girl. Yet she said she had been taken by force.

The dancing girls from the first group sat quietly to one side. Ebna had ignored the interactions of Tamrin and Ram; he could not take his eyes away from the dark-skinned girl. Tamrin watched his reaction to the girl and made a resolve.

"Our ships leave in two weeks. Ram, find two good riverboats for the girl and you. Arrange for your travel to *Sujawal*. Take four men with you. We leave in two weeks. Do not exchange a laying hen for a clutch of eggs. Go, and when you return your ship will be filled with trade items and stones. Take Ebna with you as one of the men on your boat. He can learn about this country and travel on the river." Ebna looked up when his name was spoken.

Ram leaned over and spoke to him. "So, you have become a man. Is this the very first girl that you have looked at and have desired?" He did not wait for a reply. "You will see her when we return. But now, you will be part of our small river expedition to Sujawal and have practice with the bow and arrows and other weapons. There are many ducks and wild fowl on the river. You will have a chance to shoot some for our food. The dolphin is a strange creature like a small whale that lives in the river. The people call it the *susu*. I will ask Poocho to find us a harpoon before we leave. Perhaps we can kill one and take it to Sujawal for the wedding feast. We leave tomorrow at dawn."

Ebna slept fitfully on the deck of Ram's dhow. He dreamed of the face of the dark skinned girl, her large eyes and full body and awakened long before dawn and looked across the water to the lights of the town, wondering where they had taken her and what would become of her. There were two slave girls that served his mother in Aksum and had fussed over him, even dressed him as a child. Every day they greeted him with small hugs and happy faces, a kiss on his forehead. He loved them, he had always known them, but they were more like older sisters, he thought. Yet he had always felt stirring warmth in their short embraces and teasing. But the slave girl who danced for them yesterday, owned by Poocho stirred strong longings that he could not put aside. He did not even know her name. Her eyes had told him that she recognized his eyes.

Two river dhows were loaded with skins of water, food of many sorts including plantains and mangoes. The Indus River was sluggish against them but using sails and paddles they set off toward the town of Sujawal, which was a two-day journey. The women were all put on the second dhow and given the small cabin for privacy.

Ebna was unhappy. He hated to stay on the deck in the open sun. He disliked the long pole that was given to him to push into the sand to move the boat forward. His hands were soon blistered and his skin sunburned. He sat on the edge of the boat and scooped water with a small pot and poured it over himself. Ram said nothing, simply watched Ebna, knowing who he was. His telling a secret to Adesh resulted in Adesh telling Rinta; Rinta telling Ram and in the process, other ears had heard. No one relieved the prince of his duties. All just watched and waited to see how he reacted to severe physical discomfort.

Ebna looked toward the small hut on the craft hoping that food would be served, but no one else seemed hungry or concerned. He glanced at the boat following theirs and saw that the women were sitting in the shade of a small cotton canvas, eating. They saw him looking and from a distance, one girl held up a mango and motioned for him to come and get it. That act irritated Ebna and he looked at the girl's face and remembered it, thinking that when he got a chance he would surely …Now he wondered what he could surely do. No one had ever played jokes or taunted him before; his mother was stern, but the servants were always there to satisfy his wants. He glanced back at the boat behind theirs. Two of the girls were pointing at him and laughing. Obviously they had not heard any gossip.

After four hours on the water the boats were pulled into a small bay near a huge banyan tree that grew on the bank. They tied up and the entire crew removed their clothes and bathed, keeping half submerged, their eyes closed in pleasure. Ebna joined them but had never been completely naked in front of other men before, much less women. He walked into the water with his *dhoti* wrapped around him. This caused everyone to look at him because he acted differently, so ducking down he took it off and soaked in the lukewarm water. The women waded into the water on the far side of the tree and they too bathed but none removed all their clothes. Ebna glanced toward them quickly, then came out of the water and tied his dripping wrap around his hips.

Food was provided. Two baskets had flat *tundoori* breads stacked in small piles; the other smaller basket had raw tomatoes, raw onions and a dish of ground red pepper mixed with salt. He watched as the women ate the raw onions, dipped the half ripe tomatoes in red pepper and ate this with their bread tearing off chunks with their teeth. Ebna disliked red pepper. He disliked raw tomatoes, and raw onions were new to him. He was very hungry and imitated the others who watched what he did. He wondered why so many eyes seemed to look at him, at all his actions. Some of the men smiled and whispered to each other when he ate red pepper and coughed. Ebna knew the reason. He had not been able to keep a secret, and Adesh had not kept his secret either. The burden of knowing that everyone knew that he was the prince, son of the wise Solomon made him depressed. Now, every glance, every word spoken, every command given him, his every action took on new meaning. He deeply wished he had not told his secret and not broken his promise to his mother and Tamrin to keep his status unknown. He sighed. Once a fly escapes through an open window there is no catching it.

Ram motioned for him to come and sit near him. He was braiding long strands of horsehair and wanted Ebna to hold one end, rather than holding it between his toes. He did not look at Ebna but concentrated on the task at hand, but spoke softly to Ebna.

"Even Emperors make mistakes. Everyone makes mistakes. Most promises are broken, but in your case the result of your telling Adesh has huge consequences. He sleeps with Tamrin; they talk of many things and he talked about you. He was very surprised at what he heard. He told me. I asked him if he had told anyone else and he said he had, but to those who could keep a secret. Then he laughed. Ebna, what should you do now for the rest of the trip? Should we pretend that all the crew does not know and for almost half a year play secret games? Tell me. What do you think we should do?"

Ebna watched Ram's clever fingers braiding the horsehair lariat and was quiet for a long moment. He looked up at Ram. "Tell me what you think is the best thing to do, Ram. Please."

"You must feel and understand the result of your own action. You decide what to do and what is best now. Our trip is only half over.

Now what?" Ram glanced at the boy's serious face and waited.

Ebna did not like to think about the options. Yet he did. If nothing more was said, all the interactions with everyone on the long trip would be acted out, would not be real reactions from the others. If he confessed to them all about his mistake, then he would be losing face and be shamed. He already felt ashamed of himself, but six months, even six days of playing pretend games was more than he could bear to think about.

"Listen Ebna, whatever you decide you will live with it. Your future will be affected by it. People will give nicknames to the new Emperor that you will not hear, but they will all speak. Think of such nicknames Ebna. Think hard."

Ebna's voice cracked. "When all of us are together at the village and having a meal I will tell everyone that I promised to keep a secret, that I told a friend my secret, and that broke the trust my mother the Queen and Tamrin had for me. I will tell them I made a mistake and I am sorry about it and that for the rest of the trip I am to be called Ebna as before and treated as a young servant who will do all the things necessary for this entire trip." He took a deep breath and looked at Ram's face.

"Son of a wise man, a wise decision. When you tell them, act like a man, not a sniveling child. I have had good friends who were mortally wounded in battle ask me to plunge in a sword and kill them rather than fall into the hands of the enemy when we retreated. I did so. Everyone watched my face and my eyes. My eyes were moist, but I did not break down and cry. There is a balance between being a caring man and being an unfeeling despotic ruler or leader." Ram finished his braiding, got up casually and moved to the front of the boat. "You have learned, and our people say, 'He who learns teaches'. All of the crewmembers have been put in a difficult position because they see before them the future emperor, yet they are to see a ship's errand boy as well. That is difficult. If you live to become emperor, remember this day well. Hold your council, keep your promises and know that the dearest friend, the most intimate lover, the person you trust most will act just like you did, tell what should not be told. Yes, my mother keeps secrets from me and from her other sons. She must be a 'Queen' at all times or we brothers would probably kill each other."

Ebna went to the back of the boat and watched the sailor move the steering arm. The wind was in their favor, to the east, which allowed the dhows to move sluggishly against the current. The steersman nodded to Ebna.

"Do you want to try it? I will stand next to you. All you have to do is keep your eyes up on the sail. You can't see the wind, but the sail tells you where it is coming from and how strong it is. Look over there on that rope, five wind tails have been tied. See how they all blow in a certain direction. That will tell you which way the wind blows. The rule is to always satisfy the sail. Look, if I over steer and head directly upstream the sail suffers and the wind can't catch it. So I move it back again to get the wind in the sail and steer slightly to the left, but still heading up stream." He motioned for Ebna to hold the steering bar. For more than an hour Ebna stayed aft and with his instructor began to understand and feel where the power for the motion of the ship was. Too much motion in the sails and he could not control the direction, too little and the boat lost headway.

"Ebna, it is like marriage. At times the woman at the helm, at times the man, but if the family and children are to move forward, there must be enough agreement to move with the push and the flow of life. If either is too strong it disrupts the family. On a ship there can only be one captain and in an army, only one general. Weak sons come from a home that is divided, with over dominant mothers and fathers who are absent in their love. Always arguing over the helm. Weak daughters come from fathers that spoil and favor the girls unduly. Such a house cannot move forward. Do you understand?"

The helmsman took over. Ahead there were floating hazards. Trees that stuck up out of the water bespoke a terrible storm up river, which had uprooted trees. Both dhows steered for the shore long before the floating trees approached them too closely. Slowly, the trees moved by in the current, their roots a perch for cormorants and mergansers.

A cry went up. "Susu! Susu! Look there beyond the floating trees."

Ebna watched as the creatures, larger than a huge man surfaced and blew, taking air from a hole in the top of their head. Their eyes seemed to be covered with a membrane and they looked blind, yet they moved about easily. One surfaced with a fish in its mouth. A merganser flew toward it hoping it would drop the fish. Other birds now flew to where the Susu last surfaced and landed on the water, alert for a possible meal.

Ram retrieved the harpoon he had borrowed and stood at the front of the dhow. "Try to move into the area where the birds are floating. Watch out for the dead trees. The dhow moved slowly toward the spot, the sail hardly catching any breeze. Ram stood poised. He had removed his outer robe and stood half naked, his brown, lean body now moist with sweat. As they approached the branches of the floating tree, a snake, which had been curled around the branches, slithered off into the water.

"Naga, Naga!" The women shouted. The python undulated through the murky water and headed straight for the women's boat. The sailors waited, hoping it would come close enough for them to hit with a pole or slash with a sword. It veered away and headed directly across the river and then was swept away out of their sight.

Ram stood with the harpoon, hopeful for a sighting close enough for him to impale the dolphin. To his surprise, it surfaced for an instant to breathe, directly in front of them. He threw the harpoon but only managed to strike its body toward the back. The harpoon held and the beast pulled strongly against the rope, thrashing its tail as it tried to get away. The action moved the front of the boat around toward the deeper current where it was pulled by the flow of the current.

"The anchor! Throw out the anchor, we don't want to drift too far." The anchor, a basket of woven bamboo fibers containing heavy black stones, was tied to a sturdy rope. A crewman lifted it over the side and dropped into the water. When the rope went slack the men tied it to the rear of the boat onto the pivot of the steering mechanism. Everyone watched Ram. No one rushed to his assistance. This was a test of man against a creature, a test to see which would tire first. Men from the other boat shouted encouragement, and dropped anchor.

After two spirited dashes the Susu tired and came to the surface, breathing audibly. Then from its mouth came a cry like a wounded child. Ram drew in the line carefully until the porpoise was next to the boat. Two men leaned over the gunwale, almost tipping the boat and stabbed with spears. Blood filled the water and the men shouted happily.

The boat that had been behind them was now off to the side with everyone watching and yelling across the water. Many had never seen a live dolphin before and were fascinated as the animal was carefully lifted over the side of Ram's dhow. The women's boat was carefully poled over and the men shouted at each other.

"Uncle, you have provided for the marriage feast. All the relatives will eat meat. The pots will be boiling the blubber, making ghee oil for cooking and for the lamps."

From the other boat came women's voices and happy clapping. One girl had watched Ram harpoon the Susu, standing half naked, his muscles rippling. She had watched as he fought against the beast and overcame it. She watched as he wiped the sweat from his body with a cloth and lean against the mast as the men dealt with the body of the porpoise. She watched and nodded, a happy smile on her face. The other women watched her watch and they too, smiled knowingly.

CHAPTER 8

A single word of reproof is sufficient for a wise man.

Tamrin's scribe entered all transactions, the trades, cash sales, the gold exchanged, the tons of material brought aboard each of the ships; he entered all in the manifest. Finally he entered the amount paid for the three girls, two for Ram and one dark skinned girl he said was for the Queen. This purchase, though not as lavish as for the two other women, depleted the silver bar reserves. The scribe entered all that had been lost in the ship that had been attacked by pirates. He shook his head. He tried to put all the gains in one column and all the costs in the other with estimated worth of things such as silk, cotton cloth, tooled leather bags, jewels, dried sugar bricks and strange items like smoked dried flesh from the river porpoise, a delicacy that was prized in Aksum by the wealthy. He noted that Tamrin had agreed to purchase sixteen large burlap bags of this dry smoked meat, and wondered if he was aware that the profit would balance his costs.

Tamrin could read numbers in Gi'iz but was not literate. He was able to write symbols for most of the trade items. Tamrin had an unusual mind for details. He could tell Bahbey his scribe, almost the exact items that were on the various ship manifests. He knew what each ship held and importantly remembered the merchants who cheated or gave short weights. Bahbey brought his scroll to Tamrin who sat under an umbrella at the rear of the largest ship.

"Bahbey, are we going to get rich on this voyage?" He laughed as he asked, answering his own question.

"Master, the loss of the cargo from our largest dhow was a great blow. The ebony wood and elephant tusks alone would have made you a profit, without the exchanges of all the rest of the fleet of ships. Treasure was found. Yet this trip you have agreed to buy the most costly items, the three girls, which means you will only break even if sales of the items you take back find a good market in Aksum. It is difficult to estimate, master, but the gods were not on our side this journey."

"Do you see the white hairs in my beard and the hairs on my head? Most of them are from this trip. Perhaps Ram should take over and I should find a quiet place above the harbor and simply rest. I have served the Queen, regarding her son Menelik, and now I should serve myself. Some have advised me to simply take a journey to the inland of Ethiopia, travel all the way to the mountain that has snow, see the great valley that looks like a tear in the earth, kill a lion or two, and marvel at the waters of the Blue Nile. But I am tired of travel. Thirty years is a lifetime, and what is my reward? Sons? Wealth? A position of respect? Bahbey, I think I will ask you to arrange to find men who are masters of writing in three languages, all who speak Gi'iz, and I will write my memoir, those things that happened, and more important, what I thought about it."

"Master, you are still in your prime, a man of great knowledge and strength. Your white hairs, each one, speak of your success. Perhaps I will explore for you when we return. I will find wise men from the east, from the west and north who will tell your story, write it down." He now laid the account book on Tamrin's outstretched hands.

"Before I do that I have a score to settle, a large score. My revenge will be sweet. There is a yellow boat with an eye painted on it, the boat of a pirate along the Arabian coast, about halfway to our destination that I wish to see. Its master will kneel and kiss my feet and beg for his life. Pirates are worse than fleas on a dog. Worse than tapeworms which eat the food in our guts, a condition worse than the wasting disease of leprosy. I have made an agreement with Poocho that will cost us all of the profit of this journey. He has agreed to hire crews for four dhows that will accompany ours to the territory where the pirates strike. Each of those boats will look like fat traders, but each will carry no cargo except a dozen bowmen and those who are expert with the sword. I have agreed with Poocho that if the pirates are beaten, that we will move to their villages along the coast, pillage everything of value, take all the women and girls and leave behind bloody chaos. All the spoils will go to the soldiers that Poocho hires, and a quarter of all of those will go to Poocho who hired them. Look, over there, see those four boats. They are even now fitting new sails and hammocks to hang below decks for the soldiers. Only food and water is being loaded, and good food, dried meats, dried fruits, rice from the swamps near Kolachi."

"Master, revenge can be bittersweet. What if the pirates burn our ships to the water line and take all we have? They are masters of fighting and their small boats with oarsmen and sails move about like water bugs."

"It is in the hands of the gods, which ever ones we all pray to. The scriptures that are read daily to our queen have the words of the One God. 'Revenge is mine sayeth the Lord. I will smite them with a rod of iron! An eye for an eye, a tooth for a tooth.

I am a jealous God.' Let us learn from the ancient writings. Poocho showed me a new weapon that came down through the silk route, down the river to Sukkur and Kolachi. It is from Chin, and called the Hubei crossbow. It is a strange bow that is like a cross on a handle and shoots short darts. This cross has a copper trigger that releases the dart. One type can reload quickly and shoot two darts in the time it takes to shoot one with the long bowmen. I have bought one such bow and the soldiers on the other ships will have both long bows to shoot fire arrows and cross bows to overpower the archers on the boats which are generally smaller than our dhows."

Tamrin's eyes were intense. "There is a poison that Poocho spoke of. It is ancient. He read this to me from their ancient Sanskrit scripture. *Jalam visravayet sarmavamavisravyam ca dusayet,"* which translates to "Waters of wells were to be mixed with poison and thus polluted." Indians are poison masters. He showed me the darts of the crossbows. On the shaft of special darts there is a small groove and in it is placed the dried poisons of the Hindush, including dried cobra venom. Even if the warriors barely wound the pirates, they will soon die. Truly I want revenge. The scourge of pirates, parasites of all merchants will be avenged. Others will hear of the reprisal and think carefully about flying the Ethiopian flag with the lion upside down! In this only my name may be known, Tamrin the Merchant defeated the pirates of lower Arabia. All of the longbow arrows will be coated with the poison. Even a flesh wound will be lethal. "

The river dhows returned from the marriage ceremony. With monsoon winds beginning, and the favorable flow of the river, the expedition made good time and arrived two days earlier than Tamrin had expected. Ram and his two new women were ferried to his own dhow. The dark skinned girl was taken to Tamrin's dhow and put in the care of Adesh, the beautiful castrated one.

Adesh and the girl took an immediate liking to each other. She loved to cook and relieved Adesh of kitchen duties, but she also loved sweets and with the Indian gur from the hold, she produced pastries and sweets, and drinks flavored with pomegranate juice. Tamrin had decided that Ebna would travel the return journey on Ram's dhow and learn how to use the crossbow. Two additional crossbows had been purchased so that all the crewmembers would learn to use them well.

While they were in port the first monsoon rains came. The skies opened up and water poured on the ships in sheets and made its way into the holds. Servants were sent to the bilges to drain out the water, and in three days, mold began to appear on slippers, belts, shoes and even leather water carriers. Then, abruptly the rains stopped, yet the wind from the southeast blew hard. This is what Tamrin had been waiting for. The eight ships under full sail left the harbor and sailed into the Hindush Sea, their sails taut. Tamrin assigned three changes of watches at the steering arm. Men not working slept, unless the brass gong was sounded to come to deck. Adesh was busy and exhausted. It was his duty to climb the wet masts and tie down sails, unfurl others and make sure all ropes were neatly coiled like cobras in a basket. Wind in the sails meant following seas and the person at the helm had to keep constant watch against a huge swell that could engulf them.

They made good progress in the windy weather, but paid the price of exhaustion. In three days there was no let up and the dhows literally flew across the water. The last in line was the dhow captained by Rinta who was instructed to keep the convoy together and not let ships lag behind. Rinta, high strung and often impatient, herded the ships ahead of him like a shepherd dog, insisting that all the ships carry two stern lights, and if these were blown out, they were to be lit again. The caravan moved toward Aden and all the men became more alert. The soldiers prepared their cross bows and weapons, but kept hidden behind canvas sheets strung across the decks.

Tamrin's face was stony, his eyes hard, and the crew avoided him. He seldom had angry moods, but the crew could see that he was thinking of revenge, of killing, of stopping the pirates once and for all. He walked quietly on the deck and inspected the weapons of the crews. In front of the dhow was a line of other dhows, all moving with the wind. He looked at his flotilla and knew that each of his sons and the crewmembers were prepared for a battle.

A small sail appeared on the horizon ahead of Tamrin's first ship. Then as quickly as it had appeared it seemed to vanish beneath the horizon. Tamrin knew that the pirates were waiting behind the small peninsula that was ahead of them. On all the dhows the pots of tar were boiling. All the sailors drank deeply knowing that during a fight there would be no time to quench thirst. Tamrin looked at the dhow ahead of his own to see if he could see Ebna, but the figures were too small. He thought of the Queen's words, that the lad needed to become a man, to experience work, hunger, thirst, and perhaps danger. Now Tamrin regretted that he had not kept the lad on his own dhow. Injury to Ebna never entered the mind of his mother: he would become a man on the journey. The Queen herself knew about war and fighting, but had never been in the fray of an attack herself and had never witnessed the gory mess that a sword made of a face or the horror of an arrow protruding from the back of a man.

The plan that Tamrin had made with all the dhows was that when the first pirate scout appeared, each dhow would join the others and sail forward in a rough semi-circle and remain within shouting distance of each other, or at least near enough to be able to hear the ships' bells. Tamrin's ship bell was the largest and its tone easily recognized by the others. The fleet would hear three loud rings, and at that signal all sails would be raised on the masts for maximum forward speed. They would wait for the fight to come to them, for the pirates to move toward them and make their threats. From past experience Tamrin knew that the leader of the pirates would first send a warning to heave to, or be burned to the level of the water. His own ships would use this sign as a signal to let the sails go slack so that they would become smaller targets for flaming arrows.

Their fleet of dhows moved forward with the wind strongly behind them. The pirates would have to come to them at an angle, quartered against the wind, which would slow them and make them less maneuverable. Tamrin avoided coming too close to the land to avoid the sand bars and reefs that took as many ships to the bottom as the flaming arrows of pirates.

The first village they passed looked peaceful. Small boats bobbed at anchor and people stopped their normal activities to watch Tamrin's boats sail past. The second village, the largest, was devoid of dhows and other sailboats. They had moved off and were waiting like jackals waiting for hares.

Tamrin was caught unawares. He and his lookouts were watching for sails on the horizon, but the pirates had taken down their sails, and only the sticklike masts bobbed up and down on the seas, often hidden by the swells. Tamrin's ships passed the pirates' boats that were waiting to the west. Then to their surprise, the pirates' boats hoisted sail and were now behind Tamrin's fleet, moving quickly toward them, aided with the strong wind.

Alarm bells were sounded on all the dhows which lumbered along, heavy with cargo as the pirate boats approached. There was no warning this time. The smaller and quicker boats approached the dhows from behind and immediately began to shoot fire arrows at the sails. Tamrin sounded his alarm with the bell and all the sails were furled. The attack was not silent. The attacking boats carried drummers, and the sounds of drums were like constant thunder as they approached. The nearest boat had a large eye painted on its hull.

Tamrin's crewmembers had strapped chest and body protectors of leather on the front of their bodies. These body armors seldom stopped an arrow fired from a longbow at close quarters, but they prevented many deaths. Adesh did not wear a protective leather apron as he scampered up and down the masts. He perched high and shouted to Tamrin about the approach of the pirate ships, pointing to the boat that had the drummers, perhaps the leader of the group. Four fire arrows arched into the sky toward Tamrin's dhow, all aimed at the same target, Adesh. To Tamrin's horror one arrow struck the boy directly in the chest and he fell to the deck, the tar arrow still smoking. His beautiful face, eyes open, stared directly into Tamrin's face, but Adesh was dead, impaled with a flaming arrow of death.

Tamrin placed his hand on the face of the boy and remained there, still and bowed over while the fighting raged around him. His eyes filled with tears but his face radiated hatred and resolve. His hand trembled as he reached down and closed the eyelids of Adesh's beautiful face.

Now the four men with cross bows and poison arrows all aimed at the same target, the drummers and the longbow archers. Three arrows found their mark, but at the great distance did little bodily damage. One pirate sailor was hit in the leg. He pulled out the dart, held it up for other crewmembers to see. They laughed as they prepared to fire four more fire arrows at the dhow, now close by. Again the darts rained on them like wasps and screams came from the men who had been injured in the first volley. They staggered around on the deck and held their wounds, feeling the first effect of the poison. Two drummers were hit and their thunder abruptly ceased.

Tamrin's dhows, with sails furled, bobbed like corks as the pirates approached. Burning sails, screams of pain, and the mayhem that is war, falling bodies and wounded men, blood and fire and the sound of conch shells being blown, terrified the women on the second ship. The black girl on Tamrin's dhow cowered in the protective shelter on the deck until a flame arrow crashed into its roof. She ran out, climbed up, and pulled out the arrow, tossing it overboard. She beat out the fire with her wrap-around skirt. Then she saw Adesh's body on the deck below her, and crying with a loud, anguished scream, jumped down and went to the body of her friend, slumped over it and collapsed in tears, a black shiny naked back against the bloody deck. Tamrin ran to her and pulled her into the shelter.

Only two of Tamrin's smaller dhows, those with shallow draft, were able to brave the sandy shoals that protected the pirate's village from the larger boats. The larger dhows attacked the pirate boats relentlessly. Soon all but one was burning. Most of their crews were too ill from the darts' poisons to work at putting out fires. The two boats with shallow draft unfurled their sails and moved toward the pirate village, little more than a group of about fifty grass-roofed huts. Yet, with long bows the sailors were able to launch burning arrows into the village. One after another of the grass roofs caught fire. Women and children ran screaming and shouting, trying to pull valuables from their homes, bedding, fishing gear and food. The crews, tired of battle, pulled away and joined their sister dhows, extinguishing fires still burning on their ships. The Hindush boats moved to the beach area, intent on taking their spoils-- the women and female children, and the goods they had salvaged.

Five of Tamrin's sailors had been killed during the battle,

none from swords, all from the pirate archers' arrows. Among the dead was Tamrin's third son Aaghaa, whose mother was of desert lineage. A falling spar had struck him during the battle. His crew mates undressed and washed his charred body. They gathered and dropped ashes from the sail that burned him into the sea. Then seawater was poured onto him, and his body dropped into the sea with the others who had been killed. Tamrin, stern faced, witnessed the burials at sea, then turned and walked to the front of the ship where he quietly wept for Adesh and his son, vowing that this would be his last journey.

The return to their homeport near Aksum was somber. Red flags flying from each of the dhows signaled the arrival of Tamrin's men. Long before they moored the news traveled to Aksum and to the Queen of Sheba. Her son had been spared, but Tamrin's losses were great. Usually the unloading of cargo was a time of feasting and happy shouting. Now as the ships were unloaded one after another by slaves, the mood was somber. Many glanced away from the wounded sailors. Wives and children gathered and much weeping was heard in the streets of Aksum for their dead, never to be seen again. From each sailor killed, a talisman had been taken for his family: a knife, a hair comb, an ornate belt, even a pair of Hindush sandals. This was all that the families had as reminders of their dead fathers and husbands.

Widows sat in their courtyards at night, stared into the fire, and would not be comforted. Their lot was now in doubt within the family. Would a brother of the dead husband take them to become wives? The middle-aged widows now anticipated a life of labor within the extended family. Some of the dead men had four wives, and all of these sat together mourning their loss, as well as their uncertain future. They knew their husband's property would be taken by blood relatives; that they could be left without a mite and that they would rely on others to leave portions of a crop in the field for them to glean, fallen fruit for them to pick up. Most wept because their children were now fatherless, and to be a fatherless child meant their share of the household wealth would go to the next male relative in line.

Tamrin mourned for three days before he asked to meet with his queen in her stone palace. He walked into her meeting room and looked around, then saw her sitting on a low couch toward the far wall with her son Menelik. Both turned, sad and serious, to face Tamrin, who remained quiet until Sheba spoke.

"Thank you for bringing me back my son Menelik. He has changed. He has seen death, has felt the sting of the scorching sun, has been challenged and has responded manfully. He has also felt the sting of shame at not having kept his secret and of losing face. This too is a lesson he will never forget. Rulers must keep their council. His grief for the death of Aaghaa and his friend Adesh is great. He was telling me about his bodyguard Desha and how he had died while shielding him from an arrow. He too will always know the meaning of death and the loss of one dear and the value of living and having another morning to greet the god of the sun." She held out her hand.

Tamrin did not take her hand. "My queen, these hands are still remembering the blood and gore, the feel of death, the feel of the bodies hefted over the rail into the sea. Later. Later. I am here in your presence and that is my only joy today. I have lived to return with your son and with that to renew my pledge of honor and fealty to you. Today and for a week to come allow me a time to mourn, to fast, to greet the rising sun and to worship the setting sun god in honor of my safe return."

He turned to face Menelik. "Ebna, the reality of death is hard to learn. You learned to kill beasts to eat, but to see men in their prime die and look at the surprise in their face as death reaches for them, that lesson is the hardest. Young men think they will live forever, yet death may come at any time. You have learned Ebna, that death is as close as the arrow that flies by night. From death of a close friend comes humbleness, and the question, 'Why was it not I?' Our people say that to die in the glory of combat for one's country, is honorable. Those who say this have never rubbed against the misery of pain, suffering, loneliness and terror that the messenger of death brings. When I buried my son, my loyal crew members, my cabin boy at sea and saw their bodies sink away, I was struck by the mystery of life, the mystery of our conception, our living and then nothingness. Mystery! Ebna, I do not think they died because their time had come; that it was set in the stars. No, they died because an arrow killed them."

The Queen looked at the two men she loved more than any others and could hardly bear their grief. "My faithful Tamrin, rest now, honor the sun god and then return when your mind and heart are able. I will have a small feast prepared for just the two of us and we shall drink wine from grapes grown from the vineyards of Solomon. There is yet a great challenge for you and my son. Menelik, you shall return to Solomon and learn from your father and bring back the best from that kingdom. You, Tamrin, only you can guide him to Israel and once more return with him to Aksum."

Tamrin bowed his head. "I have no Benarsi scarves. My gift for you this time is not a silk carpet. It is a slave girl; a dark skinned Indian lass of great beauty, pleasant attitude and sorely in need of a loving motherly face. Her name is Bakht. She will serve you with her life." He clapped, and the girl walked in, knelt and held her head low, terrified of the Queen. Sheba touched her and with one finger lifted her to her feet.

"Bakht, I need your help. You will live with me and take care of my needs. I will take care of your life and promise that when

I am old and have white hair, I will care for your children as well." The girl did not understand the words, but she understood the expression on the Queen's face, a smile much like her own mother gave her. She avoided Menelik's eyes.

The Queen turned and left Tamrin standing on a carpet he had given her after his last journey, a carpet from the Hindush made of silk with hues of purple and blood red on the paisley patterns. The girl rose and followed Tamrin who led her to his household where he would put her under the care of his Hindush wife, the mother of his son Ram. There she would learn how to serve.

PART 2

CHAPTER 9

A good friend always loves, but a brother is born for adversity.

The Aksum palace of the Queen was unusually quiet. As Tamrin approached, riding his own Arabian stallion, a mare whinnied inside the palace stables. The effect was instant. The stallion's head went up and he whinnied loudly, snorted and became agitated, forgetting that he had a rider. Tamrin slapped the beautiful beast on his neck with his hand twice before the horse responded to him. It had the habit of raising and lowering its head when it responded to commands, either from Tamrin's heels, the reigns, or his voice when he used his given name, Abtar, the strong one.

"Abtar, you have work to do today. No mares for you. You are going to run full speed with me to the seacoast, then back home again. No mares today." He patted the arched neck in front of him. Again a mare whinnied and Abtar's ears moved to pick up the sound. Tamrin kicked him in the ribs and the horse ran forward rapidly, its head moving from side to side.

Tamrin gave the reins to the keeper of the imperial stables. "Don't take off his saddle. I will not be here long. Give him a drink and put honey in the water so he drinks it all. Put this powerful one at the far end of the stables in a stall. One of your mares is in heat and her calls are like those of the siren, only stronger. Be careful. He is powerful."

Saba sat on a low leather stuffed seat. She waited until Tamrin was at the entrance to the garden where she sat, and then only did she acknowledge him, silently with a tiny wave of her fingers, encouraging him to enter.

"May the god of the sun shine on you. May your reign..." he began but was interrupted by her laughter.

"May all your wives and concubines bear you a legion of sons Tamrin." She pointed at a seat. "When you send a messenger that you wish to see me I know it is serious or you want something or that you are getting senile." Saba's smile was crooked and he noticed a few grey hairs were visible in her long hair being braided by a servant girl.

"I have been planning the next expedition. This time it will be different for Menelik. He has the beginning of hairs growing under his nose. His voice is low and his gait uneven because he seems to be growing out of his skin. I think he is now twenty years of age?" She nodded. "Yet, I am sure that you see his father's eyes and his father's thick brows and his nose to sniff out what is sweet." Tamrin often spoke words that had two meanings.

Saba smiled. "Yes, Solomon will be amazed. He has a host of children, both girls and boys, young women and young men, but from what I observed, in spite of his wisdom he had a hard time remembering who was who and came from what mother." Now she laughed. "His nose was impossible to ignore. I seldom saw his eyes; they were usually shut in ecstasy." She made a face. "Have you ever seen among a flock of chicks, one which is totally different from the others and wondered why?"

"I have. Yet among the many children of Solomon that I observed, not one had the long ear lobes that are like yours, long enough to caress the central part of the jaw. Not one except Menelik. He is yours without doubt. I spoke to the mid-wife when he was born and we both noted how this feature resembled you. But more striking is his nose, like the prow of a ship that dips in the waves. A hundred artists have drawn Solomon's nose. It is his trademark. The wise king who nose." He kept a straight face, waiting for her to praise his witty remark, but she retorted with one of her own.

"Nine hundred women speak little of his nose. They speak of his manhood. Some have called it the 'mark of the beast'. Menelik is Solomon's son and will be recognized by the women in his court."

"I have been looking at the maps that were drawn by various sailors, those from the Hindush, from the shores of the great desert of nothing, the tradesmen from the land of Ishmaelite. My own scribes and scribes of the Midianites copied these maps. The finger of the sea that is between Amelek, Edon and Midian, really a gulf, shaped much like the Hindush lingam, the phallus they worship; this gulf is the quickest and best way to move to Israel, to Judah. At the end of the gulf of al-Akaba is a town called Hazema, which has a huge camel market. So, with a fleet of six dhows and well-trained sailors with bows and arrows, newly smelted iron swords from Kedar, we will fight off the pirates; create terror by burning their seaport towns and sail northeast to Hazema. Then we will travel over-land, our ships protected by half our group anchored in a small cove I have seen. The journey by sea will take one moon, the rest of the journey by land to Solomon's empire a matter of two weeks by camel caravan. I will send a message with Solomon's captains who are here in our port, that we will seek one hundred camels when we arrive."

"So you want to make most of the trip by boat, rather than by camel through Egypt? I think you are wise. Our first trip was very difficult, even though I was much younger. Camel travel was hard even though there was a tent above my head and a support for me to lie down and sleep. Egypt even now is at war with Assyrians and should be avoided. Will Solomon know about your coming?"

"Riding the waves in the harbor below us, here in Adulis, are three of Solomon's trading ships that are heading north along the Arabian coast from the Hindush carrying trade goods. I have made excellent trade with them for Nubian gold, which Solomon desires for his temple. They brought spices and woven silks from the Hindush of high quality. These are now in my own warehouse. I will send sealed messages by each of their ships' captains to Solomon about our plans to bring his son Menelik to Israel again. I will request that he send six of his own ships to join with ours in the gulf of al-Akaba to insure Menelik safety. We should set sail in three months when the seasons change and the strong monsoon winds find their way here. Three months to prepare. During this time I would like to have you order your son to learn at least two skills of war, fencing with swords or cutlasses and the use of the new cross bow that came from across the *Himal*. Instead of a being a passenger this time, he will be a skilled warrior and perhaps lead a few men of his own on the ship that transports him."

"Why not have him be on your own dhow? That way you could watch out for him better?" she asked, not convinced that Menelik was ready to lead warriors. "What if I paid one of Solomon's ship captains to take Menelik with him and save you the huge burden of traveling, watching out for Menelik and fighting off pirates?" She did not sound as if she believed her own words.

"Respected and wise Queen. Solomon hires these boats to move his trade goods. Along the way each boat captain finds a number of ways to get wealthy while serving Solomon. I would not trust one of them with my pet dog. They fly Solomon's flag but from the gossip I hear among other traders, Solomon will be fortunate to make a fortune from their trade. He wants the gold, the special woods, ebony, *shittim* and, worm wood, for his temple. When we were there, the servants in Solomon's palace spoke to us about *shittim* wood that grows here and on the Arabian coast. They told me that the Ark of the Covenant was made of *shittim* wood, the carvings of the angels on the top of ebony and the base, of cedar from the hills of Lebanon. His visitors bring lavish gifts to him; he lives lavishly. But he is not a businessman. For all his wisdom, he has two weaknesses: wealth which he did not earn by his own sweat and tears and a huge flock of women in his haram. Solomon is easily affected by pillow talk. His wives serve a dozen gods, and Solomon placates them all and serves these as well with his generous offerings of sacrifices, animals by the hundreds, and gifts to the priests to placate many gods."

He looked at her face, her eyes half shut, her mind far away. She did not look pleased. "He is of the tribe of Judah and his temple is to the One God, who is very jealous."

"Enough about Solomon's wisdom. I think he was very clever in his deception of me. Imagine, a drink of water that I took, gave him the right to me. Not wise. Clever. Yet, in spite of it, I miss the man. He had a certain attraction. I think it was his closed eyes. You are right; Menelik should not travel with strangers even if his father hires them. Speaking of a flock of chickens, I must remind the keeper of the livestock to find two new cocks. Twenty hens is simply too many for one. If I put a new cock with ten chickens in a pen near the old rooster, he will lose weight from strutting and mounting. I strolled among them yesterday and saw that four hens had the feathers of their backs and heads almost worn off. Favorites!"

The Queen, in spite of her lovers was lonely, often by herself and depressed by the condition of her foot and ankle. In spite of her beauty she saw herself as deformed. Tamrin knew that when she was with Solomon she had used depilatory substances to remove the hair from her legs and genital area to please Solomon who abhorred hairy women. In fact it was rumored in the palace that many of the women in his harem were mere girls with little body hair. She looked in the brass mirror frequently and was content with her thick eyebrows, a dark dusting of hair under her nose, and dark hair under her arm pits.

Tamrin observed the Queen closely whenever he visited. He was sorry that he had been so harsh about Solomon, and knew very well that the Queen of Saba would never wed, though her court was filled with young handsome men. To wed formally would be to formalize a husband as a somewhat co-equal and this had its many problems. The Queen wanted and kept strict control over all her wealth and would never share such details with a husband. She grilled her accountants about her treasures on a weekly basis and visited the warehouses and locked vaults to look at the gold and treasures. She knew all the animals within the palace walls.

Tamrin now saw that she caught herself in a daydream and looked up at him and nodded for him to continue.

"The ship for Menelik is the one with my best captain. It is a medium dhow with two sails and moves quickly in the water. It will be the lead ship and the rest of the fleet will follow. I have learned something from the pirates we fought. They have small, fast dhows with shallow drafts and raw silk sails that can be raised quickly. On my ship, directly behind the first ship in the fleet, there will be four of these smaller boats rigged and ready. If there is trouble with the lead ship and the gong warns of danger, these four boats will be lowered to the sea with block and tackle and carry flaming arrows and cross bows. This is my new strategy. I think it will work, and word will get around. Even the crews of Solomon's ships can see what we are now planning and building. The word has traveled along the coast to beware of ships that carry the Ethiopian flag with the lion. Tamrin the Trader's ships are to be avoided like a nest of hornets. Our use of poison on arrows has marked our ships as ruthless defenders. Solomon will hear about our plans as well. One last word about Solomon's captains. They are hired men with their own agendas. Edomites. I do not trust them. They are wealthy because of their trade for Solomon, but they are also rich because they hold for ransom some kidnapped family members of rich men along the coast. Imagine their joy if they could hold Menelik for ransom. Sly people, the Edomites, going as far back as Esau their great, great, great, grandfather. I do not like their gods, which require the bloody sacrifice of people. Their history is one of deception and brutality, yet they surround the courts of Solomon and fawn on him. Their women are often stunningly beautiful and Solomon's harem has many of them. They have clever tongues and band together. I do not trust the Edomites. If I may say so, I think Solomon is unwise to choose them to do his business."

Saba had met many young women during her stay with Solomon. She had heard the gossip and had been amazed at the ease with which the Edomite girls moved from one part of the palace to another. She glanced up at Tamrin and frowned. He was now pacing back and forth in front of her. He stopped abruptly. "While we are gone you must be protected. A month before the trip to Solomon I will take you to Hodeida port and escort you to Marib to your winter palace there. You can enjoy the dates and produce from the gardens at Marib. The dam there is a wonder to behold now and you should be in Marib a part of each year to keep your kingdom on both sides of the Red Sea unified. Marib! You have many trusted servants there who would die for you. Sabaeans, each and every one, all loyal to you and your kingdom!"

She picked up on his enthusiasm. "The sound of Marib, my Sabaean people, these are sweet on the tongue, sweet as pomegranates. Yes. I will inform my generals to make plans for guarding the Aksumite kingdom while I am gone. A strong front here will deter those who are fighting to the north in Egypt. Yes!"

She clapped her hands twice and a maid of unusual beauty came out to the courtyard and stood quietly. "Send my cooks to me. Tonight we will feast in honor of Tamrin." She was about to dismiss her, then saw the look on his face. "This is Surati, my newest slave girl, a gift from the Chief of At-Tur on the Arabian coast, near your home of Hodeida. Her companion is the dark Hindush girl you brought to me on your last trip. She has changed from a gangly girl into a tall and rather spirited young mare." She laughed. "But Surati is a virgin. Many of my visitors who have seen her have already made enquiries and offers for her. But I thought that she should remain in my court until Tamrin the Trader returns from a successful journey to see Solomon."

"Your majesty is most generous, but look, the hairs on my head are turning white. However, however, it will make the journey more memorable and my return more urgent, that is, to see your face." He bowed. She laughed happily.

"Tamrin, even the very old Ethiopian Honey Badger loves honey cones, even the infirm men love honey mead liquor, tej, even the lame and infirm, salivate when their cooks prepare the Hindush sweet called round honey ball, *gulab jamin*. I doubt if the journey will dull your appetites." He bowed again and stared at the tiny feet of the young girl in front of him. Her toenails were stained red with beet juice. Was it an omen? Red skies and red toes? He looked up and saw she was blushing.

The largest room available to Tamrin was the meeting hall in the palace of the Queen in Aksum. Its walls were made of sandstone that were plastered with lime and decorated with designs from Nubia, Hindush, Egypt and Arabia. Large cedar shutters enclosed the window openings, which were along three of the walls. These were thrown open and provided light and importantly, a cross breeze that came from the distant sea. Tables in the room were normally placed around the perimeter. Many of these were large and ornate. The most ornate came from Hindush, which had leg supports that resembled elephants, realistically carved to the point of inserting small carved ivory tusks. One table stood out more than the others because it was jet black, made entirely of ebony. Its surface was smoothed and then covered with a varnish made of pinesap mixed with the oil of the seeds of lin or flax plant. Many thin coats of this varnish had been applied to the top and legs of the ebony table. The Queen, for special functions, used it with great pride. Because it was very heavy and hard to move, its feet were placed on flat copper plates, which could slide across the stone floor without damaging the wood. One of the tables, a complete contrast to the ebony table, was made of bamboo wood slabs that were planed flat, joined with *meska*, Gum Arabic, at the seams, and polished with multiple coats of oil derived from the heads of small whales, a very fine oil that did not become rancid.

Tamrin walked with his entourage around the perimeter of the room admiring the tables and giving accounts of each to his sons and six of the dhow captains. Next to him walked the tall and light skinned Menelik, the Queen's son. Tamrin's great delight was wood. Wood of any kind. Sheba knew better than mention any thing to do with wood, or she would get a long lecture about where the wood came from and how it was used to build ships.

"Ship builders learned many of the wood-making skills from carpenters such as those who fashioned these tables. Wood becomes dry in the air, cracks and disintegrates easily if left unfinished. Our ship builders use many large pots of the flax seed oil called *lin* and gum *meska,* to coat the exterior surfaces of our boats. You remember I took you to a grove of acacia trees, which had been scored with a knife. Remember the gum we pulled off and chewed?" They looked at each other and smiled. "Bitumen tar from the pits is also used to coat the surfaces that will be under water and between joins. Even then, seawater eventually erodes the wood because of the small barnacles that attach to the ships that are always in the water. Look at this ebony table. There is not one like it in the kingdom. Each of the boards is two hand spans across and twenty hand spans long. I learned that the trees that were felled to make this table may have been four hundred years old or more. Ebony trees grown in many parts of the Aksum kingdom, but few are as huge as the tree was that was felled to make this table. This will take eight of us to move to the other side of the room nearer to the window openings so we can have light."

Even with the might of the eight young men, four on a side, it was difficult for them to lift the massive black wood table, and it slid on its copper runners. "Keep it up! Don't let it rest on the floor as you move it."

Slaves brought two long benches and placed these next to the table as the men settled down and found a place to sit.

"*Tej* first. Let us drink the sweet honey wine as a sweet omen to the trip we are planning. The men filled their clay cups and drank, eyeing each other over the rims.

"Menelik, take a cup to the window and toss an offering to the sun god. Toss the wine high."

They watched as the ritual was carried out. Menelik outdid Tamrin's orders. He took a mouthful of wine and blew it out like the spray from the breathing hole of a whale. He did this three times and when he turned around his face was damp and sticky. The men slapped their hands on the table to celebrate his sacrifice. A slave brought a bowl of water and Menelik washed his face and hands and sat down at a place next to Tamrin.

Tamrin spread four maps on the tabletop, each beautifully drawn on vellum or papyrus. All of the men leaned forward to look at these and began to point at various locations mentioning trips they had taken.

"Look at the four that have been spread next to each other. The cartographers did not seem to agree on the shape and size of many of the features. Look here. The Gulf of Aqaba is like a small finger on this map, like a thin feather on this one and here, it is drawn with strange undulations. Nonetheless, each of us can agree that these charts will be helpful in our journey to Israel. This map on vellum was obtained from one of Solomon's ship captains. It marks five points on the western shore. Look, here is *Sharm al-Sheikh,* near the southern tip of the Sinai Peninsula. All of us except Menelik have been there." He looked around the table and the men acknowledged with head nods.

"We need to have clearer lines, a larger map of the port of *Sharm a-Sheikh.* Such a strange name, Bay of the Leader. Perhaps some sailor named this, centuries ago, and it has kept the name until now. Do our maps show a bay? No! So, each captain will choose one of his crew who is good with writing to draw the outline of the bay, the placement of the multiple reefs that are to be avoided. An Egyptian cubit, which is twenty eight digits, used as a measuring reed; four being the length of a very tall man, provides a way to know the width and breadth of the city as well as the span of the entry to the bay. All such information will be written down as we travel, and at the end of our journey we will compare our estimates and have a composite map drawn up for future use by sailors yet unborn. Artists like to draw the face of the Queen of Egypt, of the pyramids, but we shall draw the shape of the sea and the land for future generations." He looked around at the serious faces of the captains and his sons.

"I see on these maps that each of the five cities along the Gulf of Aqaba seem to be about the same distance apart. When we traveled there three years ago, it seemed to me that the distance between *Dhahab* and *Wasit* was much greater than the distance from *Wasit* to *al-Aqaba* city. How can we know the distances? This is important to sailors?" The captain of his smallest dhow had his finger on the map as he spoke.

"As the crow flies is different from how the ship sails. We struggle against currents, wind speeds, terrible dust storms at sea so thick they are blinding, and the amount of barnacles on the bottom of each ship hold us back, many things. But each of us will record our own travel time and record these as well as the wind direction. Then when we return again we will compare and have our own mapmakers draw up the most accurate map of the Red Sea in the history of the world, the Gulf of Suez and the Gulf of Aqaba. We will make many copies and each of us will carry these in our own ships. Look, there on that blank wall we will place vellum maps of our travels for all to see." Tamrin's face was beaming, excited, almost like the face of a man who views a beautiful woman.

"Our future Emperor, Menelik I," he put his hand of the young man's shoulder, "will know not only the cities of Aksum and Marib, he will know the city of Jerusalem and bring back maps from their kingdom from the archives of his father, the Wise One. We all, around this table here will set the history for Aksum, for Ethiopia with pride. Our land is already far ahead of other nations in astronomy, in mathematics and geography. We shall excel in making the best maps of our world all the way from the Hindush, the Indus River and even south of that to the great bay of the Hind, the eastern coast south of Ethiopia of what the Berbers' call Rebu. The Hindush people speak of the sailors that came across the sea to their coast to the south, the Malagasy, who speak of an island nation as large as the nation of Midian. Yet no maps exist. Our trips will be different. We will record all of our travels and have maps drawn for future people. Ethiopia is the leader in learning and will be the leader in map making of its journeys and great histories will be written about our people!" He looked at Menelik again. "Our future leader will understand about the world, about weather, about how people in other countries live. He will bring back from the courts of Solomon treasures that exceed gold or silver. Treasures that are to be written in books of the future about gods, even what his father calls the One and Only God, and how that god is to be worshipped." He smiled and pointed out the window at the brilliant sun, now almost at its zenith.

"I salute the Sun God; I greet the Moon God and the gods of the stars that lead our ship. This journey will open our minds, and perhaps, even our imaginations. Personally, after this journey I would, as my last journey, travel south farther than any have traveled along the coast to the place called *Malagasy*. We have much to do to prepare for our voyage taking place a lunar month from now. I will visit each of your ships before we sail to see how each captain and crew has stocked provisions, weapons and materials for sailing."

The men attacked their food, roasted lamb with okra, eaten with fermented breads. They drank and shared stories. Once again Tamrin spoke, playing with a coin he held in his hand.

"Solomon was wise to create a small coin called a shekel, which though of little real value, not being more than the weight of one hundred and eighty barley corms, was used to barter goods. We have our obsidian coins, our salt bars and silver and gold bars of different weights to use for buying things, but one idea of the 'wise one' that you must explore and return with is how the Kingdom of Aksum can strike its own coinage for trade, particularly small items. No common man has a silver bar, no farmer has ingots of gold, but the farmer has produce, which can be weighed. Why not make a substitution for actual things, to approved coins like the Israeli *Gerah*. It is much easier for a merchant to carry a hundred of these small coins than two hundred small patties of dried salt, or circles of copper wire. We need something that every trader will recognize and value. Now when we trade goods, we will learn to deal with value of things in symbols that will be approved by me, or the Queen as having value.

"Solomon may have gone astray with his stable of women but his accountants and agents dealt with wealth better than we do. If I had a letter that stated that Saba, Queen of Ethiopia, promises to pay me three gold bars on my return, could any of you use that the very same letter to obtain, say, a wife, a farm, a ship? If the letter was kept by my eldest son and if I died because of accidents on such a trip, could he receive the gold?"

All of the men began to discuss the idea excitedly. His eldest ship captain, Esau, spoke up. "Tamrin, the letter itself would be the same as gold. I could say to the Queen that you gave me the letter for certain goods or services and she would give me the gold and take the letter. We already use letters of credit for some of our purchases. Why not standardize these? We must learn about this from Solomon's court. I heard that he received six hundred and sixty six 'talents' of gold from our Queen on the first journey. What is a talent? What does it look like? Can we make one?"

Another disagreed. "It will not work! How can a coin represent real value? Such a system would take trust that there is value. Trust by everyone would be necessary or the system would never work!" He leaned over and asked Tamrin to let him handle the coin. He turned it over and over and shook his head.

The merchants drank strong coffee and argued about Esau's idea. Most of them said they would not trust those who used such things as a piece of papyrus to have the same value of gold. It was ridiculous. Others shouted that it depended on who wrote the paper and if it was authentic. Another shook his head and argued that he trusted his wife more than he would a paper that promised talents of silver. A gong sounded and the room became quiet.

Makeda, Saba the Queen, was announced by a young pageboy. She entered the room, leaning on the shoulder of a beautiful dark-skinned slave girl, the gift of Tamrin to her from his previous journey to the Hindush. Makeda limped, but the men did not focus on her deformity; they stared at her face, at the beauty of her body. Her face was a map of joy and sorrow, of curiosity and impatience. Her eyes traveled from one man to another sizing them all up, estimating how they would serve her. All stood at her entry.

She nodded and looked at each face around the table. The men bowed. "Would that I were a man. Would that when my mother bore me that I was a son! My very self, my infliction limits my motion, my choices, my strength of muscle. I would exchange my royalty for the freedom of joyous, exuberant strength and youth. But the gods have chosen. I am what I am, your Queen and ruler. You all are my arms, my eyes, my strength and my joy. I will await you on your return from Solomon and each one of you will meet me privately on that return to tell me of what you found and what you bring back to our great Aksum, to Ethiopia. Each of you will have your own reward. I will make a special reward of gold to the captain of the ship that brings back the secret treasure from Solomon's temple. I did not see it, but was shown drawings of it, the Ark that was kept in a secret place, a box carved of shittim wood in which treasures are kept like the tablets of their god's ten commandments. Menelik, your father may wish you to have an exact copy of it made to bring back to Aksum. This is your special task. The Ark of the Covenant. It has supernatural powers.

"Menelik, you go on this trip not only as a member of the crew but also as future emperor. Never forget your heritage and who you are. Son of the Wise One, return with the knowledge of how Solomon's Great and Only One God is approached, how he is served and how pleased. I hear there is real magic in their holy symbol, the Ark of the Covenant, that it draws their great spirit that supports them. Think about this when you are there Menelik. Perhaps ask your father to show you the Ark."

She turned toward Tamrin. "I have gifts for Solomon, not of the kind I brought him the first time. I am not a naïve virgin. I will make the package for you to take to him. Only he will understand and remember the items that I will include. My scribe is already writing a letter that I dictated to him yesterday. It is good for Menelik to meet his father and learn about Solomon's kingdom. It would not be good for Solomon to see me now. Eighteen years, or is it twenty, wears hard on a woman, though I have borne no more children. But when I look in the reflecting copper mirror I see one quite different from the girl who was seduced by Solomon.

The men were dismissed, all except Tamrin and her son.

Her face now held an expression of distaste. "I will say no more about your father, Menelik, than he knew many women, but he knew little about any one of them and less about their feelings and desires. Tamrin, you have a large stable of horses and camels. Some of them you like better than the others, but your liking is because of how they satisfy your travel needs, your pride in riding a spirited stallion, your joy in showing off a string of running camels, the likes of which few others could dream to possess. Possess. That is the word. Solomon possesses much, but little as well. In his stable of women he has favorites, but few of the hundreds are really a friend, an adviser, and a person who understands not only pleasure but pain."

She left the great meeting chamber. The men stood and looked away, not wanting to see their monarch walk with pain in her leg. Tamrin looked away because he knew she felt a different kind of pain. Yet he felt proud. Perhaps in her entire entourage only he was a close friend and advisor, one to whom she told the secrets of her heart. Lover, no, but loved, yes.

The ships, anchored in Adulis bay seemed to swallow up half the produce of the small port city. Butchers prepared the carcasses of flayed goats and sheep, cut in half, spread out and covered with salt from the mines at Massawa and ground anise, then smoked in sheds for two weeks. These were hung in the bowels of each of the ships. Dried fish from all the vendors in the market were purchased and as their stocks grew thin their pockets grew fatter as they raised the price. Huge sacks of raisins and dried plums, flagons of wine, pots of vinegar, and cooking oils made from the tallow of sheep, which would last for months without becoming putrid or rancid; all these and more were brought onto the ships. *Marula* fruit and dried seeds were brought on board. It had a strong tasting nut which were the comfort food of the wanderer, both on land and sea. The *marula* fruit was a favorite of elephants, particularly when the fruit had begun to ferment. Drunken elephants staggered about after gorging on the fruit and nut together. Added to this were coffee beans from Mocha, which would be ground by the cooks in the small galley on the decks of the ships and then boiled until the black liquid was as thick and strong as dark syrup. To this the prized and expensive honey was added. Without coffee for the crews the expedition would be deemed a failure.

Exchanges of all kinds were made; shark's teeth, cowry shells, silver rings, jewels, coils of copper all became items of exchange to purchase goods. But this required hours of bargaining and discussion until agreements were made. Seller and purchaser alike were afraid of being cheated, afraid that a jewel was in fact not a sapphire but quartz with a blue color.

One said, " Last year I took an emerald in exchange for an Arabian stallion. The man disappeared. Later I found another who had done a similar exchange. We found out that the object was only crystallized green sand from Mesopotamia, a place called Molda where natural jewel-like clusters can be found. If I meet that man he will regret that he cheated me. Lightening melted colored sand for a stallion!"

Values for all commodities rose daily. The cost of an amphora of distilled wine doubled in two weeks. Merchants knew that the supplies for the ships would come from the Queen's treasury in Aksum. The taxes they paid yearly to the Queen's agents, in small ingots of gold, coils of copper, shark's teeth and cowry shells for doing business would quickly be regained. The Queen also exacted tribute from the kingdoms around her in the form of talents of silver.

Small boys played their games near the ships, waiting for handouts from the sailors, cleaning up the spilled foods, pilfering what they could. The boys became businessmen, bringing half grown kittens to sell to the boat owners. They brought dry unleavened breads that their mothers made from wheat and barley flour, anointed with oils, packed flat and tied seven to a bundle. They knew the cooks on the ships had little time or patience to grind grain and make bread. Hundreds of dried flat breads were easy to store and became part of most meals for sailors. Though hard as rock and taking good teeth to chew, the hard bread business boomed in Adulis and even Aksum, a three-day journey over land. To keep the foodstuffs from being eaten and polluted by rats and mice, cedrus wood barrel containers were obtained from merchants. These containers were ten spans tall and five spans wide, made of thin planks of reddish cedar wood bound together by bands of copper with a round wood base and a round wood lid. Coopers in Aksum busily made hundreds of casks and barrels in anticipation of the sailing of the fleet of Tamrin. No other container on a ship is more useful because it resists moisture and keeps out vermin and insects, particularly cockroaches and ants. Boxes of the same material were made for the sailors to store their own personal supplies. Hammock makers, frequently small boys, wove strings into sleeping hammocks, invaluable in crowded quarters on a ship to provide a comfortable night's sleep for sailors.

Camels lumbered along the hilly terrain from Aksum carrying heavy loads of dates to Adulis. These were sold to the street merchants, who in turn sold them to the ships purveyors.

Scribes wrote down all the items that went into the storage areas of all the dhows. This journey was subsidized by the Queen herself and was better outfitted than most. Tamrin the merchant became involved in most of the transactions; in fact he had to sanction each. Thus, every night merchants came to him introducing their goods, how much they cost and how much would be given to Tamrin to store in his own warehouses as middleman for purchasing supplies. He was often distant and cool in these transactions, as if they meant little to him. Yet, in the end the offer of a silver bar, or two barrels of dried meats would help him make his decisions. Tamrin was one of the wealthiest men in Aksum because of his ability to weasel the last 'coin' from a purchaser in a bargain, and then demand a gift that would sweeten the transaction. In fact the word for bargain meant, *a sweet deal*, for Tamrin the Merchant of Aksum.

In almost every sailor's home, the last night was one of feasting and revelry. The women, wives and children of the sailors served the men but their eyes were full of tears. Most of them had friends whose father, whose husband or brother had not returned from a journey, and all knew that they would have little attention from any man during the trip of months. Children would be born during this time, crawlers would become toddlers.

Tamrin's wives and women as well as the women of Aksum had more freedom than their Arabian or Israeli sisters. His wives traded in the markets, traveled to other households, met other men and developed sexual liaisons, often as openly as their men did. Many jokes and stories developed around these affairs. Men could only sleep in one bed at a time, and when they had five wives and four concubines their women developed clever networks and ways to meet with a passing trader, a handsome cousin, and a wealthy cloth merchant. Ancient Aksum was known for its pleasures; enhanced by *tej,* made mellow by *qat* and dreamy by the smoke of hemp in water pipes. These were a happy people, a volatile and dynamic society which encouraged open laughter and talk, hearty physical contact and also, quick tempers and bloody revenge. The kingdom had men from both the Arabian deserts and the Ethiopian highlands bumping shoulders in the streets, and each of them carried the *jambiya,* a curved, long bladed dagger tucked into his waist band. These were kept razor sharp and highly prized. A father would often pass one to his eldest son, with a handle made of rhinoceros horn, the most coveted material.

Debtors had reason to fear their creditors if they did not repay, both in coin and kind. Yet the streets were filled with shouting children who had the entire city as their playground, running in age-set groups from the markets to the fields, from the sea coast to the hills with caves. Age-sets, children born within the same year became friends and 'brothers' for life. Such bonds were stronger than those of siblings, who themselves were caught up in goings and doings with members of their own age group.

Tamrin's many households had such age set groups of children within the family and tied to the family. Tamrin himself had been a leader in his own age group as a youngster, but his frequent trips and movements away from Aksum, Hodeida and Marib dissolved these bonds, as did deaths and sickness.

Tamrin was worldly wise, world traveled, and world respected, from Jerusalem to the Hindush River, from the highland of Ethiopia to the shores of the Blue Nile. He was a cosmopolitan of his time who spoke four languages with ease, sat with kings and Queens at dining tables and dined with poor merchants and sailors alike. Tamrin sought after women but in truth, cherished only one of his wives, Kali, the fair woman from Hindush who seemed to breathe in and enjoy life with Tamrin like no other person. Her advice, her conversation late at night while sitting on the flat roof of their house, gave Tamrin comfort and security. She seemed to be of his own flesh, of his own mind, and she in her independent and spirited way did not fear Tamrin, rather understood and supported him, but balked as well when he forgot her own needs and ignored her advice. Yet, the other wives of Tamrin were not close to her, she born in foreign soil so far distant, she who spoke the language of the Hindush, she who walked with the air of a Queen, even when carrying out the garbage basket. She carried a newborn on her hip every two years and her home was filled with laughter and joy now that the new slave girl had been brought to her who spoke her own language. Shanti became her daughter.

The day before setting sail with the fleet to the Gulf of Aqaba, Tamrin visited each of his four extended households. The children pulled on his fingers, asking him to bring them back a special gift, which he agreed to do. His wives wished him safe journey, knowing that he would stop first along the Arabian coast at Hodeida his birth place home and visit his fifth wife and family there. He made his rounds, as he had done a dozen times before and they wished him the blessing of the Sun God, during his travel in the daytime, and the Moon God and Sirius when he was at sea at night. Finally he went to Kali's compound, but she was unable to meet him because she was in a time of confinement with her menses, so she sent their eldest daughter who handed Tamrin a strange crudely made copper coin which had punch marks on it. "Mama said it is called a *purana* which she thinks means old and wise. She told me she got it from her grandfather as a child, who wished her to become old and wise. Mama said, return to Aksum, Tamrin, and live your life in peace here, become old and wise." The girl laughed and ran back into the compound. Purana. Strange name he thought. Perhaps when I return I will show this to Sheba, our Makeda, the Queen, and talk about how Ethiopia could also have a currency, a strange lump of metal that would mean as much as a dozen chicken eggs or six cakes of salt.

CHAPTER 10

A woman who lacks discretion is like a pig with a jewel in its snout.

Tamrin changed his mind. He decided at the last moment that Menelik should be part of his own crew. He was like a father to the young man and they spent hours talking, reading and exploring when they were in Aksum. Tamrin already missed having someone to talk to about other things than food, babies and horses.

Menelik had his servants carry his six bags of possessions, which included gifts to his father.

"Why did you change your mind, Tamrin?" Menelik asked.

"Well, the trip will be long and tiresome. There will be many hours and days when we are in strange water where there will be no wind in our sails. I thought it would be a good idea for you to be on board to play *dara* with me and see if you can ever beat me at it." He laughed.

"Tamrin, you know very well that you seldom win. We do have draws, but you must admit that in the last three games the draw was in my favor." Menelik tried to keep a somber face.

"Well, that was one reason. The other is that you can help me keep the daily log on this ship. Your writing is better than mine. So you will be in charge of that. We will need to talk about what should be entered into it. And finally, your mother." He paused for a long moment. "Your mother wanted me to keep track of you when we are in one of the many ports of call we will visit. She thinks that you will be swept away by some beautiful woman on the streets who will work with her pimp and capture you as a hostage." He tried to keep a straight face.

"What does that have to do with my being on your ship? My mother has already been putting the dark slave girl in my path at home. Practically every evening she is the one who brings me a drink to my rooms. Tamrin, this is one area that you do not have to be alert about. You could get one of your crewmembers to learn some of the skills of body massage like Audu in the palace. Imagine, every day after a hard day climbing the mast to have a massage with sweet smelling oils and then a dip in the sea. I will make you a bargain. I will not fall into the arms of a beautiful woman unless she can be invited onto the ship to spend the night with me alone while we are in port. I dislike the atmosphere of brothels. But, when we are in your home port of Hodeida, one of your young daughters could be introduced to me and perhaps…" He tried to keep his face serious.

"You are very creative, Menelik. I think we will leave out an on board masseuse, but I will consider finding you a young woman in my hometown. I know just the one. Perhaps, if you two get along, on the return voyage you could bring her back to Aksum and begin your own harem." He patted Menelik on the back. "My daughter. I have to tell you that she has high standards!"

"How high are her standards? Can she be seeking someone higher than the next ruler of Ethiopia?" He kept a straight face, but Menelik saw he had touched a raw spot.

"The strange thing between men and women may not relate to wealth, high position, authority, princely pride, it may relate more to what we are doing now. The ability to be with a person and enjoy not only body massages, the union of sweaty bodies in bed, but a strange mystical bond like lightening that is the mind. Something like it happens between men and men as well, an immediate bond, a desire to know more about the person, a feeling that without the other person's presence there is an empty space. With all four of my wives I have such a bond with only one, the woman of my own race, tongue and family with whom I feel affection and trust. I have avoided the word love because it is used by most of us for sex." Tamrin stared out to sea.

"I will wait for lightning to strike. In the meanwhile I would like body massages and yes, I will be happy to meet the young woman in Hodeida. Is she beautiful?" Menelik played with the frayed ends of a rope as he spoke, raveling and unraveling.

"In short, yes. But only in my eyes. Such matters are in our hands, but matters of the heart, of desire, of companionship are in the hands of the god Moloch, the most demanding of deities." He saw a laborer stagger under a load, almost ready to drop it. "Menelik, quick, run and help the man with his burden. Here we stand talking while the rest of the world is at work."

Without hesitation, Menelik ran to the man and helped him set the load of amphorae on the deck. He helped him arrange the containers of wine on the cross beam across his shoulders, then helped him as he balanced across the gangplank onto the ship.

"Are you ill? Your body is wet with sweat. Perhaps you have the illness of bad night air. Follow me when you have stored your jars in the hold." He waited until the man returned. "In the market is a hakim, a Hindush old man who sells medicines. Take these cowries and tell him I sent you to get the bitter bark of the 'sweet worm wood' tree from the Chin. It has helped many who traveled on the silk route to Hindush. It may help your fever." He handed the man ten small cowries. The man bowed twice and left the ship. Menelik went shopping as well and found the medicine man and returned with his own purchases.

"Menelik, you did well. You reminded me of one thing that I usually forget. Take this papyrus note on which my name is written and the number fifty. Go to that same Hindush medicine seller and purchase the same medicine for all our ships. In the bays of the small villages in the Gulf of Aqaba the night air is often hot, and the mosquitoes torment us. Also purchase bitter oil from the medicine man to ward off the bugs."

Menelik hurried away, knowing that the ships would leave in the evening when the tide turned. The northeasterly monsoons had begun and would continue in the gulf for most of their journey. But the winds within the eastern parts of the Gulf of Aqaba were as fickle and unpredictable as were the temperatures of the water and the heat blasts of wind from the Midean coasts.

They sat sipping small clay cups of strong mocha coffee, thick and sweetened with honey. Three of the men chewed *qat* , which seemed to loosen their tongues and their feelings of good will toward each other. As they spoke, they would reach over and embrace a shoulder, or even put their joined fingers to their mouths in the symbol of a kiss. Two of the men held hands, friends since childhood. Menelik was the youngest, and enjoyed the sociability, which was so different from that within his mother's palace. Men with men! What a different scene than men with women. They spoke of the red moon and many omens. They laughed at the sailor who was terrified by the strange red moon, telling him he was still a child. No sooner than mention was made of the red moon, dogs began to howl.

The earth made a cracking sound, then a rumbling tearing sound and began to shake. "Outside! Quickly! To the open streets." Tamrin was pulling Menelik with him and they could hardly stand because of the moving ground under them. They reached the street, an open area made for an outdoor market. They stood and watched as the very building in which they had been sitting toppled, the large lightly mortared stones falling inwards because of the weight of the flat, plastered roof. All around them buildings fell, stones rolled and there were screams of pain.

"The ships! We must go to the ships and lengthen the ropes running to the anchors. A wave, high as a house may come into the bay. A large bell hung on a wood frame in the center of the market area. Tamrin ran to it and rang it ten times, the signal to all his sailors and captains in Aksum to prepare for an emergency with their ships. He waited, and then rang ten loud clangs on the bell. It was fashioned from copper and had a clear high pitch when hit with a stone mallet.

They ignored the mayhem around them and rushed down to the port, got into small rowboats and headed out to their ships. Men shouted at each other, encouraging speed. Tamrin stayed by Menelik's side and encouraged him to help.

"Untie the rope and let more line pay out so the boat can rise on the wave. Here the wave will not come crashing, but be a huge smooth mound of water as high as a house. Hurry!"

One after another their captains and sailors tended the ships, and then they rowed to other craft moored on their anchors and shouted to the sailors to lengthen their anchor lines.

Tamrin and his crew remained on the biggest dhow and waited. They looked at the port city of Adulis, at the broken houses, and the collapse of multi-story buildings. They listened to the screeching of people, babies crying, dogs howling and people blowing on conches. It was a scene of utter mayhem.

They were anchored hundreds of cubits from the land, well away from the small corals that tore many ship bottoms. Then it came! There was no crashing wave or surf; the ship they were on was elevated, lifted up and up as if by the hand of the god of the sea, the lord of the cosmos, Varuna. Tamrin actually spoke the name aloud now. "Varuna protect us!"

On his many trips to the Hindush he had learned of this important god of the cosmos and the sea, *Varuna*, while trading with the dark skinned people from the *Sindh*. *Varuna* lifted all the small dhows up and up and the water slid under them and their anchors filled with stones were for a moment lifted as well, then settled back and held against the bottom sand. The surge moved into the narrows of the bay and onto the low-lying town of Adulis. The water streamed down its streets, filled the cavities left by the tumbled buildings and crashed inland, foaming and tearing any loose object in its path. Animals, horses, dogs and people were swept away.

The men on the ships waited until the water flowed back again into the bay. Then they got into their small rowboats and rowed furiously into the port of Adulis. They tied up their small craft and each hurried in different directions to the houses where their women and children were living.

For six days the people of Adulis searched, rejoiced, grieved and pulled their families from the wreckage. Many had been saved because of the way the houses had been constructed. Most of the roofs were flat, supported by wood beams across which lath and plaster had been placed. The center room of each of the houses was supported by one large post, like a tree trunk to which the beams were attached. When the stone walls collapsed, many were saved who were in their central rooms because of the wood post which allowed the roof to sag around it, but did not fall. Stonewalls and partitions collapsed, and many were killed and buried under these.

Tamrin and Menelik left Adulis and rushed by horse, a day journey to the Queen's Aksum palace, called *Dongar*. They were appalled at the damage. Most of the perimeter walls had collapsed except in places where the wall had interior clay brick buttresses. The palace was built in a rectangular shape with a major entrance, gated and guarded, an exit gate at the back which was kept locked from the inside with a slide bolt easily reached by a person inside, but difficult to get to from the outside. Along two sides of the open courtyard the living quarters were built, three rooms opening to each other with interior doors. Here were the Queen's personal quarters. Across from her were rooms where Menelik and other male relatives stayed. In the center of the large courtyard was a structure made of cedar and *shittim* wood. A ramp led up to a platform one storey high. It was Saba's favorite place to sit and rest, to play with her pet duiker, which had been raised by her when a hunter killed its mother. He had presented the tiny antelope to Makeda as a gift. The servants had designed rags immersed in milk to feed it. The red flanked Duiker seldom left Saba's side and frequently hopped onto the seat next to her. She kept treats for it in her bag and fed it special greens from the royal garden. It followed her everywhere within the palace. No dogs were allowed within the palace walls. Huge guard dogs were kept tied near the main gate and exit gate outside. These vicious animals were an effective deterrent for thieves at night.

 At the time of the massive quake, Makeda and her Duiker and two hand maidens were sitting on an elevated wood platform inside the palace courtyard enjoying the breeze coming from the distant Red Sea and the Port of Adulis, a day's journey away. Next to them was a built up area, an altar that had steps going up two sides. Here sacrifices of various kinds were made to their gods. The earthquake did not disturb this structure. The quake leveled most of the other rooms of the palace. She and the girls screamed and held to the supports of the wood platform and watched in horror as the entire stone palace tumbled to the ground. Sections of the outer wall stood. Adobe-brick buttresses from the inside had supported these. Other servant quarters attached to the palace wall were numerous. More than fifty living quarters collapsed.

Menelik and Tamrin rode into Aksum in the evening. Their horses were exhausted, as were they. The earthquake had hit Aksum hard. There was such widespread destruction of the city that they could hardly recognize where they were. They approached the ruins of the palace and saw huge crowds gathered around, many pulling rocks aside, still searching for family members or possessions such as metal pans, knives, black shiny pottery that was so highly coveted for keeping water cool.

Palace guards recognized them and relieved them of their horses.

"The Queen? What about the Queen?" shouted Tamrin.

"She was saved by the duiker and the gods of the sky. Her viewing and sitting platform in the center of the courtyard was wood and it was spared. She is still there, now shielded by large blankets that have been attached to the structure to give her privacy. Until new quarters are built, she says she will remain where she is. She says it was the *Shittim* wood that saved her. She keeps talking about Solomon's god and the Ark of the Covenant that was made of *Shittim* wood, and that her escape from the earthquake was because of this. Already she has had scribes come in to write a new law that forbids all cutting of these trees, except for the use of royalty." The guard breathlessly gave the news.

Tamrin and Menelik climbed up the wood stairs to the platform to find that Makeda was asleep. The maids encouraged them to come into the shaded interior and sit on cushions on the floor until she awakened. She whispered that she would have coffee prepared for them. Strangely, it was the whispering that awakened the Queen.

"What secrets are you telling each other?" she shouted, still facing away from them.

"Only that your merchant and your son Menelik are sitting right here!" She shouted with joy.

There was a long silent moment as the two men stared into Makeda's weeping face. She held out her hands and they came and sat next to her cot and held her hands momentarily. Then she placed her hands on the two heads near her, one with streaks of grey, the other head with black curly hair, almost a mane. She could not speak for a long moment.

She spoke to Tamrin first. "Thank you. Thank you for guarding my son, Menelik, son of the Wise Man. You are more than a trusted servant, Tamrin. You are my right hand and my eyes." She turned to Menelik. "Menelik, the gods have been kind. I shall kill many oxen and goats on the altar, there in front of us to give thanks. The first sacrifice will be to Solomon's One God, whose laws reside in the *Shittim* Wood Ark of the Covenant. The others, to the gods of the sky, the stars, the moon and the sun. Perhaps one or all of them will know of my thanks and joy." She embraced her tall lanky son, and then turned to Tamrin and they smiled at each other.

The warehouses that stored Tamrin's ivory, ebony, honey pots, sacks of Hindush spices had collapsed, but the walls fell outward, the flat roof onto the goods. Tamrin walked around, paced to and fro muttering, 'Cactus is bitter only to those who taste it.' Bitter! For three days a hundred slaves worked to clear the rubble. Tamrin called for the cutting of *Shittim* wood for the palace and planned to have the royal storage units all made of the desert wood. For a day's journey around Aksum, men searched for the largest trees, cut them and hauled them back to earn some profit from their sales to Tamrin. News of the need for this wood now spread and in the mountains of Ethiopia, in its valleys could be heard the cutting of trees with stone axes. His own trade in large ebony logs and the new use for the acacia trees soon stripped the land far from Aksum of these precious woods. Most were cut for timber at the very time they were flowering.

The Queen appointed a score of men to supervise the design and construction of her new palace, on the very foundations of the destroyed palace. Designs were brought to her and Tamrin. Walls that had not collapsed had been heavily buttressed internally with clay brick supports. This became a part of the new plans for an enlarged and new palace that could withstand some earthquakes. Structures within the outer walls were similarly made and entire rooms were to be constructed of the desert *Shittim* wood. Hard woods were cut for miles around until the land was bereft of large green trees.

The smoke and aroma of burnt offerings filled the air as hundreds of oxen were killed. The meat was distributed to families whose homes had been destroyed. Food was brought into newly made market stalls from nearby gardens and farms. Animals of all kinds were tethered and for sale. The value of food, especially meat increased. Before the quake a bull could be purchased for a shekel of silver. After the quake the same animal could be sold for ten times the amount. Traders remained straight-faced and stern as they became wealthy from the poverty of those who had lost their homes and belongings and the sale of animals for sacrifices.

Treasurers of the Queen warned her to be careful with her generosity because the royal coffers needed to be kept intact. There were yet payments to be made to Egypt for travel into their land, as required taxation or tribute. Tax collection was the answer. Much of the tax was collected in kind; animals, metal, grain, and the tax collectors' own storehouses soon began to fill.

Tamrin's planned travel through various coastal Arabian

countries would be of high cost because of tribute, and gifts of gold to bring to Solomon, which would nearly exhaust the wealth of Aksum. So tax collectors were sent out but their work was difficult. The common man of the kingdom was burdened by taxation, they said. They explained that there were always poor people, dying people, suffering people in every empire on earth, and that the poor would always be present. How would they collect from the poor? To collect from the rich, the landlords, was almost impossible because they had power, and they disdained the tax collectors, yet pledged allegiance to the Queen. Those whose homes were destroyed would have nothing to give. The collectors complained, but they went out, knowing that their jobs depended on the good will of the Queen and that they would become wealthier.

Two generals of her army requested audience and presented themselves with low bows and remained prostrated before her until she gave them a signal to approach. They were as different as the sun and the moon. One was tall, fair skinned, with a large hooked nose and big rough hands. The other short, broad and powerful, dark skinned and stood legs held apart like pillars. These men had protected her kingdom. The taller, Ibrahim, had accompanied her to Solomon's kingdom with Tamrin.

Ibrahim was the spokesman, eloquent and quick with words. "My Queen, the empire is in peril. News of this devastating quake will reach Egypt, Nubia and even the Hindush. A weakened country will entice those countries that are greedy and those who have scores to settle against Aksum. We must have a show of strength. The gold of the kingdom is needed to make new chariots, buy more horses, and purchase the best weapons, shields, swords and armor for our men. We must, even now prepare a foray against our nearest neighbor to the north to capture slaves and demand tribute from them. Their ruler, if at all possible should be captured and brought to Aksum to grovel in front of you. If we do not show our might now, soon, other nations will attack Aksum in its time of grief and sorrow, its time of devastation. The journey of Tamrin to Solomon can have a good result. They must not see our present weakness. Gold. The military needs much gold. We will send ten of our dhows with soldiers to accompany him on his journey in a show of strength."

She raised her hand and cut him short. "I understand and I am happy to be served by such loyal soldiers. You shall have some gold to prepare your army. This is our first priority. I have seen weakened animals attacked by their own kind. A limping dog soon becomes a dead dog. We have been a silent kingdom that is coveted. We are now a grieving kingdom that is limping. Prepare and bring me your plans and it shall be done." She had no alternative but to agree. "I will curtail the building of the new palace. Military might is foremost for Aksum!"

The generals now lowered their heads so their necks could be seen. They glanced at Tamrin, and lowering their heads to Menelik, walked backwards to the portal and departed.

"Tamrin, the quake has shaken loose the kingdom's honor. Last night I decided that I will move my court to my palace in Marib and show unity with that part of the empire. Let us plan to leave in a week. Prepare your ship for my travel. Menelik will travel with another of your captains. We should not be together. Yet the two ships must remain close at all times. After we arrive in Hodeida you can arrange for the camel caravans to take us through the *Tihama* to *Marib*. I long for the little bananas the size of fingers that you brought from Aksum and planted in Marib. They do better there than here, and the reddish colored ones are the best. Then give me sweet dates and the breezes from the desert at night under cloudless skies. Most of all I want to get away to the desert retreat to escape the gold hunters. Think about this and help me, Tamrin. How does one stop the tax collectors from having sticky fingers? How does one ensure that the weapons the generals seek are in fact needed and actual purchases, rather than going into their coffers? Weakness and tragedy are the poisons of the empire. How can I check on all these men, especially our short vicious general, Umdin? "

"I will think about it. Brothers will cheat brothers if there is gold to be gained. The generals know very well that they are now the strength to defend, and even fight aggressive battles against weaker nations. They are our problem, they and the collectors of taxes who enslave the people with their own greed. I will think on it."

For the rest of the day the Queen had visitors, dignitaries who came to pay homage and respect and hear the gossip and news. Small chieftains from little kingdoms around Aksum, part of her empire, brought gifts and came to see the devastation of Aksum with their own eyes. They were met at the border of the city by soldiers and escorted to the Queen under stern guard to present their gifts and hear her words.

CHAPTER 11

If you see that a town worships a calf, then cut grass and feed it.

Aksum bustled with an army of people, tradesmen, carpenters, woodcutters, and builders, seeking employment from nearby towns, to rebuild the stone buildings that had collapsed. Workers planned new homes with frames of wood on the inside, buttresses on the outside and courtyards where citizens could gather to prepare foods and to gossip. Traditional buildings of stones piled on stones for walls were now only used for fences and animal shelters. All the newer buildings included revised designs to help residents survive another earthquake.

Early the next morning the Queen's watchmen stopped an old man from entering the collapsed outer courtyard of the Queen's palace. He was the caretaker of the park around the massive obelisks, the massive Stellae that were the pride of the city. He had come to report the Stellae had collapsed. The largest, which had been completed only three years before was the height of three buildings and made of limestone from a quarry four days journey to the south.

He kneeled before the Queen. She told him to rise and approach. "Arum, come closer. Why are you weeping?"

"Our great stone obelisks have fallen over. The tallest broke into three pieces and is lying like a dead pigeon on the ground. For your honor and your glory, Queen Makeda, I humbly request that you once again commission the construction of even more massive obelisks, broader at the base and mounted on a stone platform that is embedded into the earth. The honor of our country and your throne calls for us to begin to act now. The cost will be high. Much gold will be needed to obtain the massive stones from distant quarries. Thousands of men will be hired to move the blocks from the quarry to Aksum." He bowed again.

"Arum, I will order oxen to be sacrificed at the park. Gather workmen to push the broken obelisks together to form a platform. On these will we kill the sacrifices and burn the carcasses to the god of the earth. We have been busy with the gods of the sea and the sky and have neglected *Medr* the earth god. How jealous these gods are. We do not see them. In fact we forget their existence until they are offended. They are like a jealous wife who screams when her man seeks out a younger more beautiful woman. Screams, and then plots to create subtle shifts in the balance of the home; gossips until the entire house quakes with hatred. Arum, we will remember you at the Park of the Kings. You can hire stone cutters in the quarries to prepare even larger Stele, but we will not move them until I have seen them myself during the next rainy season."

She called to have Tamrin meet with her again, to delay their departure for two weeks so she could take care of the business of her kingdom, sacrifice to the gods, visit her treasury and have the banker give accounts of her riches. Yet, through all this she gained strength, her eyes were sharper, her actions impatient and her appetite for sweet things insatiable. Her scribes wrote orders to stone masons, wood carvers, generals and a hundred merchants. Her scribes wrote to the accountants of her treasury to prepare for a visit and an audit of the kingdom's wealth. Auditors to be sent out to monitor the tax collectors, bearing her sealed orders, would be chosen carefully so that they were of a different tribe than the one they were auditing. Solomon's trading ships in the harbor were given letters from her to deliver to messengers at Aden, and taken by runners to Marib to prepare for her coming. She informed the people of Marib that their taxes would be increased, but only for the landowners, not the tenant farmers. All around her, people marveled at the power of the Queen and many of the wealthy and noble became upset.

Aksum was suzerain over a number of small tribal lords in a wide area of Ethiopia. Usually the Queen left the collection of tribute and taxes to her appointed staff and simply had an annual report and one visit to the treasury. She called in twelve of her tax and tribute collector supervisors. This summons was taken very seriously. Usually, none of these men saw the Queen and if one or another was called in it was because of fraud, stealing, or rumors of corruption that came to the ears of the Queen. Huge wooden racks were built at the edge of the city and from the crossbars criminals would soon be hung and left for days in the hot sun to rot. This was a deterrent against theft, which was a treasonous act if performed under the Queen's aegis. The men dressed up in their finest, many wearing huge lion skin hats, a sign of their valor, having killed a lion with a spear. Vultures circled as the men entered Aksum, passing punishment racks along the road. The bodies of four minor clerks caught stealing small amounts of silver from the treasury hung swaying in the breeze.

The day of reckoning came, and the weather boded well for a session in the central courtyard of the palace. The Queen sat on a round, hand carved chair with no nails or joins, made from a single huge hardwood tree. She sat high and straight on cushions placed upon the platform customarily used for sacrifices to the gods. More than fifty men gathered in front of her, each chieftain with guards and servers, slaves holding buffalo-tail fly swatters, and others with small canopies to shield their masters from the sun.

A small tent-like canopy shaded Sheba's single seat. Her retinue squatted behind her, ready to serve at her command. She nodded to a huge Nubian slave, and he struck a gong, silencing the crowd. She waited, but while she did so her eyes roved over the men in front of her. To her right and slightly behind, sitting on a silk carpet given to her by a Hindush raja, was her son Menelik el Hakim, who remained attentive and quiet. For the first time, he had a jambiya under his belt, the handle made of rhino horn and gold. He too let his eyes scan the faces of the lords of the tribes of Aksum.

The Queen sat tall. "Are the gold mines closed? Are the silver mines only in Egypt? Are the common people, the vast hordes that live on the slopes of mountains, in the green valleys, are they now invisible?" She stared at each man, and each caught her eye, and then looked aside in respect. "Common people who dig like squirrels into the earth and draw gold from the dirt, have no idea about the real value of what they mine. Pay them more, enough to buy an extra cow, a camel, another wife, and they will all bring more gold to you. Gold cannot be eaten, but finding gold can be rewarded with gifts from your coffers. Make it happen! There are some faces here that will not be seen at our next gathering. I have big ears for little pieces of news about each of your kingdoms. *Big ears and many to whisper.*"

Again she looked at the men. "Perhaps I have misjudged. The gold may well be coming in, but you have not had time to bring it to Aksum, to the royal treasury. Listen well. Your position of suzerain control, to tax, to require tribute, is only because of this throne, this great empire, Aksum, of whom I am Queen, and of whom my son, here, will be the first king, Menelik I, when he returns from his trip to visit his father. I will accompany Tamrin to Hodeida on this journey and spend four moons at the other palace in Marib. Such a meeting as this one will be called again at that time, as well as a durbar of our military might much like those Tamrin has witnessed in Kolachi. You will be invited to send members of your military might to march past the new Emperor, Menelik I, in the new chariots you have asked to be built. I will review them."

Menelik stared above the heads of the men standing at attention rigidly in front of his mother, many now perspiring because of the hot sun, their heavy clothing, and lion mane headdresses. The Queen had prepared her son for this moment. He stood proudly, keeping an expressionless face.

His voice did not crack. It had a strangely deep tone for one so young. "Upon my return, there will be a durbar celebration and each of you is to attend my coronation. Before that date, while Tamrin and I travel and my mother the Queen is at her other palace, each of you will meet with the chief scribe and the keeper of the treasury and review your record of tribute to this kingdom for the past five years. Aksum is a mighty kingdom, only as strong as its leaders and people. We are the pride of Africa, and we will remain strong through our might of arms as well as our riches, our gold, silver and hundreds of thousands of beehives that make our honey the most coveted in the world. I will return to a sweet meeting with you all." He stepped forward to the edge of the Diaz.

"We have selected two names from among the twelve of you who work in the outlaying kingdoms and chieftaincies. Each of you was allocated a number, the order in which you were to make your presentation to the Queen today. We have selected two numbers from the twelve by having a priest pick them. Numbers six and eleven are those randomly selected. Step forward!

Two of the tax collectors stepped forward, fear written across their faces.

"Number six." The man bowed his head. "Number six while you were here to report to the Queen a group of twenty of the royal soldiers was sent to your village, to your own personal home and even your own bedroom. You reported that you were able to collect only a limited amount of silver from your people and that you turned all of this into the Queen's treasury. Is that correct?"

The tax collector, a man with white hair wearing a simple robe bowed again and nodded and said "Yes, Royal Prince. Yes."

The Queen's men found nothing in your village, home or bed room except your own personal things. Thank you for your work. You may step back."

"Number eleven, our men visited your home as well, in fact both of them. Did you report that you had received limited gold this year, that your people were poor. You turned in six gold coins and some silver coins. Is that correct?" Menelik looked the man in the face until the man lowered his eyes.

"Yes, my lord Prince. That is correct." He bowed his head again.

Menelik reached deep into a side pocket of his full robe and pulled out a small sack the size of two fists joined together. He held this up. "Have you seen this bag before? Is it yours?"

The man sank to his knees and looked at the floor, nodding yes.

"It was found in your second home buried under the water pot." He then stooped over and poured out many gold and silver coins on the carpet. Everyone craned their necks to see what he had done. "Today as you rode into the royal area of Aksum, you saw scaffolds on which four men were hanging. These were scribes who cheated and stole. Our law is clear. Give unto the Queen what is the Queen's for her work in the land. The penalty of royal theft is death. Today you shall hang from one of those scaffolds and all who are in the land can see and be warned."

The man in front of him was now groveling saying, mercy, mercy, mercy. Four soldiers had to carry him out of the room. The Queen was looking to her right and carefully wiped her eyes on the sleeve of her robe.

Menelik faced the army generals. "Our army is strong, but by the time I have returned, it will be stronger. Each chiefdom will send two hundred of its strongest young men to Aksum and train them to use the most modern weapons and learn the rules of warfare. Our army will be stronger by thousands by the time we return. I will review this new and young cohort as soon as I return."

He looked at the expressions on the faces of leaders in front of him and shouted, "Aksum! Aksum!"

He smote his chest in pride. Each man held out his shield and smote it with his spear handle. "Aksum!" they cried out at each thundering strike. They continued to strike their shields, grunting out the hunting call of the lion, "Uuu, Uuu, Uuu."

A lavish feast had been prepared. Fifty oxen had been slaughtered, tej wine was brought out in huge black clay pots, the fruits of the land were spread on cloths, and young slave girls set out silver plates and sharp copper knives. The feast began, but neither Menelik nor his mother the Queen took part.

A week of feverish activity followed the meeting of the chiefs. They, with their retinues, headed home with much pomp and fanfare. Tamrin and his crew made the final preparations for their travel in Adulis. They checked the ship, furled and unfurled sails, coiled lines, while smaller boats moved among them like water beetles, bringing goods, transporting slaves and crewmembers. Yet even now the wails from those who had lost their family members could be heard as people took bodies outside the city to be buried.

Because so many walls had collapsed, the survivors had trouble with one of their ceremonies, cutting a hole in the wall of the dead person's home, moving the corpse through the small hole, feet first, and then taking a winding trail to the burial ground. The hole in the wall was to be sealed shut, making it impossible for the dead to find their way back home. Consequently, they would wander forever in the land of the dead, leaving the living to their own world. But in some cases, the earthquake or the tsunami had destroyed entire families, causing neighbors to drag all the bodies far out beyond the limits of Aksum to bury them in mass graves. There were no remaining walls through which to move the dead.

Tamrin and his crew finally met again after doing all they could for grieving families. Adulis the port city would have to rebuild, and this time with the grim knowledge of what an earthquake would do to walls of stacked stones, and what a tsunami could do to the sea level village. Houses built on a small rise behind the city fell during the earthquake, but were spared the flooding water. These families were the first to begin rebuilding. Higher level terrain became the choice place to build. Poor, desperate folk rebuilt in the same places near the waterfront, hoping the jealous gods would not seek revenge on the city again soon.

All the dhows rose and fell on the swells at their anchorages, facing in the same direction like restless racers at a starting line. Oarsmen rowed small boats out to them to bring messages, and finally delivered senior crewmembers.

Tamrin and Menelik climbed the rope ladder to their dhow, stood on the deck, and looked first at the seven dhows anchored nearby, then at the dimly burning oil lamps of a hundred struggling merchants. Tamrin walked to a large bell, undid the clapper restraint and rang four ear-piercing clangs against the copper. Each of his fleet responded with the same signal. Then the first ship rang one bell. Men unfurled sails, pulled up the heavy basket anchors, and pushed long poles with paddles at one end against the sand bottom to move the ship into deeper water away from shore.

Unsteady winds caused the men to continue paddling and pushing as the dhows slowly made way out into the Red Sea. Each ship in turn followed the pattern of the one before it. Tamrin's ship, the largest, was last, with the greatest number of sails and two masts, but it was heavy and slow and would follow the others like a fat hen follows her chicks. Shipmates and people ashore blew conch shells and beat huge upright drums in celebration of the departure. A red moon rose over the sea, illuminating the surface of the water with a pinkish glow.

"What does it mean Tamrin? Why is the moon red in color?" asked Menelik.

Tamrin bit the inside of his lip, thinking before he spoke. "It is the moon of the goddess of the sea and sky, Buk, according to the keeper of my horses. But the reddish moon may just mean that somewhere out there far away on the land there is a huge fire burning and its smoke is in the sky, or perhaps we should take note, there may be a windstorm across the Arabian deserts and the dust in the sky warns of winds and blinding dust on the sea. The gods are so hard to understand, and I wonder if they understand us. I think we can see the sun and the moon because they are big and bright, but can they see us, specks like fleas on a huge elephant? I don't know. I think when we slaughter animals to sacrifice to the gods and then eat the roasted meat, we fill our bellies, but the bellies of the gods remain empty. We can take no chances with the gods. I have seen, however, that the priests get fatter and richer, and they make the rules. There is not a single priest I trust. They claim to be keepers of the gods, but they are hollow as a sounding gong."

Menelik laughed. "My mother says that Solomon's god can hear people talk, even understand what people think. That is a better way. Just think about the goddess of the sea and then she will think about our ships and our travel. I think about why my mother was bitten by the pet jackal and became lame. I really think that no god or goddess made it happen. It was because she kept a wild animal and tried to take away the food it was eating."

"Well, Son of the Wise One, you may have spoken wisely. I always remind myself to see things around me, people around me, events that occur and think about those, think about what is before me and what happens, instead of some people who quickly look to a god or a goddess. When I was a child, every time there was something broken in the house, my mother would shout, "Tamrin!" After a while I became the house god of accidents. If I heard a spoon fall I would soon hear my name, Tamrin! Sailors drown while at sea, not when they are sleeping in bed with their wives. Farmers pick the *marula* fruit if it gets ripe, not a day before or after, because if they don't, monkeys, elephants or birds will get to the fruit before them." Tamrin and Menelik both laughed.

The sea became choppy during the night. Sailors who were not on duty or at the steering arm slept on mats on deck to catch the breezes. Tamrin was a light sleeper and the ship under him soon became part of his awareness, day or night. He sat up, looked at the dark sky. Clouds obscured stars.

Tamrin walked to the sailor at the steering arm and they shared greetings. "Keep the wind to your back," said Tamrin. "The sails tell us that southeastern winds are prevailing tonight. The water tells us that to the south there has been a storm. The clouds and sunset above us warn us of weather to come." He stood closer to the rail and looked at the water streaming by the side of the dhow. "We are moving well. Ring the bell two times.

Let us see if your fleet is close ahead of us." He took the steering arm and the sailor ran forward to the huge bell and struck it two hard blows. Far in the distance they heard an answer, two faint sounds of a bell being struck. Then silence.

"What does it mean Master Tamrin? Only one ship answered." The sailor stretched and scratched his head furiously.

"Think about it. What could it mean?" answered Tamrin.

"Only one ship is close enough to hear our bell. Or, the sailor on duty fell asleep. Or the wind blew the sound away." He looked up at Tamrin in the semi-darkness.

"Or, four of the ships are much faster than we are and are far in the distance. The sound of our bell did not reach them. Ring five bells to ask if the ship leading us had communication with the one in front of it."

The sailor rang five times, this time striking the metal bar with force. In the distance the ship responded with two strikes. They too were beyond the range of sound of the rest of the fleet.

The entire bell ringing alerted the rest of the crew. Menelik overheard the conversations. "I think the other ships have sailed off the edge of the earth. We are sailing on a huge water plate."

"Menelik believes in strange gods, gods of jackals and of the end of the world. We are all heading in the same direction, Menelik, so warn us when you see the water pouring out over the edge of the world." Tamrin's remark brought laughter from the rest of the crew. Menelik was pleased by the reaction of his crewmates. He was one of them, not simply the Son of the Wise One.

"The sleep siren calls me into her arms. I will awake when the small gong announces the next watch." Menelik returned to his mat but could not sleep. He saw the face of his first love who had died at the side of the road, the young girl with the crippled body. Her voice and her eager face had imprinted on his mind so strongly that now whenever he saw another young woman, he tried to compare her to the beggar girl. Then he thought about the young woman from Hindush who now served his mother. He had come upon her as she bathed at the edge of the water. It was not her face he remembered now. Restlessly he covered himself with his robe, disturbed by his arousal. Perhaps, he thought, Tamrin would find him that same girl in Hodeida.

The seas became rougher and the crews lowered all but one sail, simply keeping the ship into the wind. Salt spray drove the sailors to seek cover under the deck cabins and roughly constructed shelters of canvas. The cook started a small fire in a metal stove set in the firebox out of the weather and heated water with ground coffee beans to make the men a sweet, thick brew served in tiny cups. The sailors passed around hard bread, the main diet on board.

Dawn came with an overcast sky. No ships were in sight ahead. Now the course was almost due east, with the wind sometimes beating ineffectively against the sails. Men talked about Hodeida, its markets, street markets filled with freshly caught fish, merchants with bamboo cages holding various birds, including green parakeets with red rings around their necks. Merchants sold delicious foods from individual stalls. Brothels with dancing girls and women musicians along Sharmatu road enticed the wayfarer to come and drink coffee, chew *qat* and meet the girls.

Tamrin entered the conversation. "When we were in the ports of the Hindush in Kolachi, the merchant Poocho took us to see their brothels. The discussion, of course, was about women, wives, slaves, concubines and prostitutes. I was surprised that in the Hindush language there was a word similar to the one we use here in Aksum for prostitutes, a word that is used in Hodeida and Marib as well. It is sharam, which is usually connected to prostitution. But Poocho used the word to mean shamed, demeaned, of low esteem. Perhaps words travel from country to country with traders such as myself and become part of another language. *Sharam.*

Menelik nodded. "I think you are right, Tamrin. My mother still uses words she learned when visiting Solomon. *Shalom.* She uses it every day when she meets new people who visit her. She wishes them peace. But I have heard the same word, or something like it among the sailors of our ships. I think you use the same word, Tamrin."

"Of course. I was in the courts of Solomon as well, but I grew up in Hodeida and among Sabaean like myself, there is a word that is almost the same. I agree with you, Menelik, we traders and merchants are like bees that fly from flower to flower and bring pollen on their legs and hairs that make for new fruit. Our African bees in Aksum speak many languages." He smiled.

"Bees! Do you remember the time I got stung when I was playing in the almond orchard behind the palace? Six stings." Menelik rubbed his neck.

"I remember well. You were into everything and were in trouble so often that your mother assigned a full time companion to watch out for you. Bee stings on your neck made you so sick you almost died, Menelik. Honey. Sweet. *Halwa.* We are carrying many flasks of it on board now, taking it to the court of Solomon as gifts. More important, our trade item stored near to where you hang your hammock is bees' wax. The scribes in Solomon's court treasure wax more than we do. I think wax is used in Jerusalem for hundreds of things. They even collect tribute from some countries in wax. So, with the honey we will bring wax. When I was in Egypt I learned that they use wax when they mummify their rulers." He was shaking his head.

"Some day when I become…" he paused, "…you know, when my mother dies, I am going to collect wax from all over the country and it will become our most important trade item. Ethiopia is already known for its honey. We have more honey hives than any other country in the world. But we use it all up in our *halwa, tej* and coffee." He sounded very wise now.

"Good idea, Menelik. But add ivory and gold to your list. A little gold is worth more than a lot of wax. Now in Nubia and Kush their mines are producing gold and they have little means to trade it except through us, Aksum. Solomon has a great hunger for gold, but Saba's visit to him cleared out much of our Ethiopian gold. I think she did not get a bargain. Your father Solomon gave her you. So you are the gold boy." He held out his hands, palms up toward Menelik. "She was tricked. That was unwise of Solomon. Wax! A good idea."

"So what will we bring back that will make up for all the gold my mother brought him? What does Israel have that we want?" Menelik got up stiffly and stood at the rail and watched the water slide past the hull.

"Power! Fame! Information! Olives. Holy artifacts."

Everyone in the group laughed. Olives. One sailor piped up. "Our ship will be empty when we return. Fame is light. Power is invisible, and olives taste terrible. Tamrin, there must be something better. Will only the priests benefit from holy artifacts?"

"When I was in Jerusalem all the power that Solomon had came from his One God. They have an Ark that is powerful, containing the stone tablets that his god wrote upon telling people, commanding people, to do and not do certain things. 'Thou shalt not kill!' If Ethiopia had the Ark we would have Solomon's power. If we have the Ark we will be famous. If we have both of these we will return with a ship full of olive oil, the best oil for medicine, cooking, making paints, mixed with wax as a sealer. We will wax eloquent if we get artifacts."

The Queen with two of her handmaidens came on deck to

move to the rear of the ship where a canvas concealed a toilet. Everyone was quiet and listened to the sound of the water passing under the hull. The clouds in front of them lifted and stars became visible. To their left, the North Star shone brightly and to its left the mariner's beacon star. Tamrin raised his hands and pointed to the star. His other hand pointed in the direction of the ship's motion. "We are on track. Tomorrow we will be nearing Hodeida. Menelik, you will eat goat stew and drink tej and meet Miriam!"

"It's all right. You don't have to set me up to meet a girl. If I see a girl I like I will find out about her myself."

"When you get back in the court of Solomon in Jerusalem, the importance of the name Miriam will become known to you. Ask your father about her. While you are at it, ask about Moses, and Aaron his brother. Miriam was an ancient leader of Solomon's people when they were freed from bondage in Egypt. On our return trip you can tell me the story."

The women returned to their crude cabin, the maidens supporting the Queen to help keep her balance on the moving deck. They did not acknowledge the men who kept quiet until they passed.

"When you went to Jerusalem with my mother, she stayed with Solomon. Did you stay with anyone?" Menelik tried to keep a straight face.

"You ask a difficult question. Remember, that was eighteen, or was it nineteen years ago, at the time you were conceived. Since you ask, yes, I took a young and beautiful girl and she returned with me on the journey back home. You will meet her in Hodeida soon. She is the mother of Miriam of whom I spoke. You are like a ferret, digging into the holes of my history." He put out his hand for Menelik to grasp. "Six months! I was with your mother's group for six months. Now you are going to ask where that wife came from."

"I was curious of course, but I knew you would tell me even if I did not ask. All right. Who?"

"Solomon had a huge village of people who were called his wives and concubines. They lived in a section of Jerusalem that had a wall around it, but the women were not captive, nor did they hide themselves, yet they lived together because they all had one common bond, your father. One of his wives at that time was a Sabaean woman, a captured slave girl. She had a daughter who is your age now, the daughter of Solomon. Like her namesake, she is a wonderful dancer and singer. Of course I was invited to the feasts and saw her many times. She is the mother of Miriam who was born in the same month that you were born. When I returned with your mother the Queen, our last stop before heading for Aksum was Hodeida. That is the home of my family, my parents, my brothers and sisters. That is where I left my new wife, and that is where Miriam was born." He was laughing now.

"I am trying to figure this out. I am a son of Solomon. Your wife is a daughter of Solomon. Miriam is her daughter by you, thus she has Solomon's blood; like a granddaughter. Your wife and I are then half brother-sister because of Solomon. You are your daughter's father. Is she my cousin? How would you get related to me? Miriam carries Solomon's blood and so do I."

"Now you understand why I want you to wed Miriam. If you have children, our families will be bonded in a royal triangle. Solomon is royalty. You are royal. The children are tied to both royal families. That is a strong bond. Strangely, your mother the Queen never had another child, and from the time you were a tiny baby, I became as your father. It is very complicated." He put his hand on Menelik's shoulder. "Of course you will find your own women. I understand. Every man does except the Hindush. They find wives for their sons in families like themselves, who worship the same gods, who have similar businesses, and thus families are forever glued together. I will tell you a secret that is not really a secret. I now have four wives in Aksum, one in Hodeida. Yet I have had many concubines. I have lost track of many of them and their children. Ethiopian women are very independent and also become attracted to other men and move into new households. When I spoke about Miriam, I was not thinking about your having a concubine, a girl to make babies with and leave behind. I was thinking of the triangle that I mentioned."

Tamrin lay on his back and looked up at the mariner's star, the North Star, the Milky Way, and felt as if he were drifting in the heavens.

"I have been talking to one of my wives too much. She believes that parents should be involved in actual marriages because two families get involved, get tied together."

Menelik whispered now. "Did my mother have anything to do with your idea of having me meet your daughter Miriam?"

"No. We have had a good arrangement all the years I have served her. I try never to surprise her, but respond to her questions, look out for her needs. On the other hand, Tamrin the Merchant is frequently surprised by your mother the Queen. Her mind and ideas are very busy and she asks about everything and everyone in her kingdom, except my relationships with my wives and concubines. No. Your mother did not put me up to this." Tamrin sighed.

"Solomon likes riddles. You had better prepare yourself to ask him one or two riddles. He will ask many from you. Your mother was the one who got him started with riddles. She is full of them as you well know." He paused.

"Here is one." Tamrin talked with a half voice.

"There was a green house. Inside the green house there was

a white house. Inside the white house there was a red house. Inside the red house there were lots of babies."

Menelik laughed. "I don't know. Tell me, Tamrin."

"I will tell you after you meet Miriam. You have to come up with two riddles for me that have real answers. I will try to solve your riddles. Here is a problem. Why do people bow down to their rulers and their gods?"

"I can answer that one. Because the rulers and gods are to be respected and feared." He smiled knowingly.

"Why don't they just clap? Why don't they scratch their heads? Why don't they just say hello?" He was shaking his head. "What is special about bowing?"

"I know. Because the rulers want them to. Or, because…tell me Tamrin."

"You never guessed the first riddle. I will tell you that one. It is so easy. Watermelon!"

Tamrin and Menelik washed with seawater as they stood on the back deck. Menelik was lighter in skin than Tamrin whose Ethiopian and Arabic ancestry revealed his Negroid features. His graying hair was tightly curled, his skin the color of walnuts, and his face revealed more Gala than Menelik's. He stood eight spans tall and had a powerful build, sturdy legs and strong square teeth that were in places chipped or discolored. Menelik was as tall as he but fair-skinned. He had straight white teeth, straight brown hair and a generous nose resembling that of his father Solomon.

While the men washed, they laughed as they threw calabashes of water on each other. Each had his personal pumice stone with which to rub off the hard skin on heels and feet.

The future Emperor Menelik was not handsome to behold, nor did he have an air of wisdom about him. Rather the expression on his face seemed to be one of curiosity, or sometimes even surprise. Tamrin looked at Menelik, sizing him up, a gangly youth for whom the world was one huge maze to explore. He could not imagine people bowing down to him.

"So, did you come up with an answer? Why do people bow to their monarchs?" asked Tamrin.

"It is just like dogs. If a bigger or more powerful dog meets a new smaller dog in a pack, the new dog falls to the ground and exposes its vulnerable belly and throat."

"I like that. The neck is a vulnerable place, so to expose it is to be very humble. What about this? Staring. Direct eye contact without lowering the eyes is a sign of aggression in most animals. If you meet a lion on a path, look to the side, stand still, do not stare at it in the eyes, which means aggression and may make it attack. Also, looking in the eyes is an act of intimacy. One does not create immediate intimacy with a monarch; rather one allows the monarch to make the next move. Lowering the head down and staring at the floor is a stance of humility. Look at me now!"

Menelik was surprised. As soon as his eyes looked toward Tamrin's face, Tamrin lowered his head quietly and looked at his shoes. "Tamrin, don't. I get the point. You are like a father to me. I have known no other. I should bow to you."

CHAPTER 12

No one knows what the dawn will bring

The sun seemed to leap up from the edge of the sea, blazing yellow, shimmering across the water. Porpoises played alongside the dhow, moving at twice the speed of the ship, then diving and circling back. Water birds of all kinds flew across the top of their dhow, heading from mainland shallows to island feeding grounds on the horizon. A small bird with a black beak landed on the top of the mast and took a free ride as the boat moved toward the shoreline.

Tamrin walked aft to the steering arm and took it from one of the sailors. "Stand next to me and learn how to come into this port. There is a bay. See the low hills there, the rugged coast of rocks piled high one on top of the other, then beyond, hardly visible now are three houses built high on these rocks, three stories high and painted brown and white. Those are the markers to head for. The wind is not helping us much but we can struggle sideways against it, though it tips us rather strongly."

The dhow slowed without winds directly behind its sail, but the slower motion did not seem to disturb Tamrin. The deck was tilted to one side and sailors took care not to leave objects on the deck, or lose them.

"There are sand bars that reach out into the mouth of the bay, and two of them have formed over shallow rocks. They can rip out the bottom of a boat easily. The rocks are hidden by growths of coral and sand, but that is where fishermen from my village of Hodeida come because sardines and anchovies gather here. The birds will tell you if they are being bunched together by the dolphins and reef sharks." In the distance the outlines of low houses built on the edge of rocky hills could be seen.

"How many people live in your birth place, Tamrin?" asked Menelik.

"Tens of hundreds if you count those that have moved back beyond the rocky areas and are farmers, planters of coconut and date palms. You will see the extensive palm tree groves later. Even among this population there are divisions, there are spaces between dwellings and settlements because of feuds and small wars of the past. Blood feuds never seem to end. Revenge taking is the sign of a man. To leave a blood debt unpaid is the sign of a coward. So houses and settlements are scattered here and there, and of course there is the problem of race. Racial groups segregate themselves; Nubians on one side, Sabaean on another, Arabs and people from inland, those who left Marib and settled here own the vast groves of palm trees. We are a restless people, but a proud group if any outsider threatens us. Then we all join to fight an intruder. Already our approach has been noted. Look, high on the rocks, there are two poles with colored flags."

Menelik was excited, and a little ill at ease. He had no weapon now and he had never ever struck another person in a fight. Listening to Tamrin, he became concerned about his own safety. "Tamrin, you said you would teach me to use the cross bow and the long sword."

"We will practice both when we get to my village. Young

men of your age will teach you those as well as fighting with the jambiya. I suspect that one of the first gifts you will receive will be a curved dagger. No man walks without one." Tamrin maneuvered the ship in a wide tack to gain distance to the north. The sail luffed, then snapped and filled again as the ship moved in a more northerly path.

It took two hours to move into the opening of the bay. The water here was fairly shallow and it was low tide. Four of the sailors held long poles that had flat hand-like bars attached to the end to help push against the sand. The dhow moved toward the anchoring area slowly, the sand almost touching its bow.

"This is actually a good time to come into port. The water is calm, though shallow. At high tide there is often a surge of water, which moves the boat about making it difficult to control. The old saying, 'Crawling is sometimes better than a full run', is very true when it comes to moving ships. Better to creep into your docking birth and not ram another boat or the dock, if there is one. We will anchor well away from the small wood docks because our ship is too heavy to be supported by them. Small boats will come out to unload our trade goods and necessary possessions." Tamrin sounded excited.

"Do you know how to swim, Tamrin?" asked Menelik.

"What a strange question. Of course, all sailors must learn to swim. If you live near water you use the water for business and for pleasure." He now looked at Menelik critically. "Of course. You are a land child. You have never learned to swim. Well that will be another skill you will learn while we are here for a week. A son of Solomon must know how to swim, though I doubt your father knows."

Look Tamrin, there are three of our ships anchored there, just about at the north edge of the bay." As he spoke, ships' bells rang five times, and Tamrin's ship replied with five loud gongs of the metal bar. They were united, and they were home!

Two members of the crew got ready to throw out the anchor. It was of Tamrin's own design. Heavy round rocks were packed tightly into a basket-like frame made of palm fibers fashioned into rope and woven together. Tamrin noted that the Hindus had added an additional feature to their anchors, long heavy copper ingots, sharpened on each end, thrust directly through lower third of the basket anchor. Four of these ends protruded from the basket like claws. Not only did the weight of the stone-filled basket hold the ship's stern in place, but the metal dug into clay or sand beds for additional prevention of drag and drift. The drawback was if the ends got stuck into submerged roots, waterlogged wood or stones.

Menelik walked to the front of the ship and watched the men handle the anchor. It was on a small box on the deck next to a railing that could be removed. The rail was removed and the men shoved the anchor overboard, careful to let the rope ride in a grooved hardwood crosspiece. Setting the anchor looked easy, but Menelik wondered how many men it would take to hoist the heavy basket of stones onto the deck and back onto the small wood platform behind the rail.

Already a number of small craft were being rowed out to meet them, two of them from their own fleet. Menelik recognized two of Tamrin's sons and waved to greet them. Tamrin rolled out the rope ladder. Sailors crawled up the clumsy device, swaying and unstable, exerting brute strength and balance to climb.

" To the swift is the race, and the prize. We have been here for two days waiting for you. What news?" shouted Sita.

"Only gossip. Menelik has been talking about my daughter Miriam and is dying to meet her. One of our crew ripped his toe nail off and the food on board was miserable." Tamrin laughed.

Menelik was always taken by surprise when someone joked

about him. In all his young life in the palace no one dared to show such familiarity or disrespect. Yet Tamrin did the same with other crewmembers and his sons. But Menelik looked uncomfortable and did not know how to respond.

Sita added to his misery. "The Prince is not ready for such sport, Tamrin. He is but an overgrown boy. Leave him alone."

Menelik walked to Sita and looked down into his eyes because he was half a head taller. He stared into Sita's eyes in mock aggression and did not smile. Sita looked away. "The young lion has fangs!" He extended his hand and they clasped each other's wrists.

Tamrin, on a huge beast, led the line of fifty camels. He sat on a small saddle tied to the camel's back. The Queen's camel, a neutered male, had a seat formed over the single hump which had an umbrella placed to shade her from the scorching Arabian sun. Directly behind her rode two soldiers with long bows and swords, and behind them two camels with the other women. Tents for camping and supplies followed behind on a score of camels, and following up behind them rode ten armed soldiers not tied into the caravan who could move about quickly if necessary. All the rest of the beasts were tied from the saddles with ropes to the nose ring of the camel behind. Their trip to Marib would take fifteen days, a trip the Queen performed frequently. Messengers were sent ahead to small villages and oasis in the Tihama through which they were passing so the citizens could prepare for the arrival of the party in the late evening.

Dismounting was difficult for Sheba because of her disability. A small wicker step was carried on one of the camels onto which she could take two steps to the ground. Tamrin stopped their travel frequently. When the women wished to relieve themselves, they would display a red scarf on the saddles of their mounts. Privacy was a rare commodity on such a trip. The desert sands had few trees, few natural shelters. So the women carried blankets to hold up to shield each other from view. The men, during such times, made themselves busy adjusting straps, checking loads and refraining from talking or joking.

Qat was in abundance, both for the men and women. The green narcotic leaves were kept moist in a pot on one of the camels. At each stop, fresh green leaves were passed to all the travelers. For the women there was the additional treat of *Afimi* for cramps, headaches, boredom, and discontent. Tamrin had learned that greater distances could be achieved each day if the smell of opium pipes wafted over the caravan from the mounts on which the women rode. Because of the pain in Saba's foot while walking, she had little discontent on the journey.

A messenger riding a fast camel was sent ahead to Marib to warn the caretakers of the palace and the citizens of the city. Three days prior to the arrival of the caravan this messenger arrived in Marib, showing off by having his camel run through the palace gate at full lope, shouting in falsesetto ululation, alerting everyone within earshot. Women picked up the ululation and clapped their hands, small children ran around joyously knowing that soon there would be special food for them from the Queen's palace. Dogs barked, donkeys brayed and an old beggar with a small drum began to beat it in a dance rhythm.

Soldiers hurried to clean up their barracks, prepare their dress clothing, locate their weapons and see to their sharpness. The cooks in the palace had been waiting and had already gathered staples, barley and millet; red palm oil for cooking, spices and dried meats. Now in the excitement of imminent arrival of the Queen live animals were brought into the temple for slaughter, and from the extensive palm orchards, dates of every kind brought in. New bores were made in the palm wine trees and straws placed into containers hanging on the trees to collect fresh palm wine, which in three days would ferment to a potent, and pleasantly fizzy brew. Queen Sheba was coming! The Queen would soon stay in her palace. The city prepared as a bride prepares for the bridegroom.

In distant Hodeida, Menelik was given a spacious room in Tamrin's home. He had not been to Hodeida since childhood, and a great fuss was made over him. He bathed with fresh water scented with jasmine perfume, wore new clothing and joined Tamrin's extended family for the first evening meal.

A large cloth was spread over a woven mat, cushions surrounded the area, and as the family and their royal guest sat down, again the women in the household ululated and clapped. Food was set on large copper plates on the cloth and many dishes were set out and put in front of Menelik. Different women had prepared separate dishes, and they peeked around the partition, watching Menelik taste each one, waiting for his reaction. At this first meal he would always be the first to take a bite, to dip flat bread in sauce, to quaff a drink of fizzy palm wine. He made a great show for each dish, pretending to swoon with the aroma and wonderful taste. Raw sliced onions were piled on a leaf to be sprinkled on the stew. He made a face of distaste. The women, gathered around to provide the food and clean up the floor on which bones were tossed after the men had pulled the meat off with their teeth: they laughed and shouted to each other, commenting about Menelik's appetite for goat meat and making comments about what results that would have on his performance in bed. A musician played the five stringed *Oud* as the meal began.

The men of the family joined Menelik and began to eat with eager appetites. Specialties of all kinds were on the cloth. Such a feast was meant for a king. Finally after all had belched comfortably and were sitting back against their cushions, other musicians entered the room and began to play. A girl dressed in a gauze-like dress, her face half covered with a veil began to dance, slowly at first, almost as if waking up. The beat increased, as did the frequency of her steps. Her hands swept to the sides and above her head and she began to move her hips and her abdomen, slowly, then more quickly to the rhythm of the drums. Menelik did not realize it but he sat with his mouth open. He held his breath as the girl danced, when as if by accident the scarf slipped from her face and she danced with her eyes closed, swaying and stamping her feet. As she came to the end of her dance abruptly, the musicians also stopped their music with one loud slap on the skins of the drums, a climax. She happened to be directly in front of Menelik al Hakim, Solomon's son. She opened her eyes and stared into Menelik's eyes face, as a hungry leopard would stare into the eyes of its prey. She did not smile. She stared at him openly for a few seconds, which seemed to draw Menelik to his feet. He stood in front of her, unaware now of the room, the place, and the time. He reached his hands up to his brow and touched his fingers above his eyes and lowered his face to the level of her own.

She spun around and departed, leaving Menelik standing. He looked at the staring men around the eating cloth and squatted down again. "Is the dancing girl a slave?" he asked the man next to him.

"No, lord, she is the daughter of Tamrin the Trader of Aksum who is taking the Queen to Marib. Her name is Miriam. Her mother is a daughter of Solomon, your father."

Menelik busied himself with martial arts. Three men trained him to use the long bow and the cross bow for close in fighting. A swordsman trained him in the use of the long knife and *jambiya*. When a goat was to be killed for food they brought Menelik to the kitchen area so that he could cut its throat and spill the blood, and using his *jambiya*, cut off its head with one stroke. Menelik, living in the palace in Aksum, had never been present when an animal had been killed, yet meat was his favorite food. Chickens, ducks, pigeons, desert bustards held in cages, all went under Menelik's knife. Soon the sight of blood did not disturb him; in fact he became expert in the use of the curved dagger.

The long bow was Menelik's favorite weapon. Contests were held with his trainers to see who could shoot an arrow the farthest, and who could hit a tied goat on the first shot at fifty paces. The men mentioned lion every time they used the bow, even if they were shooting at a goat. They promised that they would hunt the ferocious beast as his last test of valor. Each of his trainers was an expert with the broad spear. This was Menelik's most difficult weapon to use. It required a strong upper arm and very strong back.

One morning his three trainers took him to the extensive date palm grove. They stood and watched as a young man about Menelik's age slipped a leather belt around the tree trunk and all the way around his own back, placed his bare feet on the trunk of the tree, hoisted the belt a foot higher and pushed up with his legs, again and again until he was at the top of the tree. There with a deft stroke of a knife, cut the large cluster of dates hanging from a dangling stem. Then with amazing agility, feet on the trunk, the belt sliding on the trunk the man made his way down to the ground. He handed the belt to Menelik.

Menelik was amazed! He had never done manual labor in his life. That was for the slaves to perform. He held the belt, frowning and asked his trainers why the young man had given him the belt.

"Lord, there are two reasons. One, every man who lives in the desert knows how to obtain his own food. Palm nuts, coconuts, dates and other fruit are high up. Monkeys do not starve. We do not starve. Every man learns to climb before he uses the spear. We say, one who has not climbed a hundred palm trees may not throw a spear." He bowed his head in respect.

"All right. I think I understand. Now, what does getting dates have to do with spear throwing? Let me throw the spear a hundred times instead." Menelik looked at the climber, the rippling muscles on his upper back and upper arms, the palms of his hands, which were hard and calloused. He began to understand.

On Menelik's first try, the young man followed him up the tree in case he slipped. Menelik was clumsy and uncoordinated as he tried to move the belt up and push with his feet at the same time. By the time he was to the top of the tree his legs were shaking. He reached over with the curved knife to cut the fibrous stem of the oil palm cluster and was amazed at how hard it was to do this, keep his balance and lean to the side as he cut. His efforts to move down were awkward and the belt frequently slipped. His trainers stood at the base of the tree with smiling faces.

The leader, a very tall dark man, a cousin of Tamrin, spoke. "Every day you should climb ten trees and help them harvest the palm oil clusters. Yasha will be your companion and teacher. After your hundredth tree we will make a feast. The next day we will begin to throw the long spear and learn how to use it for close-in fighting. The long spear with its broad blade, sharpened to a fine edge, is the most advanced weapon men have devised. It is accurate at long distances; a hit on an enemy usually means death; and it is an effective weapon against a man with a sword or dagger. Best of all, it is a staff when you travel. All men carry the *jambiya* and the *sabarbahah*, spear taller than a man. Add to this the light shield made of woven basket canes and a man is prepared for war and the lion. Many men have fallen under a lion attack, holding the shield in front of them as the lion leaps, bracing the spear into the earth, which impales it when it lands. You will see in two weeks. The desert lion is like the lion of the Hindush lacking a huge dark mane. It is lighter and more agile, and the male hunts with the females. You will see. The lion of Ethiopia with its black mane lets his many females do the hunting, then takes his fill both of the meat and of them." They laughed. "The lion from the desert of Hindush and Arabia usually only travels with one female and her cubs. They raise the cubs together."

Menelik's fifth day climbing trees was the worst. His arms ached, his back was sore and he was irritable. Not wishing to join in the evening meals he ate alone. Strangely, during the last three days of climbing palm trees the exercise seemed easy; his reflexes made the ascent look like an easy task. The trainers were present during his hundredth climb. He descended and faced them, a large smile on his face.

News of his accomplishment had spread to the women. Another large feast was prepared and once again Miriam danced, this time facing Tamrin the entire time, moving her belly and hips in amazingly erotic positions. At the end of Miriam's dance, Menelik stood and handed her a small palm leaf, folded into a little package. Inside the package he had placed a blood red ruby that Tamrin had brought back from Kolachi on their previous trip.

On the occasion of giving Menelik the ruby, Tamrin had said, "Menelik, this is what I gave to each of my four wives in Aksum before there were marriage agreements made. A blood red ruby speaks of fire, heat and virginity. The girl can only accept it if she has never known a man carnally and if the family, her father, is in agreement."

Miriam held the small package in her hand and felt through the wrapping with her fingers, then looked up at Menelik and smiled. She turned quickly and ran to the women's kitchen.

Ululation could now be heard as each of the women began to waggle their tongues in front of their teeth and shout out with piercing notes of pleasure.

The next day Menelik's trainers and his coach, the young palm tree climber, stood in an open area near the beach. Each man carried his own spear. Menelik held his new spear proudly, surprised at its heft.

"We all can recognize our own spears because our name is marked on the wood. Each of us will see how far we can throw it. See the leaves in the sand. Try to throw beyond those," said Tamrin's brother.

No one cheered. Each man took his turn, the tree climbing coach next to the last, and Menelik last to throw. He watched carefully as the men ran, skidded to a stop and flung their spears which arched high and became embedded in the sand. Most of the spears fell close to each other, except for the spear of the tree climber. It stuck into the sand a good body length beyond the others.

Menelik did not like this competition because he was afraid of not winning. He was worried about his image as the future ruler, the stories that would be told. He feared failure, yet he coveted winning. He ran and threw while his body was still in motion, his bare feet skidding to a stop. The spear arched high and landed almost in the center of the cluster of spears, but farther than three of them.

The men smiled broadly and raised a clenched fist at Menelik, a sign of respect and approval. The tree climber sauntered to his own spear, pulled it out of the sand, held it up high and made a strange high pitched sound like 'ow'. There were three more tries. Each time the young man threw the farthest, but on Menelik's last try his went beyond the young man's. Again, news spread to the women and they happily gossiped and prodded Miriam.

"His spear is long! His spear is strong. His spear will draw blood." They shouted and joked and she entered into their pointed gossip with words of her own. "Oh, but the target must be known by the spear handler. The target will be moving and very small." The women howled with laughter.

A month passed quickly for Menelik. The third week was the lion hunt. Six men accompanied him, all on racing camels. They moved into the desert to a huge *wadi* that ran from the hills all the way to the ocean. Though it was the dry season, there were a few pools of standing water and the men stopped and looked for signs of lion. At the second water hole there were multiple lion prints. An entire pride had come to the pool to drink.

The camels were left with caretakers and tied a distance from the pond. Six hunters were now on foot, each holding a spear and a woven shield. Their best tracker followed the spoor of the lion. The sun blazed down on the men and they dripped sweat. Menelik followed three elder men. Next to him was the tree climber. They did not talk as they moved forward, half crouched over. Menelik became terribly thirsty, but saw that the others did not drink from their small leather water pouches.

Lying under a *marula* tree in its dappled shade were four lions, a female and her half grown cubs and a male. They were panting because of the heat. The men were able to move in fairly close because the wind blew toward them. All at once the lions stood up and faced them. The male let out a low growl, but one of the females crouched low, her tail moving from side to side, her face a huge toothy snarl. All the men held their spears lightly and their shields as high as their mouths. The men continued to move forward. The female lion, now accompanied by the male, rose to running position and charged, expecting the men to flee. The men waited until they were ten paces away and all three in the first line threw their spears. As soon as they threw they moved aside for the next three men. The male lion had two spears through his chest and back and was thrashing on the ground, growling. The female was untouched and in a flash came at the men and leaped. They held up their shields and as the female fell in her leap toward the first man, he fell back to the ground, covering his body and sticking the spear in the ground in the space between his arm and chest. She landed on him with great force, her claws unsheathed, reaching for his head, but at that moment the spear pierced her chest and she somersaulted beyond the hunter, biting at the spear handle. Two men, Menelik among them, stood ready with their spears and faced the other younger lions. Menelik was breathing rapidly. He held his spear and shield at the ready, waiting for the next charge. The two younger female lions, not yet fully grown, slunk away into the grasses beyond the tree.

The man who had suffered the first attack still lay on the ground, groaning. He was not bleeding but bruised where the shield had slammed against his chest, breaking two ribs. His companions urged him to drink water. One had a bundle of qat in his waistband and gave this to the wounded man who began to chew and swallow the juice of the leaves.

The lions were skinned, and the skulls placed on the end of spears and carried over their shoulders. It took two men to carry one skin on their spears between them. When they arrived back at the pond where the camels were tethered, they bathed in the muddy water. The camels became agitated and pulled against their ropes furiously because of the smell of the lion skins. The men left the skin bundles near the camels who spat, snorted, and stared at the rolled up skins and heads, but eventually calming down, realizing the skins did not move.

Their caravan approached Tamrin's compound at dusk. Small children ran out screaming and shouting. The two skinned and gory lion skulls were dumped on the ground, and the children ran forward, lifting the heavy lion heads up and dragging them toward the dwellings, shouting and screaming as if in pain. This started the women's celebration; all came up and faced the hunters. As a group they ululated and danced, hands in the air.

Menelik and his tree climbing coach came last, helping their wounded companion get down off from the kneeling camel and supporting him as he walked toward the compound. The entire community rose up, shouting and screaming while looking at the wounded man. Still other danced and sang songs of victory. Elderly men left their beds and staggered around inspecting the lion skins, listening to stories that grew by leaps and bounds, and telling taller tales of their own bravery and prowess with lions, and their sexual conquests with women. Soon goats began to bleat as they were dragged behind the kitchen to be slaughtered. One fat-tailed sheep made no sound as it approached its death and the killing knife.

Menelik lay on his mat and stared at the ceiling, watching a pair of geckos mate. They were hanging upside down on the ceiling, and at a given moment, the female lost her hold and the pair landed on Menelik's cloth near his bed. Menelik didn't move. The geckos didn't move either, for a long time. Then, as if in a hurry to meet an appointment, the male dismounted, ran across the floor, up the wall, and hid in a large crack. Menelik did not kick the female away. He was curious. How long would she stay still, as if paralyzed? She fell asleep, and so did Menelik.

He awakened abruptly at the sound of footsteps near his door. He sat up, saw the gecko had left, and then went to the door, his *jambiya* in hand. To his right where the lion skins were stretched across a frame, a hyena was standing on its hind legs trying to reach the pelts. One of the hunters shouted and the beast left, loping away on its shorter hind legs, making a soft crying sound. Menelik went outside and tried to arrange the frames so that no beast could reach them. He returned to his room, took out fresh *qat* leaves left for him under a damp cloth, and sat on the doorsill staring into the moonlit courtyard. Someone had left the gate open allowing the hyena in. Menelik walked over and closed the wood gate, placing the locking rope over the top of two high bars.

Miriam and her younger sister had been whispering together half the night. They decided to go into the courtyard and see if any *marula* fruit had ripened. Giggling, they tiptoed out their door, made their way around the wall and almost bumped into Menelik who was standing, leaning against the wall.

He grabbed for his dagger and the girls let out a tiny scream. Miriam put up her palms toward Menelik. "Nothing! We could not sleep. Sorry we startled you." Her little sister began to giggle.

"I will go back into my room so you two can have the courtyard all to yourselves." He turned to go but Miriam again put up her hands in front of him, telling him to stop, yet an invitation.

"Please stay at least a moment. I have never even spoken to you, heard you say my name, or say mine to you. Yet you gave me a gift. Tell me its meaning. It is very beautiful." She backed up so the moonlight bathed Menelik's face.

"I can only tell you two. There are many, many more meanings that can only be told over a period of time. Meaning one. Red means fire, and that is what is in my mind and heart when I see you or hear your voice or watch you dance." He paused and cleared his throat. "Second, precious, of value, a jewel that surpasses. That is you. I dare not say more. It will take time when we are…"

"What am I to do with these meanings? Must I simply hold them, like I am holding the ruby in my right hand at this moment? Just hold to it? Give me at least one more meaning and I will leave."

"It means marriage. It means the union of our bodies." He turned and walked toward the gate and the two girls followed him.

"Menelik, we share a blood line, we share families as we stand here. Is that what you mean?"

"No. It is not proper for me to ask you openly. I have not spoken to Tamrin your father. But the second meaning is that I desire you for marriage. Upon our return from the court of Solomon, I wish to marry you. I want you to return with me to Aksum. When I return I will be called, Menelik the First, and my mother will turn over the kingdom to me. Not as a concubine, Miriam. My wife."

She stood transfixed to the spot. Her sister pulled at her hand to leave but she shook off her hand. "Menelik, will you touch my hand now?"

He reached over and not only touched her hand but held it in his own calloused hard hand, bent low and placed his cheek against the skin of her hand. He turned and left quickly.

"Let's get back into our room. Hurry. We should not be in the courtyard so long!" Her sister pulled at her arm. Miriam turned and looked up at the moon and squatted down on her haunches and pulled her sister down to join her.

"What are you doing?"

"Keep quiet. I want to be quiet and say nothing at all. Not even move. Let me be in my thoughts for a moment or two." Miriam opened her hand and the light of the moon made the ruby shine, blood red. She stared at it while her sister sat next to her. "It will be the name of our first child. *Lali.* The name our people give for red. Lali, red little one."

"What if it is a boy?"

"I will think about it then. Let us get to our room before my mother finds us out."

A hyena began its strange laugh-like call, which gave speed to the girls' legs. They fell onto the bed that they shared and hugged each other.

"Tonight was a night of secrets. You were with me but you may not say one word, to anyone. Nothing. It must be the secret that the three of us share for now. I will tell you later when you can speak of it. If I hear any gossip about this, I will…"

Her hands contracted tightly around her sister's wrist. "Secret!"

CHAPTER 13

Living is worthless to one without a home

Tamrin returned to Hodeida in an unhappy and irritable mood. For two weeks he had had no *qat* to chew and even worse, no alcoholic *tej*. His body was covered with marks of sand fleas. Tamrin was a master of ships, not a desert traveler overland on 'ships of the desert' camels. Yet he and his men were frequently subjected to the harsh realities of travel in the desert, in wilderness areas on camels or horses. Those who cared for the camels were called *Bedu*, meaning the desert dwellers. For days on end, even as many as seven days, the camels did not drink and the travelers never bathed. The *Bedu* laughed when they told Tamrin that they only bathed the newborn and the corpse at death, otherwise their bodies did not see water. Tamrin saw no fresh water and for weeks on end he did not bathe. Their clothing hung heavy on them. Sitting around campfires burning dung, being subjected to smoke that infused their clothing, their hair, their very skin made them to be one with those who lived their entire lives like this, the Bedu.

The eldest *Bedu* was a storyteller. After a meal of hard flat bread and camel's milk, and a drink of fermented camel milk his tongue loosened. "You see these camels? They are a gift to us from the deserts of *Afric,* when the first men on earth lived. Men and animals came across the land to the swamps that Judeans called *yam suf* that separated our deserts from those of the *Afric* during a great drought that lasted for two years. Our camels are like those in the deserts of *Afric.* I traveled to Kilwa in Jebal Tubayq on the eastern border of Jordan and saw with my own eyes the caves and the carvings of camels that our first ancestors made. Camels are like our children. They live for forty years and become used to one man, like a woman gets used to one man." They all laughed. "A camel during its entire life never bathes. They are healthy and enduring. We learned from them."

Tamrin spoke up. "Yes and both you and the camels have the same smell." Again the men chuckled. "I can't imagine any woman getting used to a Bedu. That's why your men only marry very young girls and keep all other men away from your compounds. If one of your women ever met a real man from Aksum, she would never be content with a little dried up desert man who smelled like a camel."

"You are wrong. They are content because, like camels, we have huge hidden talents. We have no smell. Since you arrived from the ship, we all noted that you sailors have a very bad smell. Bedu have no smell." He lifted his arm and smelled it and smiled. At that moment Menelik farted loudly, which he always did when their diet consisted mostly of milk. "Yes! Sailors smell bad and fart like pigs!"

"At least our women don't smell like your women," said Menelik.

"That is correct. Your women smell like smoked meat. I have seen how they stand over a small fire and put incense and sandalwood shavings on the coals, spread their legs and catch the smoke under their skirts." The Bedu all laughed uproariously.

"I have heard your women wipe themselves off with camel's milk."

"I have heard that your women are like lionesses that tease the male constantly for sex, because they are never satisfied."

The men talked into the night about women among various tribes and countries they had traveled. Menelik fell asleep thinking of Miriam's face.

Tamrin's caravan gathered in front of the gates of his own courtyard. Men unloaded gifts from Sheba, fruits, spices, and even a small, baby Hamadryas Baboon, which screeched constantly. It was a gift for his youngest son. Tamrin seemed in a hurry to move on to the long overland journey to Jordan. After two days the men packed their personal goods in camel bags and left for the port, a half-day trip. As they left, Miriam and her sister watched the caravan depart.

Miriam was hoping for Menelik to speak to her, or give some message, some acknowledgment, but it was a public place and she understood but felt sad. Menelik did not turn around and greet her, smile or say a word. She watched him ride over the hill and then he raised his hand high in the air and turned his palm toward her. Miriam stood with her head up and tears ran down her cheeks. Her sister hugged her waist.

"He's telling you to wait. He is thinking of you!" Her sister looked up at Miriam and saw the tears and she too, for some reason, began to cry.

The dhows rocked on the small waves, their masts moving from left to right as people use their index fingers to say no. Tamrin met with his captains and they looked at the maps together. "Here, at the town of Sharm al-Sheikh, at the mouth of the gulf of Aqaba we will meet in two weeks. My dhow may be the last to arrive, but most of you will have arrived days before I do, so enjoy the town. The belly dancers are the best in Uz. The coffee is dark and has the flavor of the desert. The food is hot and spicy. Two weeks, and perhaps you will all get a few days in port before I get there."

Tamrin's fleet re-united as planned. Small boats came and went as they traded for supplies. They obtained fresh water, as the water in their skins and barrels was useable but now foul tasting. Rather than dump the stale water overboard, the men used the occasion to bathe. Tamrin handed each of his crew, three-leafed soapberries, *sabon,* he had learned to use while he was among the Hindush. The berry was a surfactant, that bubbled when rubbed on the skin and removed oils, but more important, many of the men had lice, and the foam when left on the hair until it began to dry, killed vermin. Tamrin used its foamy suds to rub on the hundreds of sand flea bites and camel fleabites that were common to all who rode the ships of the deserts.

The small fleet sailed the western coast of the Gulf of Aqaba to Nabq, little more than a small gulf town that seemed to be struggling to exist at the edge of the desert. The men gossiped about the inhabitants.

One crewmember had been in the town previously. "This tribe of people is strange; the men dull, seeming to have strange deformities. They protect their women passionately. We hear they marry no outsiders, and even wed their own sisters and cousins."

The crew traded a few items with boatmen who came to their anchored ships, selling fresh fish, and long white radishes. They left the next day and the fleet sailed north towards to Wasit. Here they found excellent fresh water drawn from deep wells by oxen that pulled a long bar attached to a water wheel with dippers attached to a belt. All day long the oxen walked, pulling the lever, their eyes blindfolded to keep them docile. The crew recognized the water delivery device, which was a larger version of the ones used in Egypt to draw Nile water from one level to another, but there by manpower, stepping up and down on rungs on a wheel which scooped water from a lower level.

    The men were spirited, and being far away from their homes, sought out the halls where women danced. They drank fermented camel's milk and took delight in walking on a non-moving surface for a few days, as the seas had been choppy on their trip northward. This would be their last port of call before Al Aqaba where the ships would be anchored in the cove of a bay. The majority of the crew would remain on board while Tamrin and a small party, including Menelik, traveled by camel caravan to Jerusalem. Their caravan would pass through Midian, the land of Amalekites and Ammon before entering Israel.

    Tamrin and Menelik now frequently rode their racing camels side by side, shouting to each other about the changes in the land, the native people, often dressed poorly in dirty loin cloths and flimsy shawls. They pointed out different animals and birds in the distance. Twice, Menelik dismounted and stalked a Kori Bustard, a bird so large it had to make a long run before it could take to the air. It had a strange habit that helped Menelik to shoot his arrow accurately. When initially disturbed, it did not immediately fly off, rather, faced the perceived threat with wings down for an instant, then turned and began its long run to gain speed in order to take off. It was the heaviest bird still able to fly. The men called it the flying ostrich. Its meat was superior to chicken and even mutton; it had juicy dark meat the flavor of cooked walnuts. Stewed or roasted on skewers, bustard was their favorite meal while traveling through the desert. Menelik, smiling proudly brought back his prize, anticipating the feast.

    They sat around campfires and roasted their food using wood and branches that their slaves had found for their fire. Their caravan followed a well-worn trail, used for centuries by travelers from the countries of the 'sea between land on all sides.' Over the years, thousands of camel caravans had passed and the trail was worn smooth with the many camel feet that shuffled along. Both men and camels almost fell asleep as they moved along the dirt path that was lower than the earth near it. But there was a problem, because other caravans had also collected any items for fuel, leaving the area barren. The slaves in their caravan rode away from the main group and searched for fuel. All day long they dismounted and gathered sticks, broke off dry tree branches and collected dung. Dried dung of camels and cattle made excellent fuel for cooking, particularly roasting meats on skewers. The dung fuel kept its heat and glowed red and hot without smoke, long after the flames of wood had burned away. Dung smoke kept away flies that plagued the camels and men.

To pass the time, the men shouted to each other as they moved forward. "Tell me Tamrin about the temple of Solomon. Is it like what I have seen in Aksum?"

"No. Much different. You will fall asleep by the time I am finished. So I will only tell a little, because the words of the Hebrews are easily forgotten and their zeal for ritual and sacrifice is astounding. Let me see. The temple has thirteen gates, spiritual gates for prayer. Imagine having to know what to do at each gate, some for women, some just to bring in sacrificial animals, others to enter the clearing where worshippers gathered. Each gate has a different name. You could only know them if you were a native born there. Getting up into the temple are stairs of stone called the 'Stair of Assent.'' Here is where we will enter as most pilgrims do. The temple has an Ezrat Nashim, a women's court. I remember this well because of how often I came to meet Miriam's mother. The outer courtyard was called the *Misbaeach,* a place I did not like. The people brought their offerings of animals here to be slaughtered and burned, or roasted as the priests saw fit. Blood, flies, screaming bleating goats, offal, crows, vultures and poor people coming with clay bowls to take away entrails, liver, heart and the inner parts not eaten by the priests or distributed to the poor. Really a miserable, smelly bloody place!"

They rode in silence for a few moments. "Menelik, this part of their religion is abhorrent to me. Imagine if there truly was only one god, call him Yahweh. Imagine that he chose, out of all the wonderful peoples of the earth, the Israelites to be his chosen people. The Israelites say this one god made a covenant with them. If they did what he said, then he would protect them and give then a land to live in, even help them drive out the current inhabitants of that land! That god did not select any of the beautiful black people of Nubia, nor the fair women of Egypt, not even one like Miriam, who is right now holding a ruby in her palm."

Again he remained quiet. Menelik knew that when Tamrin stopped talking it was because he was thinking about things that made him angry, or sometimes things that would cost him money. "I will speak to you about her later. Oh, yes, One God, Almighty and very, very jealous, easily offended if people served or sacrificed to any other gods, even the god of the Sun. More important, this one god wrote on tablets of stone, very heavy blue sapphire slabs. God must have made them at the time he wrote the Ten Commandments for his people and told them that if they did not obey He would punish them terribly. I was told that the words of the commandments were not scratched on the stone, or written, like on a slate, but hovered inside the blue stone and could be seen through its clear surface. I would like to have seen that. First their god wrote, 'Thou shalt have no other gods before me.'

If He was the only one, he knew that there were no other gods, so how could he say that? Why worry about it? Now this is the part that I liked about their story. When Moses and his brother Aaron were in the wilderness, in fact the very wilderness we are now crossing, the people wondered if they would ever see Moses again. He had gone up to a mountain, perhaps the one on our left. He stayed away for a long time, weeks on end. The people thought a desert lion must have killed Moses. Aaron knew how important it was to keep up the spirits of the people, so he decided to make a substitute god, a golden calf. The people were easily moved to serve one god or another. In Egypt they had done so. They had observed Egyptians and their gods."

"How could he make a *golden calf* ? Gold was scarce." Menelik was amazed.

"Well, the children of Israel had been living in Egypt as slaves. They were liberated after the terrible plagues the One God visited upon Pharaoh, even killing all the first born children. The Pharaoh was so upset and terrified he said to the Hebrews, "Here, take my gold ring, go! Here is my gold necklace. Leave us. Here is my gold bar. Take anything, but just leave Egypt! Get out. Your One God has killed my eldest son." So, Aaron collected all the gold from all the people and used most of it to make the golden calf, which he put up on a stand for the people to see. It was shiny and bright. The people bowed down and worshipped and wept, seeing their treasures in the form of an idol."

They stopped their camels, dismounted and paused to take a drink of honey wine and prepare for camp.

"How large was the calf?" asked Menelik.

"I don't know, but how large is a newborn real calf? You can carry it in your arms. I think it was that big. Don't ask so many questions or we will not sleep tonight. Eventually Moses got back and he was furious. He got so mad he smashed the beautiful magical sapphire commandments. Now the One God was upset, at him and at the people. Really angry at the people for chasing after a god made of their own jewelry. I get confused here. I don't remember what they did with the golden calf, but I think Aaron probably kept it. Think about this. They were in the desert, probably this very one here. How did they get fuel to melt down gold, to make statues? Let me see. Oh yes, they had to be punished!

He made sure that hundreds of poisonous snakes just happened to be right there among them. He would teach them a lesson they would not forget. These snakes were everywhere. If a child ran to play with his friends, he would step on one, get bitten and die. If an old man went out to defecate, he would squat down, get bitten on his testicles and die. If a woman… Oh well you get the point. The people began to die by the hundreds and came crying to Moses. He could talk directly to the One God. They called it praying. "Help!" Then He told Moses, 'Put a golden snake up on a long pole. If someone gets bitten and they look up to the snake on a pole they will not die. Suffer a lot, but survive. But when they look up, they better remember that miserable golden calf they worshipped and never have any false gods as long as they live. "Golden calf. Golden snake on a stick. Very confusing."

Tamrin lay back on his blanket, looked up at the stars, and groaned; his back was sore. He took another drink. He looked over at Menelik to see if he was sleeping. Menelik turned toward him.

"Tamrin, Solomon has served lots of different gods of his wives and concubines. Did snakes bite him?" Menelik rolled on his side and looked at Tamrin who appeared to be asleep. After a few minutes, he stretched out and decided the story was too much for Tamrin. Just as he was falling asleep, Tamrin coughed, sat up, took a burning faggot from the fire and went out to urinate, looking carefully for snakes.

"You will hear lots of stories when you get to Jerusalem. The women are great storytellers, better than I. Solomon has many sons, but one that I saw was a newborn at the time I was there with Sheba, your mother. I remember that the women passed this newborn around to each other and marveled at how beautiful he was, how his skin was like satin, how his male organ was like a small plantain, how his eyes were almost purple. His name meant angel, *Mal'ahkh*. The baby's name meant the guardian angel. When we get there I am going to see if I can find this angel like baby who would be a little older than you are and perhaps he and you can become friends. He can teach you about Jerusalem, the temple and the One God. Because his mother was from Aksum he probably learned to speak our language from her. Let's go to sleep. I will tell you about one place you can ask *Mal'ahkh* about when you meet him: the Ark of the Covenant where the tablets of the Ten Commandments are kept. We have a long ride tomorrow. Sleep and dream. Oh, now I will mention Miriam. Do you dream of her?" He laughed. "You gave her your ruby? Now you will really dream dreams."

"No!" Menelik was embarrassed that Tamrin had hinted at what he actually was thinking about at that moment, how she would look naked. "I think about her all the time when I am awake, I don't have bad dreams about her. Will you arrange a marriage for us when we return? In Hodeida? Tamrin, I want to make her my Queen. Now I will not be able to sleep. "

Tamrin chuckled and rolled on his side. "Perhaps Aksum. Why not in your mother's palace? It will be difficult for me to refer to you as son some day. I don't call Miriam, daughter either. Just Miriam. So I won't call you son." He began to snore softly.

CHAPTER 14

Mock the palm tree only when the harvest of dates is over.

The camels drank their fill of murky water and rested for the night, chewing their cuds. The air was hot, so warm that the men disrobed except for loincloths and lay around on ground sheets and tried not to move. Every motion brought on perspiration. In addition, desert sand flies tormented them. Menelik seemed to be their major target. In defense he covered his body with the thin cloth of a turban and suffered even more; they seemed to crawl inside. Day came abruptly. The sun rose above the sandy dunes like an orange ball. In the distance on the eastern horizon a sand storm raged with high winds, which threw dust into the sky and made the sun's rays less intense. The storm moved toward their encampment. The caravan was loaded and the complaining camels moved forward in a long column, away from the storm, the wind and dust at their back. The men covered their heads and faces with thin scarves, trying not to breath in the dust. It was a day of misery, itching insect bites, thirst, dust and sand, and when that cleared, hot, blazing, searing sun. Even the camels complained, moaning and groaning as they moved forward, their long lashes and the membrane on their eyes helping them to keep the sand out.

Tamrin was headed for the desert village of Hazigoth. He had been there before and remembered only one thing pleasant about it. There were deep wells with cool water. It was an oasis where the camels could be hobbled and let loose to graze under the watchful eyes of two slaves whose duty it was to keep them out of the gardens of the inhabitants. Hazigoth was at the edge of the wilderness of Paran in the land of Amalekites who seldom let a caravan pass without paying tribute. During his last journey to Hazigoth, their caravan, much larger than the small one of twelve camels in which they now traveled, had been taxed according to their numbers. What disturbed Tamrin was that the men came on racing camels, their swords unsheathed, yelling and shouting and making motions to stop the caravan and make the camels lie down. It was not a pleasant memory.

"Prepare your long bows and have your spears ready at hand if the Amalekites confront us! If they see we are armed and prepared to fight, they may well not use force but they may send men to talk to me about what we will have to pay to go through their territory. Do not fire arrows at them, but hold your weapons in full view. They are fierce to behold, but loathe to die."

"What tax will they require, Tamrin?" asked Menelik.

"Since we have only twelve camels and are moving fast, not carrying lots of trade goods, only our gifts to Solomon, they may ask for one of our slaves, one of our camels, one of our saddle bags of food. I don't know. If they smell gold or silver, they will be persistent. We will not tell them that we go to meet Solomon in Jerusalem. That would tip them off that we are carrying treasures to bring him."

The caravan moved forward at a fast pace, pushing the camels to move quickly. The camels were quiet much of the day but toward evening and their approach of Hazigoth they sensed the smell of water and moved even faster, grunting and calling to each other.

Ahead on the road was a small cloud of dust, men and animals moving toward them at high speed. Tamrin's men reigned in their animals and held their weapons. To their surprise there were only ten horses approaching at a gallop. The horsemen pulled up at a distance, not coming close in to Tamrin's caravan. They dismounted except for one man who came forward on his horse, a spirited Arabian stallion difficult to control. The scent of camels seemed to disturb the horse. The old scent of the lion skins lingered on the camel blankets.

"*Baksheesh!* Silver!" the man called out. He held up five fingers indicating he wanted five talents.

Tamrin shook his head and took out a small amber necklace, one of three he had intended to give to women in Solomon's *haram*. "*Anbar*, he shouted in Arabic. He turned to the men in the caravan. "Now hold up your bows more aggressively."

"The horseman rode the entire length of the small caravan, looking at the men and the loads they were carrying. He could see they were not on a trade mission. "Where are you going?" he asked in Arabic.

"Past Havilah to Barsheba. Take the *anbar* as a tax and move aside. We do not want to fight, but we will move forward." He held out the amber beads in his left hand, a slight, a blatant sign of disrespect and distaste to offer the hand that was used for toilet.

The man stared at Tamrin, at the group of armed men, at the disdain Tamrin held for him. He sneered, "Throw down a sack of barley seeds. Keep your trinket for the women. One large sack and you may proceed." He pointed at a camel that carried supplies.

"Throw down a small sack." Tamrin spoke in the dialect of Marib. A sack of barley was untied, thrown to the ground.

Tamrin gave the signal for the caravan to move forward. The horseman motioned to his followers who now galloped forward as the caravan passed. They were armed with swords, not bows, and stayed a good distance from Tamrin's men as they watched the caravan pass. Then one rider dismounted, placed the sack of barley on the saddle of his horse, mounted in one motion behind the saddle and they were off into the desert.

"These desert people are eager for grains, millet, barley, wheat or ground nuts because their oases are small and filled with palm trees and small vegetable gardens. They will feast on ground barley bread tonight. They are crude men who have little idea of the value of trade items. The *anbar* was worth four times the value of the grain, but these men are not traders, seldom leave their crude and wild settlements. I hate these Amalekites! Trouble makers and desert dogs!"

"You held out the *anbar* in your left hand. That made him angry." Menelik sounded worried.

"Learn this well, Menelik. Deal from strength and confidence. Watchdogs that run out snarling at you, show teeth; respect the teeth, not the snarl. They saw that we have bows and spears, but if it came to a fight, yes, they would lose men, but we would be walking rather than riding. They can move with their horses behind a camel and slash its tendons, leaving it helpless. They have agility, we have death at a distance, but they would cripple our caravan. They did not want to die trying. They saw our teeth bared and took notice."

Menelik nodded. "You played a dangerous game. This is a caravan that is different, Tamrin. I am a future Emperor of Aksum. We were in danger of being killed."

"If they knew who you were, Menelik, we would all be killed, all except for you, Menelik. You are now simply a tall, lean youth who has learned to climb palm trees and shoot arrows.

Yes, I am always aware of who you are, son of Saba my dearest friend; how can I forget? With due respect, Menelik, do not use your status to make your arm and resolve weak. Do not ever, hide behind your future or your title. None of us knows what the future holds. Today you are the youngest of our group. Some day you will become Menelik I. I will bow to you then, to your status and your title, just once, pay you my loyalty and respect. After that you will decide how you wish to address me, Menelik. If I sound angry now, it is because I am angry, at the thieves who came to tax us, at your use of your title now." He moved his camel forward.

They passed out of the land of the Amalekites into a narrow strip of Aram; Syrians, then finally into the land of Israel toward a settlement called Sheba. Pomegranates grew there abundantly and on Sheba's journey to meet Solomon now almost a score of years earlier, she had been delighted by the abundance of the fruit. Solomon then named the little hamlet after her, Sheba.

Their entry into Jerusalem was late in the evening. There was a sarai at the edge of the city, a place where travelers could move in behind walls securely, feed their camels, and have a place to sleep. Town's people brought in foods to sell, some even made small fires and cooked specialties within the gates of the inn. Tamrin paid the keeper for his people and they settled in, feeling relieved that the journey was over. Weeks on the trail had put tempers on edge, had made the men long for home and its comforts.

"We should rest a couple of days before making contact with Solomon's court. We need to wash ourselves and have our clothing washed. Most of us need our beards trimmed. We look like desert savages. We will wander in the nearby souk tomorrow to see if there are things we want to buy for our families. The Hindush are the best weavers and carvers, the people of Jerusalem are skilled in the arts of metal working, gold, silver, copper and bronze from the land of Buz." He paused and greeted one of the men with a long robe sitting in a corner of the *sarai*. He was sure the man was a priest.

"Blessings of God be upon you. Do you have any of the ancient holy writings among your possessions? My young friend here is not familiar with your history and where your people gained skills as craftsmen."

He adjusted his head cap. "From Egypt. You must remember that the children of Israel were in captivity for a long time in Egypt. It is a long story; Pharaoh's daughter pulled out Moses as a tiny baby from the reeds in a little boat. She thought he was beautiful, and probably guessed that his mother was an Israelite. She became his wet nurse. So, Moses grew up as a prince in the land of Egypt. Their writing is not like our ancient Hebrew. They write in little pictures, hieroglyphics, and Moses had scribes and readers to tell him the meaning of things. Probably he could read a little. He knew numbers and money, but certainly not in Hebrew."

"Good teacher, we are only interested in how your people became such excellent craftsmen. I am sorry to interrupt. How is the story of Moses going to answer our question?" He smiled patiently.

"Sit down with me. The evening shadows are getting long. There is no rush. Let your son hear about a little of the history of the people he is visiting, or he will not understand much about his visit, nor take home more than a few cheap trinkets." He motioned for the men to sit. "Let me see. Moses then led the children of Israel out of Egypt. I will not even go into the story of the burning bush. He went up the mountain and talked with Elohim who gave him the stone tablets with the Ten Commandments written on them. Certainly written by god's finger, since Moses could not write. He was illiterate. Most of his people were illiterate, except for a few like myself who kept tradition of our people and had learned to write in ancient Hebrew. In answer to your question about our craftsmanship there is a simple answer written in the documents about the exodus from Egypt. Moses and his people were not writers or readers, except for a few like me. I heard in the Synagogue that people say Moses wrote five of the ancient books about the Children of Israel and how god dealt with them. This is a lie. Someone like me wrote. One document says that at the end of Moses' life he talked with god and god took him up and he was no more. How could Moses write about his own going up to heaven if he was dead? Scribes, holy men like me wrote the stories, the Exodus, going out, the laws, all the others. Then some later literate scribe copied what they wrote. Please remember this was hundreds of years ago. Not one copy of any of the original scrolls exists. If we did have the original, Moses did not author it. I have read what they call the books of Moses, and there is a great difference in the style of writing within the books. Scribes improved upon each other as they transcribed and copied stories. We have copies of copies of copies. Like this." The priest pulled forward a large leather box and opened the lid and took out a rolled scroll and stroked it, almost sensually. .

"Don't you feel like bowing down to this? It is holy. Are not the letters amazing? Is not the calligraphy and the artwork on the margins beautiful? Oh, here is the answer to your question about crafts and our beautiful work in gold and silver. Here is the passage you asked. Here. God speaks to Moses about Bezaleel. It is recoded in this scroll, a small part of Exodus. He held up the scroll and began to read. 'See I have called him by the name Bezaleel the son Uri, the son of Hur of the tribe of Judah. And I have filled him with the spirit of God, in wisdom, and in understanding, and knowledge, and in all manner of workmanship, to devise cunning works, to work in gold, silver and brass; And in the cutting of stones, to set them, and in the carving of timber.' Why was God so interested in the fact that he was a son of Uri? Why did it say 'with the spirit of God,' if god is speaking? You see, the scribe who wrote the story should have said, 'my spirit' if he was quoting Himself speaking. But this is the problem that all the ancient scholars and scribes faced. They wrote as if they were god. I am going to re-write this part myself later. Remember, the people had silver and gold when they came out of Egypt and Bezaleel taught them how to make all manner of crafts.' I say that they learned to fashion crafts in Egypt, yet here the scribe writes that god taught Bezaleel. So there can be two answers to your question. One. God taught him how to make fine silver and gold ornaments and woodworking. The scribes write strange things. I will re-write, Bezaleel already knew about these things since he was a slave to the Egyptians who did this kind of work and he volunteered to do it for Moses' people." He smiled broadly and put away his scroll.

Tamrin replied, "Many of our people of Ethiopia also know how to write and read. We have people of learning from Hindush who write a language called Sanskrit, others who write a language of Sumerians, others who write our own Gi'iz, and all of these people live in Aksum. Our writing was learned generations ago from the south Semitic people. It is not crude, simple picture character writing like they have in Egypt where I have been; strange hieroglyphics that can mean just about anything. Making a picture for every idea is difficult. Egyptian scribes must learn thousands of pictures. In Gi'iz, the letters represent the sounds we speak. Our's is truly a language of the gods!" He laughed. "I think the gods all understand Gi'iz."

"I have heard of your Geez, as we call it." At the mention of Geez, Menelik looked up. "Truly, your people from Aksum are a mighty and advanced civilization, much like we are here in the kingdom of Solomon. I have met the great and wise king twice.

He too does not read or write, he is illiterate, others write for him, such as me."

Menelik yawned broadly and stretched. Tamrin turned to him impatiently. " A baby learns first to crawl, then to toddle, then to walk. We are babies here. We must find out as much as we can about this people and their habits. Sleep can come later." He waved his hand at a man selling small cups of strong coffee. "Three cups!"

"I don't know what you said to your son, but I understand well that young people are impatient about learning. They are impatient to have answers; to have food, women, and all their needs satisfied, now. But when it comes to learning the history of their people, they sleep." He laughed and reached over and patted Menelik on his knee. "Old men are good to have as companions. I honor your father for bringing you to see Solomon's court, to see our great kingdom, the magnificent temple that you should visit tomorrow. What you learn and see, no one can take from you. But you can learn also from the eyes and life of others." He patted his large leather case reverently. "The priests can teach you to read. A king should not have to trust scribes and not be able to understand what they have written. There is little difference in writing one thousand shekels or one hundred shekels. Our people know about a wonderful thing, the letter for nothing, zero."

"Translate for me Tamrin, please. I do not understand his language."

"I will tell you all he said later about Moses. But just now he hopes you will learn a lot about this kingdom and its beauty so you can take what you learn back to Aksum." He sipped his strong coffee.

Menelik asked, "I wonder why there are so many languages? It makes it very hard to trade, to move about and to understand what is happening."

Tamrin asked the learned scribe Menelik's question and he smiled, nodded, opened his leather case and began to look for a scroll.

"I am sure there is an answer, but, perhaps tomorrow, Tamrin. I am going to sleep."

"Here! Let me read to you about the Tower of Babel!" The scribe was happy and animated again.

"Tomorrow. Tomorrow. The lad really did not want an answer to his question. He just wishes that all spoke his own language. With much thanks. Tomorrow!"

"Sabbath is our day of rest. Rest another day and then you will see the wonders of all the lands under the sky, wonders in craftsmanship that rival all others."

"Many thanks honored father. Would you share our meal with us? Our fare is simple but we would be honored for you to meet with our men and speak about your One God. I have already talked to my young companion about it as we traveled; however, I easily forget the meaning of things that are religious." He bowed his head briefly.

"I will fast today to prepare for the Sabbath. Thank you. Perhaps you will be here tomorrow after our people go to the synagogue. Then we will talk again."

The chief scribe brought news of the arrival of his son by Queen Sheba, to Solomon. He was informed that Tamrin and Solomon's own son were staying in a *sarai* not far from the gate for animal sacrifices, *Shaar Ha Delek*, near the southwest section of the temple. King Solomon was surprised that he had not been sent word from Aksum about his son's visit. It was true; in fact, it had been eighteen years since Sheba had left and little news from her personally had been received. Not only that, the only thing that he remembered about Sheba's visit was that she had been very generous with her gifts; she brought much gold and silver that had been used in the construction of the temple. Then he remembered that there had been a ring returned to him from Sheba, years ago, to inform him of the birth of a son.

"Send a messenger; you know, my son by the other Ethiopian concubine from Aksum, my son Mal'ahkh. He is also about eighteen years of age. He was with me last week when we visited the temple. He should meet his half brother. His mother speaks the same language as Queen Sheba spoke and he will be able to talk without interpreter to Menelik. When you have the letter prepared, bring it to me and I will put my stamp on it. Invite both my son and Tamrin to meet with me in four days, here in my inner chambers. I am sure Sheba will have sent gifts to me and I do not want the meeting to be public." Solomon dismissed the scribe, took a drink of wine and returned to his sleeping chamber. A very young girl from Phoenicia was waiting for him in his bed.

Tamrin and Menelik entered the Temple using the front steps that led to the visitors' gate. They took their time to look at the construction of the temple, the decorations, inlays of semiprecious stones in the inner courtyards, the lavish gold plating of door handles, drapes and curtains heavy with silver threads, carved ivory figures and what interested Menelik the most were tables made of black ebony wood that had been inlaid with gold designs. The rooms were filled with the odor of incense, so strong that both of them covered their mouths and noses with scarves. Priests scuttled about attending to people bringing in animals for offerings, lighting lamps and incense and simply sitting quietly reading scrolls and chanting.

"The air is fresher outside in the market place. It is more interesting there. This place is for older men and scholars. I feel lost here. Let's go." Menelik led Tamrin back the way they had come, eager to be among the crowds of people in the market.

Menelik purchased a pair of shoes made in Hindush land, which had toes that curved up in a front tail, beautifully decorated with patterns in various colors.

"Why not wear them when you meet your father? He will be pleased to see that his son had such good and expensive tastes." Tamrin, as he spoke held a similar pair of shoes for a girl, trying to decide if he too should buy a pair to take back to Hodeida and give to his daughter as a wedding present.

"We have a full day tomorrow to do nothing. Let us see if we can find stables that have horses with carts we can rent, with the driver, for a day. We could drive up to a small town called Emmaus and eat a noon meal there and then go to the hot baths and soak for a couple of hours. There used to be a specialist who could perform oil massages as well, and another to cut hair and trim beards, even another whose specialty is to remove the wax from the ears." As he spoke, his smile became broader. "After the oil has been rubbed into your skin, the attendant takes a very sharp, but not razor sharp knife, and runs the blade over the entire surface of the skin, removing the oil and dissolved impurities. Amazing!" He gazed into the distance, his thoughts far away.

"You stopped mentioning the good things near Emmaus. I think you left out something." Menelik tapped Tamrin on the arm. "Nothing more?"

"It has been many years since I had more than ear cleaning. Let's go tomorrow. Today we will each buy a new robe to wear to Solomon's court. I shall use some of the silver that your mother is sending to Solomon as a gift."

They spent the afternoon sleeping, an unusual luxury for both of them. Their carriage was like a covered four-wheeled chariot, drawn by two spirited horses. Their journey passed through dry countryside. Grapes had already been picked and many farmers were trimming vines and removing the dried stalks, tying them in bundles to take home to use as fuel for cooking.

The baths in Emmaus were enclosed in low buildings. The water in the large open stone tubs appeared to be steaming, and they discovered that the tubs ran from one to the other. The topmost tub had a hot spring feeding it that was almost too hot to use, so they progressed from one to another, moving to the fourth tub, which had body-temperature water. There they soaked and watched others enter the bath. No women entered and there was not a section set out for women. By the time they climbed back into their cart to be taken back to Jerusalem they felt as new as when they were born.

There was a long wait at Solomon's palace before they were granted access to Solomon. He met them in an inner chamber where a meal and drinks were prepared for them. They stood when he entered. Menelik glanced at Tamrin, wondering if the man who approached them was King Solomon, because he was dressed in a simple robe and sandals.

"My old friend Tamrin! How long has it been? From the white in your hair it must be ten years. And who is this?" Menelik bowed low. "Son of Sheba, you are taller than your father. And better looking as well. Tell me is your mother well? Does her suzerain prosper?"

"My father, I bring greetings from her to you. She told me to give you this small object when we first met. I have not looked inside the cloth wrapping." He handed a package the size of an apple to his father, avoiding his eyes.

"I shall open it now. There is nothing in the world I would conceal from the entire world about Sheba. He undid the wrappings to find a small silver cup, the very one Sheba had used to take a drink of water, the item he had called 'precious'. Only he knew its meaning. In front of him stood the son from the union that he had had with Sheba. He turned over the small cup and on the bottom saw there was an engraving. He was unable to read. "It has a secret message on the bottom." He held it out to Tamrin. "Can you read what it says? Perhaps it is in your own language."

Tamrin glanced at the letters in the writing of the Hindush and smiled. "Sire, it is language of Sanskrit of the Hindush. Do you have a scribe from there in your kingdom who can read the message?"

Solomon rang a bell and told a servant to call the scribe, Hathi. They talked and drank, sharing news of Sheba's kingdom. A short but fat Hindush man entered, appearing fearful. He bowed very low before Solomon. "Up man. It is nothing. I just need you to read a saying on the bottom of this small silver cup. If the message is positive you can tell me openly now. If it is a spell or about death, do not tell me at all. Write its meaning in Hebrew and bring it to me tomorrow." He handed the cup to man whose hands were still shaking.

He read twice, then looked up at the king and shrugged his shoulders. "May I tell you now? I do not need time to understand the meaning." Solomon nodded. "It is a mystery to me. The two words, if used separately mean little. If I put them together they are, *Aavalakatti Aaush.* The meaning in Sanskrit is, 'for pleasant health, a depilatory root.' Very strange. Very strange."

Solomon's smiled widely. Then began to laugh openly. "Your mother loved riddles. This is one that is as old as you are. Only I can understand it. She is still up to her quick sayings. Imagine. Depilatory root!" He laughed again as the three men watched the king.

"Menelik, lift the bottom of your robe so I can see your legs." He pointed at Menelik's knee.

"Do you want me to expose my leg, here, in this place?"

The king nodded, bent over and looked at Menelik's leg, which was covered with thick dark hair. "The riddle is solved.

You are like your mother, a hirsute person. I had never seen a woman with," he paused, "well she cooperated and had all her body hair removed. We believe that it is healthy for women to have hairless bodies. That is the riddle. She is reminding me of my amazement, eighteen years ago, of seeing her hair."

"Yes, my mother is very proud of my hair and her own. Many of our women have hair on their arms, legs, even a bit on their upper lip and heavy eyebrows. It is a sign of great beauty, strength, vitality, health and means she will have many children." Menelik spoke so rapidly that Tamrin held up his hand to translate.

The Hindush man nodded in agreement, saying yes, yes, as Menelik spoke. He understood the meaning of the engraving now and looked at the king, perplexed. "Was she not beautiful, Lord? I have heard stories that she was an Ethiopian from Aksum with brown skin and black hair like obsidian. Beautiful!"

"Of course. Roses come in many colors and hues. But some prefer only white ones, without thorns. Do you understand? You are dismissed. The words on the cup and their meaning will remain secret. You are not to speak about it! No one will know what was spoken here today. You are dismissed. Your wisdom to read your ancient language is great. Write it out for me tomorrow." He motioned with his hand and the man scuttled away.

The scribe had been told a secret and he intended to keep it. He would not talk. He would never speak of it, but the word secret, he knew was magic. He returned to his quarters and took out his pen and a new sheet of vellum and wrote on the top the title, King Solomon and Sheba: Aavalakatti Aayush. He wrote in Sanskrit for an hour taking special care with the letters and great care with the tiny drawings on the margin. He finished the sheet and looked at it with satisfaction. This was a story that would make him wealthy. It would be sold and told from Jerusalem to Kolachi. Though employed by the king, his services were seldom used, but now he was going to be a very busy writer for many weeks, for himself. He took out another sheet of velum and began to write the story in Hebrew. He paused thinking how beautiful the story would be to be written in Ge'ez. Tamrin could carry copies back and sell it in Aksum. Yes! Yes! In Sanskrit as well! He changed the title to Sheba, the Hairless Queen: Lover of Solomon.

Tamrin and Menelik returned to the *sarai* to get their possessions and the other package of gifts that Sheba had packed for Solomon. It was not heavy, but he dared not open it, knowing that the Queen liked surprises and that whatever it was, Solomon would find out. Their room in the palace was simple, two beds and a low table, two sitting cushions and a table on which a basin had been placed with a jar of water for washing their hands.

"Tamrin, I do not mean to sound imperial, but I was surprised that my father did not pay much attention to me. It seemed like he wanted to make our meeting short. Perhaps he had other more official business."

"His liaison with your mother was long ago. It is not something that he remembers well. Remember, he is now an old man with graying hair, much older than your mother. He may have a new concubine. He may have serious matters of state, or his health to deal with. Remember, he has sons that want to take over his throne as well. There is family conflict between his son and a possible heir. I will ask around. I don't even remember his grown son's name, Jahoiakim, or something like that, eager for the throne. What is good is that you will meet one of his sons, Mal'ahkh, whose mother is of our people. He is your age and the two of you can go about the temple and the palace and the city if you desire and enjoy Jerusalem. Mal has the same status as you because he is the son of royalty, except in your mother's case, you are an only one. Mal'ahkh may have a hundred half brothers, and Solomon may not even know half their names. He has the reputation of forgetting names, even those who serve him in court." Tamrin shook his head. "Some are wise, but forgetful of names and favors."

"When you take over your mother's throne, learn well from the lessons you will get here. Oh, I have decided that we will have two ceremonies for the marriage of my daughter, Miriam. One in Hodeida; a simple family affair with the blessings of the priest of the Sun God. Then when we get to Aksum, and your mother returns, she may have a great banquet for you and your new wife and at the same time turn over the kingdom to you. She will arrange a grand affair with guests and order the killing of oxen. Remember, she has no idea that you will return with a bride."

"I am in debt to you Tamrin. In debt for caring for me from the time I was small, for taking me on the trading journey, for teaching me what it is to become a man. Mostly, I will be in debt to you for my new wife, Miriam." He extended two hands and the men clasped wrists.

The two half brothers met by arrangement on the steps of the temple. Menelik recognized him immediately. They had similar skin color, both had brown hair, but Menelik was taller than Mal'ahkh but thinner. Menelik wondered if he could climb a hundred palm trees in a week or throw a broad spear. They walked into the temple, glancing at each other from time to time, neither knowing how to break into each other's thoughts. Finally Menelik asked, "Do you have plans to get married?"

Mal laughed. "Look at me. Do I look like I am old enough to get married? I have never been out of Jerusalem, I have never been in a war, and I have never been paid even a small coin for what I do. To marry a woman is to marry debt. No. But..."

Menelik smiled knowingly. "I had not thought about it much

before, but on this trip to Jerusalem I met the daughter of Tamrin. She is very beautiful and we have talked briefly. We have an understanding that when I return I will take her as my wife. It is my first time to seek out a woman." Menelik was ashamed that he had never bedded a girl.

His friend smiled. "I have sought out girls in the palace. There are many. I must be very careful because among the hundreds of women and girls and small children, there are few men because it is my father's court. But I like two of the daughters of my father's concubines."

Menelik was in his own thoughts about home. "My mother is Queen Sheba and is now at Marib. She has no children except for me. She is not well and has a foot with a cut tendon, which makes it hard for her to walk. She is very beautiful. Darker of skin than you and me from her Nubian heritage. But she seems unhappy with her life." Menelik turned toward Mal. "Is your mother alive?"

"Yes she is alive and lives in our father's court. She and Solomon meet frequently because she knows everything that is going on among the women and they talk about such things. She loves to talk. I have been given work here in the temple. There are many priests and they are always busy with sacrifices and reading the scriptures aloud to the people. Some are scribes and write things down. My work there is to keep the area around the inner holy place clean and free of debris. Only the priests may go into the inner room where the Ark of the Covenant is kept. But they take me in with them, I am no one to them, and they have me sweep the spider webs from the walls, the dust on the furniture, even the Ark, the dead lizards that are on the stone floor. It has to be very clean. I even rub the stone tiles with lemon skins and flax seed oils so it smells good. If I learn to read, I may someday become a priest. Their work is the best. They eat the choicest meats and people give them gifts when they are making sacrifices. The people give a tenth of their wealth to the temple, to god, which also means that to be a priest is to be wealthy. My father also allows each chief priest a certain amount of silver every year. So they buy houses and land. It is amazing. Those that can read and write, and talk to god directly are the most secure in the land."

"Could I go to see the Ark of the Covenant?"

Mal shook his head. "Never! It is sacred. I can get into the room where the Ark is because they know me as the 'holy sweeper'. The One God keeps some of its power there. There are old things inside that he gave Moses; only the High Priest has seen inside. Whoever has the Ark has a direct way to approach the One God. They told me there is heavenly bread in there as old as Methuselah." They strolled along quietly. "Would you like to go into the women's court and meet my mother? Only children of Solomon are allowed, so I am sure that I can take you there without any problem.

CHAPTER 15

One who tries to hide with a dog, child, goat, or a consumptive one will not remain hidden.

Mal and Menelik spent pleasant days exploring Jerusalem, the palace, and the temple. Finally, they even made their way to the hot baths in the town of Emmaus riding on the platforms of chariots that belonged to Solomon. Menelik enjoyed such luxury, to be scrubbed down, then sit in a hot tank of water and perspire, then be rubbed down and massaged with sweet oils. "Where does the hot water come from?" asked Menelik.

"From the center of the earth. It comes up into that tank up there, like a spring, never failing, day after day, then cascades down from tank to tank then outside where the water goes into stone channels and leads down into the fields. There farmers plant special crops because the water has a color and a smell and plants such as pumpkins, squash and cucumbers seem to like it. It kills grape vines."

Solomon sent a messenger and called for the boys to appear before him. They arrived and were dressed in their best robes and their skin was shiny and clean. He motioned for them to sit on the carpet on the floor in front of him.

He was dressed simply in a single linen robe that covered his entire body from shoulder to his feet. "I have prepared many things for you to take back to your mother, Menelik. One thing that is lacking is that your mother does not really worship only one true God. I will send back with you to Aksum, two of my priests who can write your language as well as read the ancient Hebrew texts. I have already ordered our best craftsmen to make a copy of the Ark of the Covenant, exactly like the one in the Holy of Holies. Mal, you know how to keep the place in good order and can learn to read from the priests as well. It is my wish that you return to Aksum, your mother's birthplace and serve the priests. A new temple can be built there, small of course, but there, our practices of sacrificing to the One True God can happen. I am sad that your mother does not understand about the true religion. Perhaps Aksum, Ethiopia will become blessed of God."

The young men looked at each other and smiled. The thought of having each other's friendship and companionship on the return journey and in Aksum was exciting. "How would we carry the replica of the new Ark to Aksum?" asked Mal.

"It will be carried just like all the loads are carried, but in a box tied to a camel back and then later transferred to the ship. I will let both of you see the replica when it is done. There were plans drawn for the first Ark of the Covenant and we are having it made of the same materials, and two of the workmen are skilled craftsmen in wood and gave advice to the younger craftsmen. This will be my gift to your mother, Menelik."

Two weeks later Tamrin and the two young men met in a gathering hall in the palace. Many workmen were there and in the center of the room on the table there was an object covered with a huge drape. The chief of the craftsmen waited for a signal from the king, then carefully took the cloth away and revealed the ark, carved angels on the top. Everyone sighed in amazement. A gong sounded and a priest stood with a scroll and read aloud in a singsong voice to those gathered. He stood behind the replica of the Ark of the Covenant that shone from reflected candlelight. Exodus 25:10-22 *"And they shall make an ark of acacia wood; two and a half cubits shall be its length, a cubit and a half its width, and a cubit and a half its height. And you shall overlay it with pure gold, inside and out you shall overlay it, and shall make on it a molding of gold all around. You shall cast four rings of gold for it, and put them in its four corners; two rings shall be on one side, and two rings on the other side. And you shall make poles of acacia wood and overlay them with gold. You shall put the poles into the rings on the sides of the ark, that the ark may be carried by them. The poles shall be in the rings of the ark; they shall not be taken from it. And you shall put into the ark the Testimony which I will give you. You shall make a mercy seat of pure gold; two and a half cubits shall be its length and a cubit and a half its width. And you shall make two cherubim of gold; of hammered work you shall make them at the two ends of the mercy seat. Make one cherub at one end, and the other cherub at the other end; you shall make cherubim at the two ends of it of one piece with the mercy seat. And the cherubim shall stretch out their wings above, covering the mercy seat with their wings, and they shall face one another; the faces of the cherubim shall be toward the mercy seat. You shall put the mercy seat on top of the ark, and in the ark you shall put the Testimony that I will give you. And there I will meet with you, and I will speak with you from above the mercy seat, from between the two cherubim which are on the ark of the Testimony, about everything which I will give you in commandment to the children of Israel."*

Solomon rose from his chair and approached the replica, in fact, ran his hands over the gold on the wings of the Cherubim. He turned to the chief craftsman and nodded his approval.

"Beautiful! I have not seen the real Ark but if it like this then you have truly done a great service. What about the contents? Will there be a rod of Aaron in it? Will there be a bowl that contains the manna bread that fed the children of Israel when they traveled through the desert?" The High Priest raised his hands toward heaven and began to chant. He turned to the king. "The Lord will remain with the true Ark here in Jerusalem. It is His place to rest with the sons of men. No, the tablets of the law will remain here as well as the other contents, but we can make a replica of the bowl and the rods, but not of the tablets of the law. We cannot make a replica of the Sapphire stones that were written by the finger of God. We do not have such rare Sapphire now and no man can copy like the original. But we will put slate slabs in the replica and copy the words like I have written here on this parchment, so the sons of Sheba shall know the will of God." Everyone leaned forward to see the written commandments. Now the priest spoke with a deep voice, pausing between each utterance.

1. I am the LORD your God, who brought you out of the land of Egypt, out of the house of bondage. You shall have no other gods before Me.

2. You shall not make for yourself a carved image, or any likeness of anything that is in heaven above, or that is in the earth beneath, or that is in the water under the earth; you shall not bow down to them nor serve them. For I, the LORD your God, am a jealous God, visiting the iniquity of the fathers on the children to the third and fourth generations of those who hate Me, but showing mercy to thousands, to those who love Me and keep My commandments.

3. You shall not take the name of the LORD your God in vain, for the LORD will not hold him guiltless who takes His name in vain.

4. Remember the Sabbath day, to keep it holy. Six days you shall labor and do all your work, but the seventh day is the Sabbath of the Lord your God. In it you shall do no work: you, nor your son, nor your daughter, nor your male servant, nor your female servant, nor your cattle, nor your stranger who is within your gates. For in six days the Lord made the heavens and the earth, the sea, and all that is in them, and rested the seventh day. Therefore the Lord blessed the Sabbath day and hallowed it.

5. Honor your father and your mother, that your days may be long upon the land which the Lord your God is giving you.

6. You shall not murder.

7. You shall not commit adultery.

8. You shall not steal.

9. You shall not bear false witness against your neighbor.

10. You shall not covet your neighbor's house; you shall not covet your neighbor's wife, nor his male servant, nor his female servant, nor his ox, nor his donkey, nor anything that is your neighbor's." He sang the commandments, and the audience sighed.

"This replica will be packed in a container that looks like a large box to carry trade goods, the kind used for packing salt. Because of its value in gold, perhaps the King should send a strong arm of his troops to guard the caravan on the journey to the ships resting now at Al Aqaba. These two men, junior priests who speak the language of Aksum will accompany the new Ark on its journey to the Queen and teach her the ways of the One True God."

Tamrin took charge of organizing the return caravan to the

ships. This time there were fifty camels to load, adjustments to be made for the first day's march, attending to slipping ropes, the noise of a hundred men tying, lifting, ordering the camels, and even catching one stray camel that bolted toward the wilderness sands. The two brothers Menelik and Mal walked from camel to camel watching and learning. At the end of the day, Tamrin ordered all the loads to be removed from the camels and to feed and water them well. He told the amazed soldiers and camel herders that this was simply a trial run for them to learn how to prepare. There would be twenty of these loading exercises, or more as they marched toward the ships.

That night, Mal went to greet the High Priest in the temple to say goodbye. He was suffering from a high fever, but in spite of it put his shaking hand on Mal'ahkh's head and gave him a blessing. The Temple was quiet as the brothers left. Priests had returned home, no animals were being sacrificed.

The two young men whispered their plans. "Menelik, tonight we will take the replica that is in the box near our camels and bring it here to the temple. Then we will put the real Ark into it and all of the contents and replace it with the replica. No one will know. Then our people of Ethiopia will have the real Ark to bring down God's blessings on us. We can do it! I will give the guards near the camel caravan strong wine as a gift. They will sleep and hear nothing. I know how to get into the holy of holies room."

The brothers got up in the middle of the night, quietly took the heavy replica of the Ark and carried it to the temple, removed the genuine Ark and put it in the carrying box, put the replica on the stand and left the temple. Twice a stranger passed them as they carried the box back to the where the caravan was waiting. Two of the watchmen who were assigned to guard the replica had placed the trunk on a blanket between them. They were still sleeping as the brothers put the real Ark in its trunk on the blanket. Menelik bumped the foot of one of the guards who was startled and sat up, brandishing his sword.

"Who is there?" Now both guards sat up and stared at the young men in the semi-darkness.

"We are Solomon's sons. We were concerned about the Ark and came to check on its safety. Sorry to have awakened you. If you don't mind we will spread out blankets near you here and wait until morning when everything will be loaded on the camels."

"Stay. Stay. Dawn is not far away." He yawned and lay back down to sleep. Tamrin kept his word. He rang a gong at the crack of dawn for the laborers and camel drivers to get loaded for the first day of the trip. Huge clay pots of millet gruel had been cooked and the men came and filled their calabash cups and drank their breakfast. Within an hour the caravan was on its way. Tamrin's camel was now the last. Directly in front of his camel was the beast that carried the Ark, in front of that were the two sons of Solomon who rode side by side and talked constantly, shouting comments to other drivers and moving to the front of the caravan to speak to the soldiers who had been assigned to guard them.

"What if we are stopped by Hittites who will want to tax the caravan?" shouted Menelik to the captain.

"There are seldom more than a couple dozen men in their group. They have been using horses rather than camels lately. I have ordered that all our archers be prepared at my signal to shoot at their horses. Have no fear, Menelik al Hakim, you shall be well guarded."

"Why will you shoot the horses?" asked Menelik.

"A man who is walking and has no steed is vulnerable, hopeless against our camel group with long spears. When they see what our defenses are, that we will not wait to negotiate, but immediately retaliate, they will flee. Look, we carry the banner of Solomon!" The captain waved the flag and his men cheered. The brothers returned to their place at the end of the line near Tamrin. They rode knee to knee so they could share their thoughts and make the long day pass more quickly.

"The Cherubim carvings on the top of the Ark are beautiful!" said Menelik. "They look like young girls, not angels."

"Except for their wings. I really wonder about those carvings and why the One God ordered them to be made that way. The High Priest reads parts of the Law of God on the Sabbath. He always reads, 'thou shalt not make unto thee a graven image', yet the priest just read that Cherubim were to be made and covered with gold. It is confusing. Those are graven images, and because they are so beautiful, people could worship them, or even the gold plated Ark. When we get to Aksum I am going to learn from the two priests who are with us about how to benefit most from the Ark, where to put it and how to get its power to help our people of Aksum." Mal stared at the box being carried by the camel in front of them.

"We should have looked inside the Ark to see if the manna bread is still in the jar and whether Aaron's staff that blossomed and produced almonds is there." Menelik reached across with his spear on which he had impaled flat bread to hand to his brother.

"We were in too much of a hurry. I hope we can sneak a look into the Ark when it is placed on the ship that will take us to Adulis, our port. But, the manna," he chewed his bread, "it would be hundreds of years old by now. Certainly it could not still be in the Ark! Unless it is magic bread that does not rot or mold or eaten by mice." Mal laughed.

"I like your idea. There will be lots of time for us to examine what is in the Ark. I was told that the real tablets on which God wrote the Ten Commandments were written on large pieces of Sapphire that were translucent, that the letters were sort of hanging inside the blue stone, a miracle. But Moses smashed those and had to make made new ones. I wonder what happened to the broken pieces?"

Tamrin who was following directly behind the brothers overheard Menelik's remarks. He had wondered about the same thing. Tamrin refrained from getting into the conversation of the young men, knowing that if he did, they would be careful about their utterances. Many of the most valuable things he had learned were remarks made by others, or questions asked by others that had no answer. He rocked along on the camel saddle and planned for the long journey ahead.

The marriage of Menelik to Miriam, he thought, would be a family feast, dancing girls and then the 'joining of hands'. The ruby had already been given, it had been received, their hands had joined and their voices were as one. They were already promised man and wife, but the family must rejoice and the bride must receive the well wishes of everyone. Menelik and Miriam would be given their own private rooms, enter holding hands, while the women ululated and sang, and a few cried. In her last words to him in Marib, Queen Sheba had told him not to come and get her on the return trip, but let her remain in Marib for some months until everything at Aksum was back to normal and the buildings rebuilt that the earthquake had destroyed. With the new plans for a wedding, he decided that a small ceremony would be held in Hodeida and the couple would be joined there; then later a more formal affair could be set up on their return to Aksum. He would travel to Marib again and try to persuade the Queen to return with their group.

He almost fell asleep as he mused, listening to the young men behind him talk and laugh. Oh, to be young once again and to know only the joy of today, that river to cross, a mountain to climb, to hold a soft and beautiful body. The motion of the camel's swaying body was hypnotic. He dozed away, dreaming of Adulis, going fishing in the bay with its clear water, the small boat rocking, rocking. He dreamed of catching a huge stingray that always appeared when their dhows anchored, but never took the bait. Adulis bay was his recurring dream fishing, sitting on the sands and watching the sun turn red on the horizon, drinking red pomegranate juice. He dreamed of a dancing girl with toenails painted red, of a ruby.

Epilogue

Don't hold back on payments due on a debt.

The physicians bled him once again, opening a vein on his hand, which bled feebly, the scarlet life force dripping into a cup. Tamrin did not have the energy to refuse the treatment. He did not know what death would be like, but surely it would not be like this. The stingray's poison and the opium dulled his senses. The infection in his leg had poisoned his entire body. He tried to listen to the surgeons as they discussed what they should do next. Surely, Tamrin thought, death would not be oblivion. Again he dreamed, red came before his eyes…

"If we leave Tamrin the way he is, he will die, and soon. If we give him more opium and cut off his leg he will surely die. Shall we let his death be in the hands of the god of the stars and the sun, or is it to be in our hands as we operate?"

An old physician raised his hand to speak. "He is in pain. His mind has wandered far away. He has told his story. People will know his fame thousands of years from now. His engraved Stela will lie buried in the sand for others to find. Let us give him more opium and let him rest in quietness and peace. No operation, no more bloodletting. Let his life force depart. We will honor his request upon his death and have the butcher cut up his poisoned flesh to feed the rays and fishes. Thus will his flesh return to its beginning, the sea. From the sea we all come, are born, to the sea we will all return."

He reached over to feel Tamrin's pulse on his left arm. Then he felt on his right and under his chin. He looked up at the scribes. "He has left us! Tamrin's life is now on its journey to the star he held dear, the *thuban*, star of the seafarers. Look, there it is shining brightly, twinkling. It is the Dhruwa, the Hindush star of eternal travel across the seas of heaven that encompass the great waters of the earth.

"Blow the conch! Announce to all that Tamrin is taking his final journey."

Ethiopian Proverbs Used in the Text

A lame bull can easily be overcome.
A poorly built craft cannot be rebuilt
once it has been put in the water.
He who cannot walk can hardly climb.
He who lives with an ass brays like an ass.
Gossip and bragging are weaknesses of
kitchen women and insecure fools.
Better a single decision maker than a thousand advisors.
Where there is no shame there is no honor.
Do not exchange a laying hen for a clutch of eggs.
Once a fly escapes through an open window
there is no catching it.
He who learns teaches; he who teaches learns.
Cactus is bitter, but, only to those who taste it.
A limping dog soon becomes a dead dog.
Brothers will cheat brothers if there is gold to be gained.
Crawling is sometimes better than a full run.
To the swift is the race and the prize.
Watchdogs that run out at you, show teeth:
respect the teeth not the snarl.
A baby learns first to crawl, than to toddle, then to walk.
Roses come in many wonderful colors. But some
prefer only the white ones without thorns.

❈ Introduction to Glossary ❈

Where did the names and entities listed in this glossary come from? The sources are current information, which means obtainable in reference books and of course the inexhaustible font of information, the web, and my own language use. I was fortunate to have lived for a decade in Pakistan/India, to have traveled up the Indus River and visit most of the towns along it and to speak Urdu. For five years I worked in the Yemen Arab Republic as Project Director of the Ibb Agricultural Project and visited most parts of that country and became intimately involved with the local histories there. My parents worked in Ethiopia for seven years as medical missionaries, and my childhood memories are flooded with discussions, books written by my father about Ethiopia, and wall decorations of many kinds from Ethiopia one of which is in my bedroom to this day, depicting the seduction of Sheba by Solomon, and the travels of Tamrin to Jerusalem. I lived in Africa for almost twenty years and was strongly marked by this enculturation. Early travels to and fro to India and Africa were by slow boats, freighters, not by airplane, and thus many coastal cities were ports of call and places to visit, including Aden. Karachi, a coastal city in Pakistan became a vacation place, as well as a focus for some aspects of my work for the Ministry of Agriculture's irrigation management program. It was here that I traveled by dhow.

Terms and references below are modern language terms, anglicized versions of peoples, places and things I saw and experienced. There are also many terms from Arabia and Ethiopia that were used in ancient documents. The Bible! I must not forget the Pentateuch, the first five books of 'our' Old Testament, not written by Moses. This source is an excellent one for writing fictional historical accounts of famous people, such as Adam and Eve.

Glossary of Arabic, Hebrew, Urdu, Hindi and Amharic Words Used

Suggestion: Run your eyes down this <u>alphabetically</u> arranged list of entries without careful reading. This will familiarize you with terms and names used in the book, which can then later be referred to for meaning. For instance, shekel. Biblical scholars will immediately remember the word from the Old Testament. Before coins were struck, values were measured in units of various kinds. Or what about *Ge'ez, Baal, dhow?*

Aaghaa: woman's name from Nubian era

Ades: man's name from Ethiopia

Afimi: Urdu: opium for smoking. Punjabi saying: Hauke se zyadah bura kya?Afimi. What is worse than discontent? Opium, (or no opium).

Aluf: Arabic and Urdu first letter of the alphabet

Al-jadiyi: the billy goat star, Sumerian origin, Arabic

Ashterof: One of the Middle Eastern ancient gods; see also Moluch, Baal, Vishnu, Yahweh, most, Biblical god names

Aksum: Ancient city of Ethiopia at time of Queen of Sheba, her palace was there as well as important Stela

Aqiqah: tiny fish caught in the Red Sea, Arabic origin for anchovy, also called Wayra during Aksumite Kingdom

Ba'al: Old Testament reference to a 'false' god. "Ba'al we cry to thee." Canaanite deity, Ba'al, an important god in a desert area, one who brings rain

Bedu: Arabic for one who lives in the desert. Ancestors of the medieval and modern Bedouin, of African and Arabian deserts. Traditional Arabic term badawi, or badiyah all relate to similar meanings at different historic periods.

Bilqiz: Koranic name for Queen of Sheba, Solomon's concubine

Blue Nile: One of the sources of the Nile; borders on Ethiopia

Buk: Sabaean god of sea where it meets the sky.

Chandi: Hindi, Urdu name for silver

Chini: Name given in Aksum for Hubei Cross Bow that came over the Silk Route into India, from China, thence into the Red Sea and Aksum

Cubit (Egyptian): twenty eight digits extending from the palm, about 20.6 feet

Dara: a board game played with seeds or pebbles, an ancient form of checkers, term used in many African countries

Deban: a weight measurement such as a copper deban, or gold deban, 24 grams

Dehta: Person's name. Sindhi slang for one who gives, a generous one

Desta: Person's name, happiness

Dhoti: A cloth wrapped around hips and genitals, Hindi and Urdu word, loin cloth, Gandhi wore such a garment

Dhow: wood boat of various sizes and styles used in the Red Sea, Indian Ocean and African Eastern coasts. Used by Solomon for his trading fleet

Dhruwa: Hindi name for the 'fixed star'

Dongar: The name Aksum's residents called the Queen's palace

Durbar: Hindi: A walk past of thousands of soldiers and officials all in their uniforms, wearing their medals and carrying arms, a show of power

Menelik-la-hakim: Aksumite name for Menelik I, means son of the Wise Man Solomon; Sanskrit and South Semitic-Arabic origin; possible use in ancient Ge'ez, language of Ethiopia

Garib: Rudu, Persain and ancient Arabic for poor or poverty

Galigali: Magicians and Aden divers

Ge'ez: Gi'iz, Historic language of old Ethiopia derived from south Semitic origins: phonetic symbols used rather than pictographs

Ghaal: a fiery alcoholic drink in Marib

Halwa: or Halva, a sweet desert, such as carrot halva, gajar halva; Hindi

Haram: women's quarters, segregated

Hawilt: See Stela, obelisk

Hieroglyphics: Very old picture writing of Egypt at the time of Pharaohs. Thousands of pictures needed to be learned to represent different objects or actions. Later some of the pictures did represent phonetic sounds as well. The common man in ancient Egypt was basically illiterate.

Hindush: Term used by ancient *Aksumite* for Indians or Hindus who used Sanskrit and an ancient phonetic language of the *puranas.*

Hodeida: (Or *Hodaidah*) An ancient city on the Yemen coast, variously spelled

Ibb: Yemeni agricultural town in plains area

Jambiya: Curved sheathed dagger worn by many Yemeni men, Arabic

Kabadi-kabadi: chant used in wrestling in the Punjab

Kamal: celestial navigation device for determining latitude by Arabs and Aksumites, used in Red Sea and Indian Ocean, a board with strings on which knots were tied at intervals.

Kassa: A girl's name in Aksum, Ethiopia

Kebra Nagast: An Ethiopian religious history of Solomon, Sheba, and Menelik I and how the Ark of the Covenant came to Ethiopia

Khol: Black eye liner, India, Hindi

Kolachi or *Krokola:* ancient names for modern Karachi Pakistan

Kul subha: Urdu, tomorrow morning

Lal: Red like a ruby, ruby, blood red, Hindi, Pashtu and Persian use the word, pronounced differently

Lin: Linseed oil, flax seed oil, wood preservative, not for human consumptions

Lingam: Penis, Hindu worship symbol

Makeda: name for Queen of Sheba in *Aksum*

Malagasy: people of Madagascar, or Madagascar language, Indian/African origin

Mal'akh: Hebrew for angel, or guardian

Marib: Yemen city, a desert town where ruins of the Aksum era Marib dam still exist

Marula: a sweet fruit tree growing wild in 27 African countries, a sacred tree. It tastes like a peach/apple.

Mocha: A coastal area in Yemen known for its coffee, also called Sanaani bean coffee from the capital of Yemen, Sanaa

Meska: Arabic for gum or sap from two varieties of acacia trees, used to chew, mix with oils or as an adhesive. Called also char goond, or in Urdu, goand. Slightly sweet in taste.

Mukhtinath: A northern Nepali town on the border of Tibet, one entry for the Silk Route trade in ancient times that I visited in 1950.

Nub: Aksumite and Egyptian name for gold

Oud: A stringed instrument with up to five pairs of strings, played with a bow. Turkish, Arabian, and Aksum instruments differ in size and the number of strings.

Panja: Ancient area now the Punjab, where I lived, meaning five rivers

Poocho: Urdu name meaning, 'just ask'

Puranas: Indian: Ancient texts in Sanskrit of Vedas-Upanishad epic stories, narrations of creation, genealogies of ancient kings and rulers, the old classic revered cosmologies of India going back thousands of years.

Punt ta netjir: land of god, Egyptian reference to land of gold, riches, honey

*Qa*t: narcotic leaves chewed by Yemeni and Ethiopian and other Horn of Africa county residents

Quran: Koran. Arabic derivation

Ram: Hindu name for one of the gods

Roz : Daily, Roz ki roti, daily bread, Urdu

Rub-al Khali: Arabian name for Desert of Emptiness

Saba: name of ancient kingdom of Sabaean history, name given to Sheba in Aksum

Sabarbaha : Arabic: wood shafted spear, six feet long with large spear blade

Sabon, Hindi (sbun) and Urdu for soap: ancient soapberry used before discovery of soap as we know it, a surfactant, Latin = Sapindus emargenatus. Still used in India and Pakistan, effective detergent-like soaping action.

Sarai: Inn for travelers, protected by walls, Urdu and Arabic

Sati: Hindi; an honorable woman, suttee, woman who self immolates on her husband's funeral pyre.

Setu: a man's name, born with dignity or righteousness, Biblical, Seth, name used in Ethiopia and many African countries

Sharaab: Hindustani name for wine, Arabic origin

Shaar Ha Delek- One of twelve gates in Solomon's temple for bringing is animal to sacrifice. Also *Misbaeach-* a gate leading to the outer courtyard. Hebrew rendering.

Sharam: Shame, or name for prostitute, Arabic and Urdu, or in Arabic also beard

Sharam al-Sheikh: a city at the tip of the Arabian peninsula at the mouth of the Gulf of Akaba: Arabic for beard of the leader

Shekel: a unit of measurement of weight or currency in Hebrew Biblical usage, Carthage shekel coin was minted in 310 B.C.

Sher: Sher Khan: Name for tiger in Urdu, Bubbar Sher is lion

Shittim Wood: Acacia seyal- Biblical Ark of the Covenant was carved from this hard, desert wood; part of the Aksum palace was constructed with this wood, called Wachu in Amharic language

Sindh: huge desert area in north central India

Sirius: God of the sailors' and travelers' star

Shukran: Arabic for thank you

Souk: Market place in Arabic, similar to Indian bazaar; consists of many markets placed together, vegetable, leather, gold etc.

Sona: Name for gold in Urdu, Hindustani

Stela: hawilt, tall and large, engraved stone obelisks found in Aksum

Taiz: Hill town in Yemen known for excellent climate

Talent: A measurement for an amount of gold or silver: Biblical usages: 2 Kings 15:30

Tamasha: group having fun, circus-like gathering, special celebration, Urdu

Tansing: or Tensing, Capital of West Nepal

Tej: sweet Ethiopian honey wine

Tenestaline: Hello. Greeting of thanks, Amharic, Ethiopian

Tigray Plateau: term used during Aksumite Kingdom, Ethiopia

Tubla: Small drum held between the knees, Punjabi origin

Thuban: North star, Sumerian and Egyptian

Tundoori roti: flat breads baked in open mud ovens

Varuna: God of the cosmos and sea for ancient Sabaean travelers.

Wachu: Amharic word for a desert hard wood used for chests and the Ark of the Covenant

Wadi: Arabic for dry stream bed, or stream bed with water

Wayra: Anchovy fish, archaic usage in Aksum

Yam suf: Legendary account of where the Israelites crossed the sea on dry ground. Legend has it that camels and animals crossed the area from North Africa and Arabia. A saline swamp that dries up in years of drought and low tidal seas.

Annotated Bibliography of Selected Sources

1. "African Proverbs from Ethiopia-African Culture" (bellaonline) 2011. Wisdom comes in the form of sayings, which beg for cultural translation. "Happy is the man that findeth wisdom, and the man that getteth understanding." Proverbs 3:13. Solomon's words echo in the modern Ethiopian proverbs. *See Appended list for all proverbs used within the text.

2. Ali, A. Yusufu, (Translator) *The Holy Quran,* Islamic Center, Washington, D.C., (Preface 1932-1934, Lahore) 1946. There are a number of English versions of the Koran available, however, this version, written in Lahore, is clear and beautifully organized. The book, however, is now rare, but worth seeking out.

3. Authorized King James Version, *New Analytical Bible,* 1929, John A. Dickson Publishing Company, Chicago. (This was for me a significant part of my early socialization. Some parts were skipped in family reading sessions including the 'begats' and 'pisseth on a wall', 'throw her down from the wall', and 'he went in unto her'.)

4. Bergsma, Stuart, *Sons of Sheba,* Eerdmans, 1933. This short novel brings the lineage of Ethiopian ancestors to the time of Christ. It posits the message that the Coptic Church had its beginnings with Menelik I. The cross bearer, a eunuch of Ethiopia features in his story.

5. Basliel Wolde, Gabriel, "Books on Ethiopia", Virtual School of Ethiopian Studies (http//Sirius-c.ncat.edu/vses/book.html) 2011. A list of 245 books related specifically to Ethiopia. An excellent beginning for Ethiopia lovers to review writings going back decades.

6. Budge, E. A. W., *The Kebra Nagast,* [1922] at sacred-texts/com, 2011. Budge's translation reveals for the non-Ethiopian a traditional history that under-girds cultural understanding about the development of the Coptic Church, in fact even the Ark of the Covenant which is believed to be hidden away in Ethiopia.

7. Burstein, Stanley, ed. *Ancient Civilizations: Kush and Aksum,* Princeton, 1998. The ancient history of Aksum is presented with data and information from archaeology when available. Like many history books, this excellent text does not create history, simply reports what exists and does not establish myths about origins and empires for which there are slender records. Yet, Aksum as a city 'lives' in ancient times.

8. Blakely, Tomas et al., *Religion in Africa,* London, James Curry, 1994. Review by country and ethnicity of religions in all parts of Africa. Helpful cultural information to understand rituals and rites.

9. Encyclopedia of Religion, 2001-2006, Macmillan, Ref. USA, Imprint, Gale Group. An invaluable and up-to-date reference book for studying ancient religions and the civilizations from which they emerged.

10. Gorfu, G., E., "King Solomon's Instructions", 1998, (www.meskot.com/solomon.htm) Gorfu writes in fictional fashion about Menelik and Solomon, however, by the time one has finished reading the story, it feels like one has read a religious text, such as the Song of Solomon. What I enjoyed most about his 'history' are the words, "It is told that..." which moves imagination and oral history into the realm of the believable. "Other scholars have argued that some of the words used in the text are Persian, which sets the written date to the postexilic period. Solomon lived in the tenth century B C E which is much earlier than the postexilic period. Solomon could not have been the author, from some of the words being used." See: Garrett, Duane A. Song of Songs. Word Biblical Commentary 23B. Nashville: Nelson, 2004.

11. "Gulf of Aqaba" Location of facts, bodies of water, (www.worldatlas.com/aatlas/infopage/gulfofawaba.htm) The most direct route from Adulis to Al Aqaba was by ship. The entire Sinai Peninsula does not need to be traversed to travel to Jerusalem. At

times there are terrible dust storms that blow across the gulf from the deserts, making travel by land almost impossible, and by ship, problematic for sailors who must keep covered.

12. Hitti, Philip K., *History of the Arabs*, Macmillan and Co. Ltd., 1943. (My treasured rare book which was written at the time of my birth in 1932, was first published in 1937) The Arab name for Sheba is Bilqis who visited the King of Israel and brought valuable gifts to Solomon. She was Queen, not in Yemen or Ethiopia, but in one of the Sabaean posts or garrisons in the north on the caravan route. Thus Hitti suggests (page 40) that Bilqis was not Ethiopian, nor from Yemen or Aksum. This massive (760 pages) and now a rare history book, was most valuable in providing a scholarly and detailed perspective in regard to Arabian history, particularly the section which reviews how Abyssinians invaded Arabia centuries before Christ.

13. Phillipson, David W., *Archaeology of Aksum Ethiopia*, 1993-97, London, Oxford, 2000. The massive Stellae of Aksum presented a challenge for the archaeologists, but their research findings and interpretations, particularly in regard to these being dedicated to monarchs, similar to the pyramids of Egypt which were tombs of pharaohs, was most important. An account that the largest of the Stelae was taken by Italy to Rome when they occupied Ethiopia, reveals the crass chauvinism of European empires in regard to Africa or other of their 'colonies.' To this day the London Museum houses treasures from Egypt and other African nations that exist nowhere else. (At least they are preserved, rather than being ruined by wandering nomads or broken up to be sold to tourists by merchants. Anon.)

14. "191 Famous Ethiopian Proverbs" http//special –dictionary." Com/proverbs/source/e/Ethiopian_pro. 2011 The title says it all. It was sweet to find this compilation. "Cactus is bitter only to those who taste it." My own collection of Tiv proverbs published by Oxford Press, "Tiv Proverbs as a Means of Social Control,' whetted my interest and curiosity for proverbs from other African countries. These pithy sayings enhance communication and create an immediate bond to the listener. In Arabic cultures, the language is rich with statements that have double meanings, and bend the mind

around topics in indirect ways, which to most English speakers is foreign. It is not always better to 'come to the point' rather, let the listener infer the point from lyrical language, the language of the Prophet. (See Proverbs, below)

15. "Menelik I, (Wikipedia, 2011)" The account of Menelik I, who was called, Menelik la-Hakim, that is "Son of the Wise" uses a phrase which places the reader's mind at ease. "...is traditionally believed to be.." So much of ancient history is tradition, which comes to us from the minds of scribes, the creativity of authors over long periods of time, which are then accepted as 'fact'. The Kebra Nagast, a traditional account of the beginning of the ancient Christian church is held by many Ethiopians to be fact, as is the Old Testament account of Solomon and Sheba. The Muslim account is much more magical, with stories of a messenger bird, a hoopoe bird that zaps back and forth from what is now Yemen to Judah to tell him about the wonderful kingdom of Sheba. Great stuff.

16. Munro-Hay, Stuart., *Aksum, An African Civilization of Late Antiquity*, Edinburgh, 1991. One of the most helpful sources for ordering the historical sequences of the origin and development of the ancient city of Aksum. Well documented with an exhaustive bibliography.

17. Rosetta Stone: "This day in History", July 19.1799, See: History.com (Egyptian hieroglyphics were a mystery until this fragment of stone, perhaps of a stone stele, was found when the stone happened to land face up during an excavation project, was preserved, and later, because a scholar who knew Greek surmised that three languages written on the stone meant the same thing. Thus the mysterious written hieroglyphics, of ancient Egypt was understood for the first time.)

18. *Timna: Valley of the Ancient Copper Mines,* Jewish Virtual Library, (Archeology) 2011. Historically, ancient peoples who lived nine centuries before Christ had limited hard materials for tools such as knives, swords, axes and the like. Stones were used, such as basalt to provide sharp edges. Axes were formed from stone. But iron was mined in Asia Minor and spearheads and knives became a prized trade item. Steel for flexible swords was not discovered until centuries later. But, copper was available and was fashioned

into a host of useful implements, including those of war. The Old Testament speaks of this, except in the King James Version calls the metal Brass. Brass, a harder substance fashioned from copper and zinc was also a later discovery, though Bronze was made from Copper and Tin. Copper was widely used at the time of Solomon (Solomon) and was an important part of the decoration and objects of utility in the construction of the temple. Gold, of course, was used widely for thousands of years before Christ. It is hard to imagine a civilization without steel, without plastic, and without all the tools of the industrial and atomic revolution, and of course fossil fuels.

19. Raffaele, Paul, "Keepers of the Lost Ark?" Smithsonian, Dec. 2007. "Tradition holds that the ark of the covenant-containing the Ten Commandments- vanished in the sixth century B.C. Christians in Ethiopia have long claimed to have it." This is a must read. Not only does one get the Old Testament version of the powers of the Ark of the Covenant, but a review of the record of Ethiopian mythology which has become world history, through design. Steven Spielberg's 1981 film, Raiders of the Lost Ark, with its special effects and approximations has reinforced readers and viewers in the world at large that they have witnessed history in the re-making. Here again, the writer designs the belief, the artist draws the pretty pictures, and the believer of myths now feels comfy to write history.

Printed by BoD™in Norderstedt, Germany